BRITANNIA

Nicolas Heft

Order this book online at www.trafford.com
or email orders@trafford.com

Most Trafford titles are also available at major online book retailers.

Printed in the United States of America.

ISBN: 978-1-4269-3232-8 (sc)
ISBN: 978-1-4269-3233-5 (dj)
ISBN: 978-1-4269-4085-9 (e)

Library of Congress Control Number: 2010911122

*Our mission is to efficiently provide the world's finest, most comprehensive book publishing
service, enabling every author to experience success. To find out how to publish your
book, your way, and have it available worldwide, visit us online at www.trafford.com*

Trafford rev. 8/23/2010

 www.trafford.com

North America & international
toll-free: 1 888 232 4444 (USA & Canada)
phone: 250 383 6864 ♦ fax: 812 355 4082

To my family. Words can not exist to express my gratitude for all you have done. I would not be the man I am today were it not for your loving support. Je vous adore a la folie.

Mors Certa, Vita Incerta —Roman Proverb
Death is certain, life is not.

I

It was a beautiful day for battle. The sun shone brightly in the sky, the wind blew in their favor, and the lush, green grass was dry, allowing for superior maneuverability. Marcus Caius, Legionnaire of Rome in the Tenth Legion, knew this battle would be decisive. If Rome were to win the day, the entire region of Belgica in northern Gaul would then become part of the Roman Empire. Marcus was a young man who had joined the Roman army shortly before the Gallic war had begun. He had brown hair, deep brown eyes that verged on black, and although not exceedingly strong, he was astoundingly physically fit.

Marcus stared across the field toward the opposing army. It was gathering in a large rectangular clearing within the forest, several miles south of Samarobriva, a small village in northwestern Gaul. On the Roman's left flank flowed the Arras River; to their right rose a large rock outcrop that towered several dozen feet in the air, providing an excellent observation post for whoever dared to climb its treacherous face.

Marcus thought about all of the battles that had led up to this one. The war in Gaul had started four years ago when Julius Caesar had invaded Gaul for various political reasons. The war had progressed rapidly, and now the majority of Gaul was under Roman control.

It had been four years since Marcus had last been in Rome; four years spent fighting the barbarians in Gaul. He stood at attention on one side of the plain, the Gauls on the other. He could make out their large figures across the expanse. Minutes ago, the Roman archers had released volley after volley of deadly arrows from a range of roughly 125 yards, in an attempt to soften up the Gallic lines. However, the Gauls had wisely moved back into the forest a short way, and the arrows had impaled the trees and dirt rather than their intended targets. As the barrage came to an end, the Gauls had reemerged from the gloom with few casualties. Now they stood in defiance, thousands of men ready to fight against the Legions, their shouts and curses reverberating across the plain into the Roman ranks. The Gauls were tall, with rippling muscles and an abundance of blond hair, as opposed to the shorter, dark haired typical Romans with their slightly smaller muscles. Where the Romans relied on armor for protection, the Gauls did not. The Gallic soldiers found armor to be a hindrance as they slashed with their swords.

Though Marcus had fought countless times, he always felt a little sick before an engagement. Marcus looked to his sides, reassured by the might of the Legions, and immediately felt a little calmer. Ten thousand Roman Legionnaires stood around him, some in the ranks in front of him, others to his rear; countless others stretched far to his sides. Two entire Legions at full strength stood waiting, anticipating.

A wave of reassurance flashed through his body like one of Jupiter's bolts, and immediately his hands shook a little less. They had been standing here since the ninth hour of morning; it was now the eleventh. He wanted the battle to commence, for their trumpets to sound, for the ranks to begin closing in. Everyone had gotten a little action—the archers, the cavalry who had gone to scout their positions, the generals—everyone but the infantry. Marcus knew boredom was a man's worst enemy. Worse than any arrow, any spear, and any sword was a wandering mind. A split second could mean the difference between surviving a battle unscathed or getting a sword thrust forcefully into your gut.

The incomprehensible babbling of the opposing army reached Marcus despite the breeze that blew against them. Suddenly it hit him how loudly they must have been shouting to be heard upwind. Then another noise reached his ears, one he knew well. He peered over the shoulders of the men in front of him and barely made out a man on a horse, closely followed by a group of guards trotting in front of the ranks. Marcus immediately recognized the short brown hair, the penetrating stare, the Godlike appearance that demanded respect. It was Julius Caesar.

Julius Caesar was parading in front of his men, encouraging and motivating them to do their best for Rome. Marcus' view was occasionally blocked by the men's large shields and helmets, but the energy reached him. Suddenly, Caesar came to a halt on a small mound of dirt a little farther in front and to the left of where Marcus was standing and almost immediately began to speak. Marcus knew what was about to happen. He had gone through this more times than he could remember. Each motivational speech in preparation for a battle was typically the same, varied by slight details. But despite the monotonous, practically invariable speech, Marcus still listened, for one simple reason. A legion's general always addressed the soldiers who would be doing the brunt of the fighting. The fact that Caesar was speaking so nearby meant that Marcus and the men around him would be tasked with the heaviest fighting among those present, an honor bestowed upon them due to heroic deeds in prior battles.

"Soldiers," Caesar began, "brothers, fellow countrymen. Across the field stands the so-called army of Gauls. I rather call it a conglomeration of drooling mongoloids that stands no chance against us. They are led by nobility and not by men skilled in the art of warfare, as we are. They outnumber us two to one, but our bravery, our swords, and our tactics will more than compensate for this slight disadvantage." Caesar paused for effect and then continued.

"For some reason; I know not what, they apparently believe they stand a chance against us! *Us!* The greatest army the gods have ever seen! They are naive beyond reason!" There came a loud cheer from the troops and then silence as Caesar resumed his speech. Marcus watched as Caesar looked over his shoulder toward the barbarians.

"I have been told by the Augurs and Haraspices that all omens are in our favor today. The hare's liver promised a great victory, and the birds this morning circled our camp three times and then flew toward the enemy, as if followed by Pluto himself!"

He nudged his horse along and began to march down the remainder of the line.

"We, men, are the demons of the underworld! Unstoppable and terrifying! Imagine for a brief moment what they see ... I, for one, can tell you it is truly an awesome sight."

Caesar paused as the troops cheered. He looked at the faces that were staring back at him; the men who would die fighting for him, die fighting for Rome.

"These are the last of the treacherous ignorant from this region who defy the greatness of Rome. Tonight when they will have been defeated, we can begin to educate them in our good ways, our *superb* ways! We will be their rulers and they our slaves! In war, only those who take great chances obtain great rewards! And by Mars, I, Caius Julius Caesar, promise you great spoils if you but just win this battle for me, for you, for your families ... *for Rome!*"

Caesar then slammed his right fist against his armor in a salute, and the mass of troops, originating from the center where Caesar stood, erupted into a loud cheer. Within seconds, the sound rippled into the following ranks and soon, the plain was filled with the shouts of thousands of Romans. Caesar quickly spoke to his guards and, as suddenly as he had appeared, disappeared toward the right flank where he had come from.

The atmosphere was now more intense; Marcus could feel it in his bones. The wind had picked up, and the snapping of the battle standards and flags muted out the enemy voices. Or *were* they muted?

Marcus peered over the man in front of him and noticed a large cloud of dust. Marcus had learned in training that there were many types of dust clouds, two of which to watch for in particular. Low and wide meant advancing infantry, whereas narrow and tall indicated advancing cavalry. The cloud before him was close to the ground and spanned the entire length of the field, soon revealing a solid line of advancing infantrymen.

Although Marcus had seen an enemy advance tens of times, his hands began to sweat, and his jaw tightened. Deep inside, he felt a knot form in his stomach, and his throat felt as though it were being squeezed in a giant's grip. Marcus then thought of his family back home. Not of a wife or kids, no, for he wasn't married; nor were the thousands of other legionnaires spanning the Roman Empire, for that matter. A soldier was, in fact, forbidden to marry. Instead, he thought of his mother, most likely at home this very moment in her kitchen, thinking of her son. He thought of his father, who had served before him and finally retired after twenty-five years of faithful service. And then he thought of his brother, who was somewhere in Parthia, fighting. He then thought of himself, standing here on a plain with thousands of his fellow countrymen, waiting to kill or be killed. He knew he was relatively safe, safer than the enemy at least, but the thought of what would happen to him and the others if they were to lose the battle still raced through his mind. Marcus gripped his pilum, a one-time-use wooden javelin tipped with a two-foot long iron shank that, upon impact, would bend and become irremovable, even tighter, and his fingers quickly turned a pale white.

Marcus watched as the enemy formation advanced on his position. He estimated the barbarians to be fifty meters away. Soon the order would come to throw their pila, and the battle would commence. He changed his grip on his shield slightly and shifted his weight, but he couldn't find the right position; each felt a little awkward. He knew it was nervousness, but it was annoying as hell. He could feel several things simultaneously: the grass tickling his feet through his open-footed leather sandals, or caligae, the wind across his face, the sweat running down his back—everything.

His eyes were locked on the Gauls as he watched them approach, so much that his eyes burned from the strain. Then the enemy stopped and began to shout and yell. Marcus found this part semi-amusing, the incomprehensible shouting that was meant to offend them. He laughed to himself. He thought that if they just stuck their tongues out at him he'd be more insulted.

As he waited for the enemy to reach him, Marcus scrutinized the enemy's clothing. The first thing he noticed was their linen pants, which varied greatly from man to man. The newer clothing was freshly dyed and bright, while the older were rather drab, the varying colors nearly imperceptible as they all converged into a dirty earthen brown. Marcus also noted that most Gauls were topless, both a display of their bravery and a strategy to not impair their movements when they fought. Marcus noted that none of the enemy wore armor; apparently, he thought, they still hadn't learned its protective value. He continued to scan the barbarians and, already knowing that they wore jewelry in keeping with their wealth, easily distinguished who was higher ranked and thus a more important target. He noted that the richest among them wore gold bracelets and torcs, large necklaces typical of the Gallic soldier. As Marcus' eyes moved up from their heavily muscled arms and chests toward their heads, he witnessed the same horrifying practice that a majority of male Gauls employed; that of washing their hair in limewater. This, he had been told, stiffened their hair and allowed some natural protection from sword blows and, though not nearly as strong as a Roman helmet, was not to be underestimated.

The Gallic soldier's armament varied slightly from man to man, as each bought his own supplies. For the most part however, each man carried a large oval shield made of wood and covered in dried hide that was then painted in bright colors. Each man carried either a spear or a long sword that hung from his belt, formidable due to its exceedingly long length and strength.

Marcus watched as they lifted their large, oval shields, the sun reflecting off of the large bronze bosses protruding from their centers. The Gauls then began striking their shields with their swords and spears, accompanied by chilling howls and curses, creating an awful cacophony. Despite this spectacle designed to instill fear in their enemies, Marcus could not help but smile. These were his enemies, ready to tear his life out with a sword, but the panoply displayed by them demanded some respect.

Suddenly they ceased; a few voices faded into silence after the others. They began to advance toward the Roman lines at a slow walk. Gradually, their speed increased, and soon the men charged, screaming at the top of their lungs. The surging mass lacked any form of organization; the more rapid men quickly passed the slower, which left large gaps in the oncoming charge. This is the moment, Marcus thought. He knew how the battle would play out from this moment on. First, he and his fellow soldiers would throw their pila. Then they would move into close-quarter combat; Marcus and his fellow soldiers would wear down the enemy. Once the enemy began to break and flee, the Roman cavalry would charge and pursue the fleeing.

But Marcus knew it would all proceed one step at a time.

As the barbarians approached to within forty meters, the commanding officers, the centurions, began to cry out the commands.

"Prepare pila!"

As one body, the Romans all lifted their pila over their shoulders and pivoted to the right. This maneuver placed the shields between them and the charging enemy and gave the legionnaires a better angle from which to throw their lethal projectiles. Marcus scanned the advancing Gauls and spotted his target almost immediately. The man he decided upon was somewhat tall; his helmeted head rose slightly above the others'. His bare chest supported a large golden necklace that hung around his thick neck, and golden earrings hung limply from his earlobes. His muscled arms waved wildly as the man shouted orders, revealing the numerous golden bracelets that encased his muscled forearms and wrists.

When the enemy was within thirty meters, the order came to throw.

"Throw pila!"

As one body, the soldiers threw their pila with maximum force toward the enemy. The flight of the lethal projectiles created a bizarrely beautiful sight.

Marcus watched as the pila arced through the sky, darkening it for a brief moment, and fell among the charging barbarians with terrifying velocity.

The spears, a full two meters in length, impaled countless numbers of the enemy, and their bodies fell lifelessly to the ground while others ran past them, barely noticing the carnage around them. Time seemed to stop as Marcus followed his pila as it honed in on the unsuspecting Gaul, and then Marcus winced as the sharp point slit through the man's flesh with ease. Marcus realized he had just killed another man but he didn't let the thought disrupt his focus. It was the enemy or him.

Marcus quickly scanned the enemy ranks and watched as some Gauls sidestepped one murderous pilum only to be impaled by another. Countless others raised their shields in fruitless attempts to protect themselves. The six-pound pila, driven by gravity, barely recognized the shields as obstacles. Occasionally two or three men were skewered at a time. Blood spattered over the inside of the shields as the soldiers fell to the ground, stuck to their shields by an iron shank two feet long.

Before the last of the pila had finished their pernicious flight, the legionnaires had returned to their original stances and unsheathed their swords. In one swift movement they braced themselves and stuck their short swords through the openings between the shields. Leaning forward with their shields and swords to better brace themselves for impact, the Romans awaited the oncoming human wave.

Suddenly, the two cultures met in a terrifying crash as the men collided into one another. When the Gauls reached the Roman lines, the legionnaires stepped forward with their shields, destabilizing and knocking down many of the enemy's frontline soldiers. However, the legions immediately buckled as they were pushed back by the sheer mass of the human wave. The Romans were pushed back a foot as the enemy rammed into the wall of shields and swords, attempting to penetrate the impregnable Roman ranks. Fortunately for the injured, the built-up adrenaline temporarily muted the pain of fractured shoulders, broken ankles and shattered teeth as men rammed into each other.

Then, as the Romans recovered from the initial impact, they began to push their shields into the barbarian ranks with all their might. This move destabilized the enemy, and the Roman soldiers then followed up with quick jabs of their swords. The barbarians, bleeding from deep fatal wounds, crumbled. As they fell, soldiers from behind stepped over them to take their places. The Romans then again lunged with their shields and swords, slicing easily through Gallic flesh.

The Roman fighting technique was particularly strong for many reasons. Firstly, no man fought for more than sixty seconds before being replaced by the man behind. After sixty seconds, the trumpeters would sound an order to switch, and the front row would step back and snake their way to the rear of the formation; simultaneously, the second row would step up and shield the retreating soldiers. The second row, which was now first, would fight for sixty seconds, and the process was repeated.

This allowed for a constant supply of fresh men, as opposed to the enemy, who grew tired quickly from continuous fighting.

The second strength of the Roman army was their superb weapons. The Roman soldier's sword was short and double-sided, better suited for thrusting than slashing. This led to deeper wounds and consequently a higher mortality rate. The Romans also carried a large, rectangular bowed shield that offered greater protection than any other shield carried by any other army. The shield allowed protection of the front as well as a portion of the flanks. The shield was then put to use in several different tactics employed by the Roman army against their foes. One tactic, called the Testudo, or tortoise in Latin, required the Roman soldiers to lift their shields above their heads while the outer ranks turned their shields outward, thus creating an impenetrable wall of shields that protected them from arrows. Another tactic, called the hollow square, required all of the Roman soldiers to form a square, creating a strong formation to defend against infantry attacks.

Marcus, who was, for the moment, in the fourth rank, held on to the man in front of him to keep him from being pulled into the enemy mass. Due to the fear brought on by combat, men had a tendency to fight their way into the enemy formation instead of holding their place and standing their ground. The unfortunate man would then eventually, if not immediately, be exposed and rapidly dispatched. The Romans prevented this simply by having each man hold on to the man in front of him; a simple solution to a simple problem.

However, no matter how well a man is trained for battle, training can only approximate the stress, unpredictability, and atrocity of combat. Fortunately, Marcus had already fought in many battles and was accustomed to the possibility of slight changes in plans during a battle; especially when fighting barbarians. The Gauls were a crazy type. Their form of combat lacked any discipline, and cohesion between units was absent. The various tribes who banded together to fight the Roman invaders would each fight in their own manner, oblivious to the fact that this individuality would be the cause of their demise. In fact, it was this form of warfare that allowed the Romans to destroy Gallic armies with minimal losses.

Suddenly, Marcus heard the trumpeters sound the order to switch and realized he was in the second rank. Apparently his mind had wandered for one minute while he moved up one rank from where he had last found himself. As the man in front of Marcus fell back as ordered, he was stabbed from beneath his shield and armor by wounded barbarian, who had fallen and then thrust a spear up into the soldier.

As the spear was torn out of the Roman's side in a torrent of blood, Marcus immediately took his place, knowing full well that a gap could be filled as easily by a barbarian as by a Roman. He stepped into position through the wrestling forms of his fighting comrades, raised his shield, and began following the procedures on how to take an enemy's life that he had practiced in training and actual battle hundreds of times before. Meanwhile, his dying comrade was dragged backward out of harm's way to his left.

Seeing his fellow soldier being dragged on the ground like a heavy bag angered Marcus and he immediately wanted to avenge his wounded comrade. Marcus raised his shield, protecting his face and torso from the man who stood on the other side, and his eyes began to scan the ground as he searched for the unlucky Gaul; unlucky, because Marcus was bent on exacting his revenge on the man in a most lethal way.

The ground was an awful mess, covered in broken swords, shields, blood, and corpses. Suddenly, his eyes found their target. The wounded Gaul was preparing to thrust again, and this time Marcus was in the spear's path. Without wasting a second, Marcus sent his sword slicing down into the man's chest and watched as the spear fell out of the cold, white, lifeless hands onto the noxious ground. He made sure the man was indeed dead this time with a kick of his foot and then put his mind back on the man in front of him.

As he looked back up, he felt someone tug on the top of his shield, trying to bring his shield down. Marcus resisted, but the force was too strong for his left arm. After a mere two-second struggle, Marcus found himself peering into the small, blue eyes of a Gaul, inches away from his own face. He felt the man's breath on his face and the murderous intentions running through the man's body. He realized that the soldier had been pulling down on Marcus' shield with his hands, trying to get a clear shot at him. Seconds felt like minutes as both men peered into each other's eyes, each planning to kill the other. Almost as if in slow motion, Marcus watched the Gaul raise his sword, tantalizing the defenseless Roman. Then, the Gaul began to smile satanically.

Marcus tried to bring his sword up to stab the opposing soldier, but it was pressed against him by his shield. The barbarian was leaning against him and was obviously squelching Marcus' ability to move as he moved in for the kill. The barbarian was using the same tactics the Romans did, a little different in style, but the result was the same. Marcus wondered when the trumpet would blow and he'd have a chance to get out. When everyone switched position, the momentary distraction could be the key to his survival. But he had a better idea. Leaning his head back, Marcus then gave the Gaul as strong a head butt as he could muster. His metal helmet instantly broke the man's nose, and Marcus watched as the ogre blinked in shock at the realization that his nose was contorted at an awful angle. Then, filled with insatiable rage, the Gaul began to bellow, his eyes bulging from the strain.

Marcus was frozen in shock at the sight of the soldier towering above him, his nose broken and bleeding, and his eyes in unnatural positions. Again, he slammed his head into the man's face. He felt more than heard the man's face crack under the metallic onslaught. Sweat and blood now poured over Marcus' body, some his, some his enemy's. Marcus realized he had received a cut above his right brow, and the sting of the cut only infuriated him more. He tried to bring his sword up again, but he was still pinned. *Hasn't it been sixty seconds already?*

Suddenly, Marcus decided to crouch down and catch the Gaul off guard, causing him to fall forward. Marcus then swiftly lifted the rim of the shield hard into the man's jaw. The towering barbarian immediately cried out as his half-rotten teeth cracked under the rigidity of the shield. The man suddenly began to blink his eyes as the pain reached his brain and became intolerable. Seizing the moment, Marcus plunged his sword deep into the man's abdomen and watched as he fell to the ground, his body a tattered mess. Panting and out of breath, Marcus looked up at his next opponent. *You want a taste of Roman steel too?* He thought as he looked into the man's face.

Initially, Marcus thought nothing of the blue paint all over the man's body, but then it began to sink in. The blue swirls of woad, a plant that produces blue dye, covered the man's exposed body parts, and the short brown hair and bushy mustache all supported Marcus' hypothesis. In fact, this man wasn't Gallic at all but Briton. Marcus realized that this was in fact his fifth encounter with these foreign men. He knew this wasn't a coincidence; the Britons had to be supplying auxiliaries to the Gauls. The centurions cried out to switch again, but Marcus was focused on his new threat. Only when he felt a strong tug backward did he realize he was to switch.

Meanwhile, the soldier behind Marcus stepped up, and he too paused as he saw the Briton warrior. But without wasting time, the Roman legionnaire quickly slashed at the man's femoral artery, bringing him down to the ground hard.

As Marcus wormed his way toward the back, imperceptibly the Romans began to creep forward, smashing with their shields and stabbing with their swords. Soon, a narrow strand of Romans had advanced beyond the others; the reserves quickly filled the gaps. Marcus believed the battle was impossible to lose from this point. Nothing could stop the Romans once they began wedging into the enemy formations. A lot had been learned since the defeat at Cannae at the hands of the Carthaginian scum led by Hannibal. There, the Romans had been tricked into wedging but were later encircled and massacred to the last man. Now, over a century and a half later, precautions were taken to prevent such a thing from ever happening again.

Another five minutes passed before the Romans succeeded in dividing the opposing army in two. The wedge had three benefits; first it divided the enemy army; second, it prevented the now separated sections of the opposing army from communicating with each other; and third, it allowed more Roman soldiers to fight simultaneously.

As time passed and the opposing army was worn down, the Gauls and Britons began to tire from the strenuous fighting. With no reserves to replace them, the Gauls and Britons embarked on a disorderly retreat. With their flanks and rear now fully exposed to the murderous onslaught of the Romans, the Roman cavalry was suddenly given the order to charge.

Erupting from the forest, from behind the former Gallic lines, the horsemen quickly intercepted the fleeing enemy and cut them down mercilessly. Some of the fleeing warriors were impaled by the long cavalry spears, while others were slain by the long swords.

This part of the battle was always the bloodiest, Marcus knew, the moment when the pursuers hacked down the fleeing enemy without mercy. As Marcus ran after the fleeing Gauls and Britons, he was thankful that the cavalry was now in charge, and he quickly slowed to a jog, his lungs starving for air. He tried to keep an eye on the fleeing enemy when he finally stopped, but they were obscured by the pursuing cavalry and the large clouds of dust. With a smile, he wiped the sweat and blood off of his shining brow with the back of his hand.

It had been a glorious victory.

Marcus took a look at the ground around him; most of the slain were the enemy. Bent pila were stuck in the ground everywhere. Slain horses and men were strewn everywhere like pieces of trash blown around by wind.

After catching his breath, Marcus walked slowly among the dead. He guessed the ratio to be ten barbarians to every Roman who lay gloriously on the ground. Sick of the sight, Marcus leaned backward, stretching his back and lungs, then set his shield down on the bloody ground and loosened his helmet. As his mind began to slow and his body cooled down from the exertion, he smiled at the thought that the year's fighting was finally over. They had just defeated the tribesmen of this region, and the approach of winter would not allow any further conquest. Whatever he was doing, he was doing correctly, he realized, for he had survived yet again. He knelt on the grass, his heartbeat slowing, and thought of how great it was to be alive.

II

The Roman fort of Castra Constantia stood on a plot of land just west of the previous day's battlefield. The troops and engineers had cleared the land of all vegetation weeks ago; the very day the legions had reached their destination. The castrum was a classic example of superior Roman military engineering. In fact, the layout of the castrum required it be built from the inside out. At the center of the large rectangular fortified camp stood the principia; the headquarters of the Roman army.

The principia was an imposing tent that stood ten feet high, topped by a large, red, triangular flag that blew proudly in the wind. In front of it stood the Eagles of the two legions that resided in the camp.

The Eagles, or Aquilas, were the Legions' standards, the very objects the legions' existence revolved around. To lose one meant disgrace to the entire body of men who served under it and usually resulted in the disbanding of the unit. But there they stood, their bases planted into the hard ground, the golden, waist-sized eagles standing proudly at the top, their wings outstretched as if ready to take flight at a moment's notice.

Under the Eagles lay a red, hip-wide flag that draped downward and sported the letters SPQR, which stood for *Senatus Populusque Romanus,* or "the senate and people of Rome," in golden thread.

From where the Eagles were planted, stretching in all four cardinal directions from the principia, were the principal roads that lead to the four gates. The Via Praetoria ran from north to south and lead to the main gate, called the Porta Praetoria, and the back gate through which supplies entered, called the Porta Decumana. From east to west ran the Via Principales, which lead to the right and left gates, or Porta Prinicpales Dextra and Porta Principales Sinistra, respectively.

The fort, which was already surrounded by a wall roughly fifteen feet high, was also protected by a ditch several feet deep. Spaced at intervals of thirty feet, towers suitable for archers were placed. The fort was a busy place, with each soldier carrying out specific functions when not in battle. Some repaired broken shields, others sat cooking their meals of cereal grain, and others repaired the wall or maintained the ditch, while the vigilia patrolled twenty-four hours a day in three-hour shifts. Today, however, most of the legionnaires were busy ferrying the dead back from the battlefield. The dead were deposited in front of the infirmary, where the doctors and aides undressed the men and placed everything that could be reused in separate piles. The dead were then carried away to a nearby clearing where they were buried and sent to the afterlife by the camp priests. Despite the gruesome tasks carried out by the legionnaires within the camp, something far more serious was taking place within the principia.

Caesar stood front of a table, a map of Gaul rolled out on top of it. On the other side of the table stood the two commanders of the two Legions, their helmets stuck under their arms. The first was a tall bald man in his mid-forties who had a scar that ran along the right side of his face from the eye to the bottom of his nose, courtesy of a disgruntled Gaul and his sword. His small narrow eyes were fixed on Caesar, his large ears ready to catch the faintest of sounds. The second man was slightly shorter, with a slight but visible paunch and a tuft of dark hair that was stuck to his head from sweat.

"Good evening, men," Caesar began. "Please take a seat."

The two men were motioned to folding chairs that sat on a large rug on one side of the tent. Caesar, however, remained standing and stared each man in the eyes.

The first man began. "I have come to report our complete control over the enemy, sir."

The second man added, "After the battle, the cavalry ran down the fleeing and slaughtered a good many of them. We estimate the number of dead to be around ten thousand."

"Half of their available fighting forces," said Caesar, obviously discontent. "I gave orders to have no mercy with the enemy."

Neither man dared respond for a second. Then, the bald man began. "Sir, the good news is our men suffered minor casualties. We only suffered seven hundred dead and that same number of wounded."

"A quarter of my legion has been traded for just half of the enemy's forces," Caesar asked, "Do you realize that a large portion of my army is now either dead or ineffective?"

The second man, Lucius, commander of the Seventh Legion, watched as Caesar went to fill his goblet with wine.

"Our men accounted for themselves well," said the second man, running his fingers through his damp hair. "We sent, what, seven or eight of their men to their death for every one of ours?"

Caesar returned.

"Yes, but that is only a *good* ratio. I want a *great* ratio—no, scratch that, I want a *phenomenal* ratio. I want twenty of theirs killed for every one of ours, not seven. These tribesmen must be annihilated. They are like a disease that spreads if not crushed in time. If we but slay them a couple at a time they will return to their villages and re-supply their diminishing forces with others. Men, if you just pick the leaves from a tree, what happens to that tree?" he asked as he took a swig from his goblet.

Neither man dared respond, baffled by the simplicity of the question.

"Nothing," Caesar continued, annoyed at their failure to answer. "Nothing happens. You must cut at the base. It is wider and tougher, but you only have to do it once."

Both men knew not to speak for another couple of seconds while Caesar regained his composure.

"We could burn down their villages," Lucius proposed.

Caesar shook his head. "All that would do is turn other villages against us. As you may know, our enemies come from different tribes, and within those tribes, not all of the populace is against us. I don't want to anger those Gallo-Romans who have welcomed us with open arms."

"Our armies could easily defeat them all," Claudius, the Tenth Legion's commander, boasted proudly.

"Claudius, how long have you served in the Roman army?"

Claudius looked taken aback by the question. "Since the day I turned eighteen, sir."

"Then you should know that the Roman army, despite its significant advantages, cannot take on all of the Gallic men who would unite against us if we were to begin a mass slaughter."

"Besides, not all of the enemies are Gauls. I estimate that a quarter of our enemies come from Britannia, and another fifth come from Germania," Lucius stated.

"I returned from a punitive expedition in Germania with the Eighth Legion not too long ago. I'm sure they will think twice before crossing the Rhine again for the time being," Caesar assured them as he took another drink of wine.

"Perhaps, but the Britons are still coming in from across the sea."

"Yesterday, we found countless number of dead British tribesmen," stated Lucius.

"We must find a way to end their involvement," Caesar said, stating the obvious.

"We could invade their island," said Claudius. "Leave two legions to guard the straight and two others to cross it."

"Two problems come to mind. One, there's no time. Winter will be upon us soon, and we have already begun winter encampment in the north, near Portius Itius. It would be better to stay and begin when we have plenty of time available and winter has passed. And two, I can't leave my rear open to attack. The conquest of Gaul is already underway. I can't divert half my army across the channel and call the Eighth and Ninth Legions over to protect our flanks. It would take too long for them to get the message, mobilize, and then deploy to this position, not to mention that would leave all of Gaul open for rebellion."

"I understand but ... the alternative is to do nothing to prevent the Britons from crossing over and strengthening the Gallic forces. If more British soldiers cross over, our men will have to fight additional enemies, and consequently more of our soldiers will die," Claudius said.

"Besides, now that I think of it, the Ninth Legion will be continuing north, and only the Eighth could be here to assure a safe landing zone upon our return. It would be insane to debark into enemy territory on both stretches of the trip," Caesar said matter-of-factly.

Lucius hesitated for a moment and then began to speak.

"Claudius is right, Caesar, the Britons will simply amass more men on Gallic coastlines and blend into villages. With that will come more frequent and larger attacks on our forts. Not to mention more danger to our supply train."

Caesar was about to respond when an aide pulled aside the curtain shielding the tent from the cold breeze that blew outside.

"Caesar, Gallic envoys have arrived and wish to speak to you," the young man said, his big blue eyes watching for the slightest nod of approval. He was dressed in the army's red skirt and wore a light brown shirt that covered his meager torso.

"Give me two minutes," said Caesar, and the man quickly disappeared back outside. Caesar turned to face the men, who now stood.

"So Claudius, you suggest I invade the island and leave a small garrison to cover our rear throughout the winter months. Lucius, what do you recommend—the same?"

Lucius thought for a moment and then spoke quietly. "What I recommend is that you send a reconnaissance force. They could cruise the shorelines and land where it seems safe. From there we immediately begin building our fortifications from which we can venture out a safe distance, gather what information you will, and return to Gaul before the nastiest of the winter has arrived." Caesar considered the plan from every angle but could find only one flaw.

"It is a good plan indeed, Lucius, but the army will be sailing the shorelines and therefore wasting time. Without mentioning the curiosity the appearance of Roman ships on their coastline will arouse. It would be better to have a sound strategy for where we are to land so that when we arrive, we can disembark immediately and set up our base of operations."

Lucius looked baffled. "You are suggesting a recon force for ...," he paused briefly, "the main recon force. Did I get that right?"

Caesar grinned. "To the dot."

Claudius sighed; things were never easy in the army.

"Do we have the time?"

Caesar began to reply but was interrupted by the aide again.

"Sir, the guests await your permission to enter."

Caesar looked at the man and stared so deeply into his eyes the young man could not help but avert his gaze. He then took a step toward the aide, who now stared at the rugs on the floor.

"Tell them ..." he said, lifting the man's chin to look into his eyes, "that I am busy planning out my next step of this conquest. Tell them ..."

Suddenly he stopped. He had seen a movement behind the young aide, and he quickly peered around the corner, spotting two men dressed in loose-fitting linen clothing that was apparently freshly dyed. The two men were morbid-looking. Caesar regarded the first man; he was tall and skinny as a pole, and his deep blue eyes gazed around his immediate surroundings.

The second was the same height but large, like a bear. He had hairy arms, and his fingers reached his knees; his nostrils were abnormally large, his eyes as black as night, and his mostly bald head was scarred and covered in sparse blond tufts of hair. Caesar recognized what he was seeing immediately. The Gallic ritual of washing their hair in limewater stiffened it, but Gallic turncoats had told him that this practice was a double-edged sword. It was harmless in moderation, but it would lead to hair loss and scarring if done too often. This man, Caesar thought, had definitely taken it to the extreme. He let go of the young man's chin and told the aide to let the Gauls in once the generals had departed, and then sent the aide on his way. Caesar turned around and approached his senior commanders as the young man quietly left the tent.

"To answer your question Claudius, yes, we do have the time. *But* we must not let up, for we have little time to spare before it *will* be too late. Send a messenger to Portius Itius right away and tell the officer in charge that he has orders to begin assembling a fleet capable of carrying two legions. Then, I want you to do whatever is necessary to bring your legions to full readiness, fully manned and fully armed. I, meanwhile, will reposition navies from all the nearest nautical positions to hasten the crossing. I have decided that I will bring two legions wherever we go in Britannia, Claudius, as you mentioned. If we succeed, I get the credit; if we fail, you do," Caesar joked as he tapped Claudius on the shoulder, his fist hitting solid armor.

Claudius smiled back. "Yes, sir."

"As for you, Lucius, I want to know anything and everything about Britannia. I want to know how the tribes are set up throughout the island, who the major tribes are, and the names of anyone of importance within them. No detail is too trivial.

"Any questions?" Caesar asked.

Neither man voiced any.

"Dismissed," Caesar said as he set his goblet down and returned the men's salutes.

Both generals spun on their heels and quickly walked out of the tent into the strong wind. The two Gauls, upon seeing the generals walk out, entered the tent. Although in charge, Caesar felt vulnerable in their presence. He would fight anyone fearlessly, but these men looked as if they could tear off his limbs with their bare hands as easily as picking grapes off a vine.

"General Caesar," said Scarhead, "we have come to negotiate peace terms."

Caesar wasn't taken aback as much by the flawless Latin as he was by the peace proposal. The Gauls rarely talked about peace, preferring to die gloriously on the field of battle, fighting to the last man beside their friends or running to fight another day.

The Roman looked at the man and said, "Well, this comes at an opportune time. What has spurred this desire to surrender?"

Caesar knew he couldn't push the Gallic envoys too hard out of fear they would cancel their negotiations and take up arms against him again.

"We of the Morini tribes were ignorant of your ways. We had no idea as to your plans ..."

Caesar curtly cut the man off.

"Do you realize that over a thousand of my men are either dead or dying because of this ignorance of yours?"

The man's face lifted. "One thousand? We had estimated half that."

Caesar's eyes tried to penetrate through to the man's soul, but the Gaul stood strangely still, knowing he was in no danger from the Roman who stood nearly a foot shorter than he.

"Have you come to tell me your estimates or to negotiate?" Caesar said curtly, all the while keeping an eye on the other man, who had moved to his side and was looking at the food spread out on the low table.

"What are your estimations of our dead? Forget, for the moment, the wounded that will certainly die from their wounds," said the second man as he sat on a chair and began to eat some grapes from the tray on the table, making himself at home, to Caesar's great dislike.

Caesar would have killed the man for his disrespect, but he told himself that their surrender was more important in the long run.

"We had them at five thousand ..." Caesar bluffed, throwing a murderous stare in his direction.

The man thumbed toward the ceiling without averting his gaze from the food tray.

"These are good. I am beginning to appreciate your Roman ways. What do you call them?" the man asked.

Caesar ignored him and stated another number. "Ten thousand."

The man again motioned higher. *Now you're bluffing*, Caesar thought.

"Fifteen thousand," Caesar said, pretending to go along with the man's bluff.

Immediately the man stood up and approached Caesar, "Ten thousand three hundred. You know not what you speak.

24

You should consider our proposal to surrender a great step in our relations."

The bald man stepped next to his colleague and began to scratch his head. "Caesar, we have come to surrender, and you refuse us ..."

"I have not refused anything," Caesar replied.

"As I said earlier, we were ignorant of the great ways of Rome, and now we gladly turn over all of Belgica to you with our sincere surrender."

The barbarian paused for a moment. Caesar would have accepted immediately, but he did not want to convey desperation.

"Now that we are tutored in your ways, we regret having taken up arms against you lightly."

"Lightly?" Caesar snickered.

"If we had wanted, we could have easily amassed men from all over Gaul and attacked you with the largest army ever to see the fields," the grape-eater said, gesturing vaguely behind him with a sway of his arm.

"Impossible!" said Caesar. "This state has so many tribes it would take an unimaginable leader to be able to unify them all long enough to wage even one battle, let alone an entire war."

"Impossible, you say ... or is it?" the bald man interjected.

"Listen, enough with the lecture. I will accept your surrender under two conditions," Caesar said, thinking the talks had gone on long enough.

"We will listen to your slightest demands," the bald man said, taking another step forward.

"First condition is the return of one thousand prisoners. Second is your word that you will never take up arms against us again."

"One thousand! One fifth of a Legion?"

"I see you are indeed *very* well acquainted with our ways," Caesar said, looking at his nails, vividly imagining the envoy's face turning to disgust, the eyes bulging, the nostrils flaring, the lips tightening.

"I will try, but I can promise little. My prisoners will be released upon my return, but the others will be tougher. As for the second, if we wished to take up arms against you, Caesar, we would not be standing here humiliated, asking to surrender."

"You don't seem humiliated. Besides, I will ensure your suzerainty by demanding one thousand of your swords be handed in and broken, a small act to make obvious your submission."

The man winced at the Roman face that looked back up at him. He wanted to crush him, to pull his hidden dagger and plunge it into the Roman heart that beat inches away from his. But he kept his cool.

"I can't do that. We need them for defense. We need them to hunt."

"Defense? Just a minute ago you claimed the men of Gaul would want to fight only us, so with this surrender, you no longer need to defend yourselves from us. As for the hunting, I am unfamiliar with the practice of hunting deer, boar, and presumably bear with swords. Do you not use the bow and arrow? Or the spear?" Caesar asked, feigning surprise.

Caesar watched the second man approach, strangely calm, or perhaps it was the ogre who was strangely aggravated. Caesar took slight pleasure at seeing the bear of a man turn red, rage mounting inside him.

"So, have we reached an agreement?" the Roman asked, beginning to tire of the conversation.

The older man grabbed the raging man by the arm and, in his native tongue, told him to wait outside.

The human beast turned around slowly and stomped out of the tent like an angry child.

Cesar could tell the man was easily provoked. *Typical Gaul,* he thought.

"I cannot offer up the swords; they are our only means of defense. We are not highly skilled with the bow."

"In war, victors can place any conditions they wish upon the vanquished. Take it or leave it, but you must decide quickly. It is time for me to make a round of my camp."

Caesar watched as the man pondered and debated what to do. Finally, he agreed.

"Are all Romans as difficult to negotiate with as you?" the barbarian said bitterly.

"No, I'm of my own special breed." Caesar laughed, unlike his Gallic counterpart.

"I wish you a good day," the man lied.

"Same to you," Caesar lied back.

Caesar watched as the man exited through the dangling curtain and presumably met with his colleague outside. Caesar then approached the table where food and wine waited and refilled his goblet. *It has been a stressful week,* he thought, *but once again I've come out on top.*

Once the envoy stepped out of the tent and into the chilling wind, he stopped to get his bearings. His face was whipped by a gust, and a slight numbness crept in. *It's cold early this year,* he realized. *Surely the damned Romans' fault,* he laughed to himself. He took a look around him, but his friend was nowhere to be seen.

The Gaul traveled down the road that led to the front gate through which they had entered, looking between the rows of tents on each side. *Where has he gone?* He thought to himself. *He definitely can't be easily missed.* He craned his neck and peered over the Roman soldiers who crowded the streets. He decided he would go back to the tent to see if perhaps he had missed him. Turning around, he found himself face to face with his friend.

"Calidro, where did you go?" asked the tall man. "I've been looking for you."

"I took a stroll, looked at the men, thought of how I would like each of them to be sacrificed to our gods in revenge for the terrible things they have done to us. I hate them, Androvates, really I do," replied Calidro slowly.

"Same here but speak softly for Roman ears encircle us," Androvates said, pulling his friend gently toward the gate, "Out there, only the trees will hear us."

They hurried and soon passed over the wooden drawbridge that spanned the ditch. When they entered the forest and were out of earshot of the two guards at the gate and the small patrol that circled the camp, they stopped and hid in a small tuft of bushes. Androvates peered through the bushes and watched as the Roman patrol passed by thirty feet away.

"So have we officially surrendered?" asked Calidro.

"I tried to act as civilized as I could and, in the end, he accepted."

"Good."

"Yes, but he suspects us and is putting every term to his advantage," said Androvates, gazing through the scarce leaves.

"The breaking of the swords is a sacrilege!" said Calidro, his voice rising in anger.

"Keep it down! Stay quiet for five minutes and listen if anyone is following us, and then we'll go."

They waited and were pleased to realize they were not being tailed. Discreetly crawling a short distance, they then got up and began to walk at a fast pace back to their village.

"We must find a way to stash weapons aside," said Androvates.

"Couldn't we simply take the weapons of the fallen?"

"We'd be seen—it's too risky."

"Not at night. It will be a half moon tomorrow, bright enough to see but dark enough to be easily concealed."

"By tomorrow, they might have cleaned up the battlefield."

"Then we go tonight. We go get the weapons and turn those in instead of ours, which we will hide for the time being. When the right time comes, we will be ready to fight a battle they don't expect."

"You don't think the Romans would notice that the thousand swords simply vanished overnight?"

"Out of ten thousand? Hardly! Besides, it is our only chance. It would be nice if it would rain. The swords would be then be presumed lost to the muddy ground."

Androvates stopped immediately; he saw a glimmer of hope in the plan. If it did rain, the plan just might work. He glanced at the gray sky. There was definitely a chance. He smiled and looked at Calidro.

"My friend, with a little help from the gods, we might just be able to make this thing work." And with that, both men hurried to their village without another word.

III

"By Jupiter, I can't believe these Gauls don't know anything about the Britons!" scoffed a voice from atop a horse in front of Marcus.

Without lifting his eyes from the ground, Marcus recognized the voice as belonging to his cohort's centurion, Severus Atticus. The man had obviously served in the army for a long time; his no-nonsense attitude was evident in his mannerisms. He carried a large, eight-sided oblong shield, as opposed to the infantry's semi-circular shield, and a long spear. Hanging from his right side was a spatha, a cavalry sword, distinguished by its significantly longer length, as opposed to the short stabbing swords of the infantry.

Severus' face sported no distinct facial features. He was without any battle scars or other characteristics that set him apart. His frame was normal-sized, his eyes blue, his hair short and brown, but his mere presence would reassure the most wavering man. He was followed by his century of eighty men. Their task, along with nine other centuries, had been to carry out Caesar's order and obtain information on the Britons. Unfortunately, the villagers had been of very little help.

"I have never seen a group of people who speak less than the Gauls. A rock would have been of greater help than they!" Marcus laughed.

"Don't they know at least how big the island is?" Severus asked, thinking aloud.

A voice from behind Marcus spoke. "Either they are entirely ignorant, or they are withholding the information from us."

"I don't think so. I think they are just downright ignorant," said another.

Marcus looked around; temporarily lifting his eyes from the dirt road they were marching on. All around him stood the village of Samarobriva. The village encircled a hill on which stood the market, the town square, and the tribal chief's residence. The Roman detachment had amassed the town's population in the square and offered money to anyone who could be of service while others marched throughout the narrow streets asking all of the Gauls the same questions to no avail. Now, nine hours after having started, the Roman detachment was descending the southern slope, returning to camp.

Marcus felt tired; the battle exhaustion still lingered, and the patrol was not helping. Before he knew it, they had exited the village gates and entered the forest. The woods were dark, cold, and ominous—the perfect place for an ambush, the men quickly realized. Night was falling, although the stars refused to reveal themselves through the heavy cloud cover above. The darkness caused anxiety among the men, and none dared fall behind. Without speaking, the men traveled down the path, their eyes scanning their immediate surroundings, their ears straining to hear the faintest of whispers or the crack of a twig. Each man dreaded the forests, but none spoke of it.

After what seemed an eternity, the uneventful passage came to an end, and they emerged on the other side, the sight of the fort as welcome as a blanket in winter. They passed over the wide drawbridge, saluting the guards on each side. Finally, they found themselves at the principia and waited to be admitted inside.

Severus quickly spoke to the aide, and the latter curtly departed to tell Caesar of their arrival. Severus was ushered inside while the others were released from their duties. Each man gratefully accepted their dismissal and went off toward their tents to fix themselves dinner. Severus, meanwhile, had entered the tent, and he held his helmet, its red crest running transversally, and stood at attention while waiting for Caesar to look up from his maps.

"Ah, Severus. What news do you have for me?" Caesar said, moving around the table and motioning him to a chair.

"I am afraid I have acquired practically no information," Severus said, obviously disappointed.

Caesar groaned softly. "I was afraid it would not turn out the way I planned. Communications between the Britons and the Gauls is limited to the traders and further limited to the coastline."

"So what are we to do? We are no better off now than we were this morning," Severus stated matter-of-factly.

"I was hoping the soldiers could extract the information without me having to send a recon force to Britannia, but it seems I have no choice."

Severus looked at him, anticipating what Caesar was about to say. He expected that Caesar would ask him to lead the reconnaissance force to Britain, and he didn't feel like going to Britain at all. He winced as Caesar continued.

"I am going to send someone I can trust with the same mission as this morning."

Severus awaited the order to deploy to Britannia, but it never came. He guessed that he would not be sent because he was not of high enough ranking, but he still felt that fear.

"Caius Volusenus—do you know him?"

Severus took a deep breath as he felt a load rise from his shoulders.

"No, sir."

"I need you to go find him and tell him he is to report here immediately."

"Where can I find this man, sir?"

"He is one of my officers."

"Here, sir?"

"Correct. He should be out completing a tour of the camp."

"Yes, sir."

Severus saluted, turned on his heels, and quickly walked out of the tent.

Less than fifteen minutes later, under the pouring rain, Caius Volusenus entered the tent, drenched. He had large coffee-brown eyes, a crooked nose, and large square shoulders. His face looked as if it had been chiseled from stone. He walked with a visible air of self-assurance, a no-nonsense attitude, and seemed as sturdy as a tree. He stood at attention, his large chest sticking out, oblivious to the rainwater tickling his ears and back. Caesar came up to him and patted his long-time friend on the back.

"How's the weather?" he asked with a large grin and invited him to stand at ease.

"Beautiful, not a cloud in the sky," he replied, tit-for-tat.

"My friend, I have some news for you."

Volusenus smiled and looked down at the floor.

"What are you planning now?" he said.

"Frankly, I am planning a reconnaissance force to Britannia."

"And, I'm presuming you need me to lead it?" the man asked, a jovial expression spreading across his face.

"I'm afraid not. I need you to carry out a mission for me of equal importance, though."

Volusenus was visibly disappointed.

"So, what's the role?"

"I need you to go and scout the British coastline. Acquire information vital to my invasion. I need to know how big the island is and who the main tribal chiefs are."

"So, how big a detachment of men will escort me?"

"None. I would prefer for you to go alone."

"What? Are you out of your mind?"

"It'll be less alarming to the Britons if a single envoy goes instead of a whole detachment."

"These men are our enemies. They'll spear me before I make ten yards up their beach." Volusenus cut him off curtly.

"No, I am planning on sending a Gallic chief with you to help."

"One enemy to accompany me on a visit with another?" he asked, stunned.

"His name is Commius. He's a Gallo-Roman, so you have nothing to fear."

"Many Gauls have been friendly, and then they stab you in the back when you're busy elsewhere."

Caesar shook his head.

"After I defeated the Atrebates tribe, I personally placed Commius in charge. He is courageous, loyal, and has great capacity. He will help bring an example to the Britons. Together, you will impress upon the natives the advisability of trusting us."

"You trust this man with my life?"

"Fully," Caesar answered with a nod.

"I am in no position to refuse the order, but I sincerely hope you are not misguided."

"You will be back before you know it."

"Where am I to obtain a vessel for the crossing?"

Caesar nodded and took out a dyptichon, two small wooden tablets filled with wax, held together by three leather laces.

"Once you reach Portius Itius," he said, writing in the notebook, "you will proceed to the principia. There you will meet with the commander in charge; tell him he is to provide a ship for you. Tell him also that you are to be aided in any way that will assist in your mission and that you shall have command of the ship's destination to any location you please."

Volusenus nodded, and he waited until Caesar had finished writing in the wax. Caesar quickly finished, closed the notebook, and handed it to Volusenus. Volusenus, towering over Caesar, took the tablet from his friend's hands and then saluted him. He began to walk toward the curtain when Caesar called to him.

"Oh, and Caius, tell them I will be arriving soon myself."

Volusenus nodded in approval and was out of the tent before Caesar could blink.

IV

It had been raining for an hour, Ambiorix estimated. The Gallic chief scanned the muddy field beyond the thin set of bushes behind which he hid. There was little light, but he was used to it. He couldn't remember the number of times he and some followers had gone and attacked neighboring villages on moonless nights prior to the Romans invading his lands.

Ambiorix had a large moustache that joined his beard and shielded his mouth from view. He also had bushy eyebrows that helped prevent the rain from running into his cold, gray eyes. Behind him, over two hundred men knelt in the muddy ground, waiting for the order to move. They were a fearsome bunch; the running water accentuating their muscles, their faces as hard as the stone they carved, and their focus unbendable. They each remained immobile, despite the strong winds and heavy rain.

Each man had come without a weapon, not expecting to encounter any enemy soldiers on the ghostly plains. Ambiorix stood momentarily, his eyes straining through the darkness, looking for a Roman sentry. But he saw none. Discreetly, another man crawled up beside him.

"See anything?" the man said.

Ambiorix immediately recognized his son Algodorix.

"No, the Romans are not men enough to stay out in weather like this," Ambiorix whispered back.

"Then let us go and exact our revenge."

"I agree with you, my son."

Ambiorix stood and, waving for the others to follow, began a crouched run across the open. The men behind him spread out a short distance. As they found Gallic swords, they picked them up and placed them into large hide bags they carried. The Roman swords were overlooked in favor of their heavier swords. Algodorix, whose small physique naturally concealed him, stacked up swords rather quickly considering the darkness and rain. He had four swords in his sack and was straining to put a fifth one in when his father came up.

"Nice pile you've got yourself."

Algodorix spun around at the sound of his father's voice and stole a glance at his father's full bag.

"Not bad yourself," he grinned. "I've got everything I can handle, plus one."

Ambiorix smiled and looked back at his men scattered across the field.

"We will need to return again; we only have about eight hundred swords," Ambiorix said to his son as he watched his men jogging in his direction, their feet occasionally sinking in the ankle-deep mud.

Ambiorix shivered and crouched down lower, trying to retain body heat. He looked up at the sky as lightning cracked a short distance away, illuminating the field for a fraction of a second. He got up and, closely followed by his son, began to head back toward his village. Ambiorix performed cursory stops, checking on his men every twenty feet or so. As he reached the edge of the forest, he stopped and waited until the two hundred men had caught up with him. The first part of the mission now complete, he scanned the field one last time. The men disappeared into the comforting darkness of the forest, leaving only their muddy footprints as evidence of their passage.

V

Commius, a small, rotund man, stood a mere five feet six inches but had the build of a bear. His face sported a long mustache and dirty beard, and his dirty brown hair was not lime-washed. He rode his horse at the side of Volusenus, his gaze wandering freely across the path.

Commius carried a large oval shield covered in rawhide, a long sword, and a spear, and a distinctively elongated helmet topped his head. Volusenus kept a close eye on his company, but as far as he could tell, the man was true to Caesar's words.

The Roman officer placed his attention back on the path before him. He had been riding for a day and a half, closing the gap between Castra Constantia and Portius Itius. The sun had set roughly thirty minutes ago, and the pair rode silently, each man lost in his own thoughts. The moon partially illuminated their path, and both men held torches, but the pair still felt uneasy. Volusenus knew that Caesar would have understood had he halted until sunrise, but Volusenus was too eager to arrive to do so. He knew the fort was nearby, and he didn't feel like wasting hours over what could be accomplished tonight in minutes.

Volusenus estimated the port fort to be somewhere up ahead. He could hear the indistinct talking and general ruckus that accompanied an army. As he approached the fort, its form winding in and out of sight through the trees and snaking path; he felt a great sigh of relief. The forest he had marched through was known for its vicious attacks on the Roman sentries and occasionally on passing detachments, but thankfully the two men had avoided detection.

As they emerged from the forest, the Roman watch immediately spotted them, and the watch guard officer was summoned. Before the men had made it three steps into the camp, they were called for. A tall, skinny man came jogging after them from a side street.

"Good evening, men," the man spoke, stopping beside them.

Volusenus stepped down from his horse and repositioned his belt and sword.

"I am here with direct orders from Caesar to travel to Britannia, along with my assistant. I need to speak to whoever is in charge here," Volusenus said, getting right down to the point.

The man looked dazed; he had expected a little small talk but should have known better from a man with Volusenus' looks. Volusenus looked expectantly at the young man.

"This way. Our camp Prefect is Cyriacus Balanus," he said, motioning for the two men to follow him in the direction of the principia.

Before long, they reached the principia and stood outside the curtained door leading into the tent. An older man with dark skin and a slight hunch came out of nowhere and stared at Volusenus and the Gaul questioningly. Volusenus noticed the man's beady eyes were staring intently at Commius.

"We are here to see Commander Cyriacus Balanus," Volusenus said, and the small man's eyes quickly shifted to look at the tall Roman directly in front of him.

The man didn't respond but turned slowly around and walked into the tent, motioning for the two men to enter as well. The tent was well lit with candles, and a distinctive smell of wine lingered in the air. Volusenus gagged at the stench, and his eyes watered.

The inside was arranged in a similar fashion to the principia at Castra Constantia, and he immediately saw Cyriacus, laying on a bench, one hand lowering the grapes to his mouth, the other lifting the wine cup to it.

Cyriacus was a large man composed almost entirely of fat. He had large, bloodshot eyes and didn't seem to carry a worry in the world. Volusenus immediately recognized the type, the kind that made an entire career of avoiding front-line combat, the kind that gained rank by politics rather than deeds.

At first, the man did not take notice of the guests, but upon setting eyes on them, he rose to his feet. The fat man tried to straighten his uniform as he approached them, his large body swaying from the excessive alcohol flowing through his veins. His breath smelled of wine, and his speech was slurred from countless drinks.

The man broke into a sweat from the light exercise. Upon reaching the two men, he pointed his pig-like nose menacingly at Volusenus. "What brings you here at this time of night?" he asked, lacking all formal manners.

Volusenus gazed at the man, disgusted by the lack of self-respect the drunken officer displayed. He began to reply when the intoxicated man rudely interrupted him.

"What is this primitive, tasteless, uncultured *barbarian* doing in my tent?" he asked, pointing a menacing finger at the Gaul.

Commius' face changed from a smile to total hatred as the tipsy Roman swayed and smirked provocatively. Volusenus wasted no time in niceties.

"You're a disgraceful embarrassment to the Roman Empire. Our original purpose was to employ one of your vessels to transport us to Britannia, but by the authority given us by Caesar, we will now commandeer one of your vessels. I can only hope that you try to stop us so that I have just cause to use my gladius to remove the malignancy that you have become. Better yet, I should allow Commius to demonstrate his war-fighting skills on you. He is not only a true warrior but has honor and stature that you will never achieve," Volusenus said coldly.

The officer's swollen eyelids drooped partly over his eyes as they rolled between the Gaul and the Roman officer. Cyriacus tried to process what Volusenus had just said, but the alcohol interfered with the man's ability to think properly, and, as a result, he merely stood there hiccupping stupidly.

"Going off to sea, are we?" the man said with a nervous smile, suddenly trying to appease the infuriated officer.

"Well, seeing that our engineers haven't bridged that stretch of water yet."

"So ... You will need a ship," he replied, his voice trembling as he searched for a scroll with the names of the ships currently harbored in his port.

"I have the written order from Caesar himself. And besides, I do not even need to ask for your permission—this is merely an act of politeness," Volusenus said, handing over the dyptichon.

Cyriacus undid the ties of the dyptichon without dropping his eyes from Volusenus. The pair watched as the large man opened the tablets with his short, stubby fingers and began to read. He shook his head in disbelief and then tied the dyptichon closed and handed it back to Volusenus. He had stopped swaying, as if the weight of the order were balancing him out.

"I can't deny you rite of passage," he said, his blurry eyes focusing on the tall Roman in front of him.

"What ship will we be provided?"

"The *Fidelis*, a trireme most suited to face the channel waters," Cyriacus said, having run his stubby index finger down the list of ships.

"Good. I want to set sail right away," Volusenus said, turning around to walk out of the tent.

The intoxicated man moved forward, slightly losing his balance. Volusenus knew he wouldn't make it five yards before being spotted as a drunk. He looked at Commius, who was staring disgustedly at the swaying Roman. Volusenus laughed discreetly to himself. Romans were supposed to be extremely civilized, and yet the officer commanding the port could barely command himself.

Suddenly, Cyriacus stopped and motioned for Volusenus to approach. Cyriacus walked over to a cabinet at the back of the room and pulled out a dyptichon from one of the drawers. He began to scribble a message. When finished, he handed it to Volusenus.

Volusenus starred quizzically at the man as he took the dyptichon from his hand.

"I am obviously unfit to be seen in such a state. I must beg you to go off on your own to find the ship. In the tablets I have written my orders that you are to be granted full command and aided in any way."

"Thank you, but I'm sure Caesar's orders will be more than sufficient."

Cyriacus nodded slowly and curled his lower lip before saluting Volusenus.

Volusenus returned the salute and watched disgustingly as sweat ran down the man's forehead.

The two newcomers turned to exit the tent, and Volusenus waited for Commius to be outside before saying one final thing to Cyriacus over his shoulder.

"Do as you wish, but I would advise you to clean up your act. Caesar will be arriving shortly, and I would hate to see you killed because of your intoxication."

Then he exited the tent, and the two men climbed atop their horses. They suddenly heard a faint thump as the man finally fell unconscious. Commius searched for the aide and saw him sitting on a small chair by a brazier, warming his hands from the chilling wind, oblivious to his commander's unconsciousness.

"A weird man, if you do not mind my saying," Commius said, shaking his head slowly.

Volusenus laughed at the man's comment. It was maybe the third time Volusenus had heard the Gaul speak.

"Indeed he is."

"You are not a real man unless you can get drunk and go fight a battle afterwards. He couldn't have even brought his sword to bear, much less fight for his life."

Volusenus looked at the man.

"Oh," Volusenus laughed, "so that's your secret ... You fellows get drunk before a battle."

Commius looked at him, smiled, and shrugged, hesitant to reveal a generations-old secret, although his grin gave it away.

VI

The *Fidelis* was a wonderful ship, thirty-seven meters long, with a short draught that allowed for superb navigation in shallow coastal waters. Volusenus had only ridden in a boat once before. That time he had gone fishing with his father the day before he enlisted. Now, as he cut through the waves at a steady four knots, he remembered that time.

Commius, who was gazing at the stars above, listened to the paddles cut through the water. Riding a mere seven feet above the waves, he felt the seawater caress his face as the ship slammed through the large waves. They had set course at one o'clock in the morning, and the crew had been rowing for five hours straight, roughly half the time it would take to get to Britannia. Soon, early after daybreak, he would disembark on British soil.

The trireme carried two sails, one large and one smaller, to propel itself. However, most of its power came from the one hundred and seventy rowers who paddled half at a time, replacing each other on the hour. Volusenus hadn't felt so alone, so unworried and so peaceful, in a long time. As he gazed out across the portside railing, he wondered how men could do the things they did in a time of war. He remembered all of his friends who had died in combat, all those blank faces as their lives ebbed away from them.

"How are you men doing?" a voice said from behind Volusenus, pulling him back from his disturbing visions.

Volusenus slowly turned around and observed a large, heavily muscled man who wore a tattered shirt made of wool and battered-looking pants. Volusenus smiled, recognizing the ship's captain.

"Good evening Crassius," Volusenus said as he turned around and leaned his back against the railing.

"Good morning," corrected the blue-eyed man. "It's nearly six."

"My apologies," Volusenus yawned.

"My goodness, you need some rest. It will be tough to talk with the Britons while half asleep."

"I know. I've tried but I can't."

Crassius nodded and grabbed him on the shoulder. He said, "Do you realize the danger that awaits you over there?"

"I do," said Volusenus, shocked to wakefulness by a large sea spray from the bow.

"And you came with no soldiers to help fend off any attacks?"

"Caesar's very order."

The man shook his head.

"I will gladly provide some of my men if you need them. I do not plan on making my return trip without you."

"I appreciate your offer, but orders are orders."

"Not to worry, this is just between you and me."

Volusenus smiled and patted the man on the arm. "I appreciate it but I must refuse."

"As you wish. I won't insist any further."

And with that, Crassius left for the stern, where two men commanded the rudder oars, their eyelids fluttering as they drifted in and out of sleep.

Meanwhile, Volusenus gazed out toward the sea directly in front of him; he knew Britain was somewhere in the distance, but in this darkness he couldn't see her shores yet. There he'd either find his death or his promotion; at this time, he knew not which, but he'd discover that soon enough.

Evidently, the messenger had made it to Portius Itius safely, Caesar thought.

Over sixty ships floated in the harbor, and its surrounding waters awaiting their human cargo. Caesar watched from atop his horse as he trotted into the fortified port, his eyes riveted on the ships. They were truly beautiful, he thought, the mixture of mastodon ships capable of carrying over one hundred and fifty men mixed with light ships, swift as the wind, provided a strong sample of Roman naval capabilities.

All around him, soldiers stopped in their tracks and saluted him as he passed, but his mind was focused on the task ahead. The soldiers, although ignored, maintained their position of respect until the general had passed, at which point they relaxed and resumed their activities. Caesar finally arrived at the principia, where he dismounted and handed the reins to one of the guards. He entered the tent without warning, his nose and eyes straining to find anything beyond the norm.

Cyriacus had followed Volusenus' advice and had refrained from drinking wine the previous day; the room was clear of stench, and he was sober.

"Good day, Caesar," said Cyriacus, saluting.

Now that his mind was not shrouded by drink, he was visibly excited by the task at hand.

"How was your trip here?" Cyriacus asked.

"Good, thank you," Caesar said, removing his gloves and taking a cursory glance around the tent. "I trust Volusenus got the ship he was entitled to without any complications."

"Indeed, sir. He was provided with the *Fidelis*. A beautiful ship, if I may add."

Caesar simply nodded.

"My messenger made it here as well?" Caesar stated more than asked.

"Yes sir, just a few days ago. As you may have noticed, the majority of the fleet has indeed made it here already. We are just waiting for the remainder of the fleet to arrive from northern Spain and from up around the Rhine and the Northern provinces."

Caesar nodded again. He felt like asking about Volusenus but knew the officer would know no more than Caesar. He had promised his friend that he would be safe, but now he felt some anxiety as to his actual safety.

"How long has Volusenus been gone?" he asked pointlessly, already knowing the answer.

"Two days today."

Caesar was lost in his thoughts when a man suddenly charged into the tent. It was one of Cyriacus' assistants.

"Sir, fifteen vessels have just arrived from the southern provinces: eleven transports along with four men-of-war."

"Currently, what is the total number of ships at our disposal?" Caesar asked.

"Seventy-eight total, sir. Sixty-nine transports and nine men-o'-wars," the aide answered in with a slight drawl.

"Splendid," Caesar answered before thanking the assistant and dismissing him. Caesar placed his helmet on his head and exited the tent mere seconds after the aide. The general regained his horse, mounted, and began to trot down the small hill toward the port.

The vessels were dropping anchor when Caesar arrived at the dock. He led his horse around the small port and examined the vessels and the crews.

The transports, consisting mostly of biremes, triremes and some quinqueremes, could transport anywhere between one hundred and two hundred men each. They lacked any form of tower or other tall structure from where an archer could fire unobstructed. The men-of-war, on the other hand, had a smaller cargo bay but were equipped with towers and equipment ranging from archers to catapults and ballistae.

Upon examining the vessels, he was well pleased by what he saw. Before he knew it, Caesar had reached the last vessel. He listened to the gulls singing overhead, felt the cool wind on his face, and suddenly realized that he was making a daring crossing. The people back in Rome would either praise him or hate him, but it was too late now; he was too far into the game.

VII

Volusenus had managed to fall asleep early that morning, lying down on the cold, damp deck of the vessel. *That was one of the worst nights I've had in a long time*, he thought to himself. Now, he stared through semi-bloodshot eyes at the coastline. They had been following the coast for four hours, and Volusenus was still not pleased by what he saw.

They were roughly five hundred feet away from shore, and the land was menacing, as if ready to reach out and devour him. A small wave tossed spray into his face, shaking him coldly out of his morbid thoughts.

The dark waters crept up to the rocky, white cliffs; the waves splashed up in a cloud of mist and fell slowly back to the sea. It seemed as if even the water was not welcome on Britain's shore. The waves tried to climb the abrupt face and fell back, unable to climb any higher, but still they tried. Wave after wave, the water smashed unrewardingly against the rock.

Volusenus stared back down at his drawing, his etches messy and grotesque. He knew his artistic skills were far from flawless. He replayed the morning's events in his mind. They had arrived several miles south of their current position and moved slowly north. By now, they had navigated roughly ten miles from where they had first started their survey. Volusenus looked up at the shoreline again and analyzed the landscape. The hills were lined with trees, shielding the interior lands from prying eyes.

Volusenus was reminded that his mission was far from over. He had only started his coastline survey, and what remained were the tribal leader encounters and the attempts to pacify and explain his presence to what he already knew were his enemies.

He watched as the coastline drifted past him, peaceful yet menacing. He longed to regain Gaul already.

Suddenly the coast took a sharp inward turn toward the mainland. As the *Fidelis* drifted past, a long stretch of beach was revealed, perfect for a massive disembarkation. He gazed around and noticed a large, flat—or so it seemed from his perspective— stretch of ground up on the cliff that stretched a short ways into the sea. It would have to be felled of trees, but it could work.

He couldn't believe his eyes at first; it was like divine intervention. *It must be a work of the gods, who sensed my wavering determination*, he thought. The beach shone like the Pharos of Alexandria, standing out against a dark backdrop of mysterious territory. It was extremely wide and rather deep, allowing for a large number of soldiers to disembark simultaneously. The beach rose gradually, the two far ends rising a little steeper than the main beach due to the adjacent cliffs, but still nothing the trained Legions couldn't tackle. At the back side, the beach gave way to the forest, the trees giving the impression of staring over the light sand as if looking-out for its smaller brother.

Volusenus quickly began to jot down his observations and drew an arrow at a spot on his map. He smiled to himself. Only he could decipher what he wrote; but still, it was better than nothing. As the ship drifted slowly past, he returned his gaze to the tree line. After discovering the beach, Volusenus felt his spirits lift and, with renewed assurance, the Roman resumed his coastal drawing.

VIII

He had been hunting for an hour now, Ludovic estimated. His family was hungry, and they depended on his superb hunting skills to bring home the week's meals. He crept through the bushes and large trees, gently placing his feet on the ground, purposely evading even the smallest twigs. The bald man peered through the dense undergrowth, his dark brown eyes looking for movement amid the immobile branches. There was little wind, and he could hear the birds singing clearly above him. Except for his head, the man was covered in hair, and despite his short size, he could hold his own in battle with a ferocious savagery that few could equal.

Ludovic approached a fallen tree and silently crouched behind it. Slowly, he raised his head and looked directly in front of him. He knew where he was; he had been through here a hundred times at least. Every couple of days, he ventured into the forest to hunt boar and deer. He never got lost. He knew the sea lay ahead, his village stood behind him, and to the right, roughly three hundred feet away, flowed a small creek. Ludovic knew his homeland flawlessly.

Not seeing anything worthwhile, he stood up and limbed the dead trunk, not the faintest of sounds resulting from his movement. He decided he would go to the sea and plot a new course from there. He approached the cliff quietly, his hands gripped around his long spear, the bow strung loosely over his shoulder.

Ludovic was covered in woad, the blue paint creating beautiful designs over his exposed chest and face. The blue man resembled the sea, deadly even at its calmest. He reached the last of the brush before the edge of the cliff. Ludovic stepped through the last of the bushes running alongside the top of the cliff and began to follow the small path that ran along the edge. Ludovic walked nearly three feet before the sound of the birds caught his attention. He looked unconcernedly toward the squawking seagulls that circled a ship a short distance away from shore. At first, the ship did not strike him as odd, but then it hit him. Floating on the sea, under sail, was a Roman vessel. He didn't know the type, but the mere fact that it was there; navigating his waters, was annoying enough.

Flashbacks of the two times he had served in Gaul fighting those arrogant Romans raced through his mind. The Romans, he had learned, didn't enjoy anything but adding new lands to the ones they already owned. He remembered the battles he had lost, the friends who had never returned from their voyage across the sea. In fact, Ludovic had yet to win a battle against the Romans. The Briton ached for revenge. Ludovic didn't hate Romans—no, he *loathed* them.

As Ludovic stood on the edge of the cliff, his eyes welded to the Roman ship, he felt overwhelmed by a plethora of feelings. He felt anger at these people who spread like the cold; he felt defenseless at the thought that they spied on his coast and that he could do nothing; and yet he also felt a little jealousy at the thought of all their lands and the little he had. He was not chief of his tribe, yet he felt as if the burden lay on his shoulders. He quickly dove to the ground and rolled behind a bush, his chest pressed to the cold, hard ground, his face protected by the massive beard and moustache that hid the lower half of his face.

Ludovic crawled slowly across the top of the cliff as the ship navigated the turbulent waters a little off shore. His hands twitching as he clutched his spear, he followed the vessel's every move. After following the ship and cursing at it for several long seconds, Ludovic felt he had to return to his village and warn his chief. The Briton quickly turned around, jumped to his feet, and began a sprint back toward his village. The path was arduous and twisted; throughout the trail were gnarled roots and bushes that slapped and caught his feet and baggy pants, yet despite the treacherous nature of the path, the man long-accustomed to this terrain never tripped or slipped a single time. As he ran, he leaped over a small ditch, his feet landing simultaneously on the opposite muddy bank. Ironically, a wild boar ran past him, but Ludovic merely shrugged off the encounter, and, without ever slowing his pace, he reached his village in a quarter of an hour.

Between the forest and his village was an open stretch of ground roughly half a mile long, which allowed the village an unobstructed view of the surrounding countryside. Behind the village, the terrain turned to grassland and sprouted a few trees. To Ludovic's right, roughly one mile away, was a large wheat field that provided much of the village's food.

After his fifteen-minute scramble, Ludovic reached the gates to his village and quickly passed through the doorway, which consisted of a wooden frame and two large doors on iron hinges. Without even slowing for the guards, he ran up the hill to the tribal chief's hut.

The village was like many others, with its circular shape, the hill in the center, the large plaza at the top with the market, and the houses and outer wall encompassing the whole. The village's outer wall was made of felled trees, the top extremely uneven and jagged. Ludovic arrived at the top in record time, his lungs barely on fire, his heartbeat only slightly above normal. The brute of a man was awesome and seemed almost unstoppable.

He entered the hut without warning, his voice cutting through the air like an arrow.

"They're sailing our coast!" Ludovic cried as he stopped at the base of his chief's chair.

The chief, Androvic, was fairly large and composed mostly of muscle. His wrinkled face sported no moustache or beard despite his abundant wealth. He sat on a large wooden chair atop a small dais, his shield and spear hanging proudly at his sides, his sword at his waist. Androvic had himself served in the auxiliary forces against the Romans on several occasions, and he, like Ludovic and the remainder of the village's population, hated the expansionists.

Ludovic then noticed that Androvic was talking to another man, who turned to face Ludovic as well. Androvic shifted his weight and looked past the man toward Ludovic.

"What? Who are *they?*" Androvic asked.

"The Romans, sir."

The man who had been talking to Androvic turned around to face his chief again.

Androvic remained calm for a second, letting the full weight of the comment sink in before unexpectedly beginning to rage at the Romans, realizing that if the Romans were examining his lands, they would be impossible to stop. He liked a fair fight, but the Legions? They were unstoppable both tactically and logistically. Suddenly Androvic stopped, staring at but not seeing the men in front of him.

"How many of them?" he asked.

"There is but one ship," Ludovic replied.

"One ship?" Androvic repeated, as if it would clarify his incomprehension.

"Yes, sir, I believe they are simply scouting our shores."

The chief grunted in approval.

"Did they seem to have any intention of landing?" he continued.

"It's hard to tell. They are surely dying to know what these lands hide!"

"Yes, but they fear what we may do to them if they do, in fact, land."

"I say we kill them all as they land," Ludovic said, caressing his spear.

"I agree. I have had enough of these people."

"If we kill their scouts when they come, they may think twice about invading our island," the third man said, inviting himself to the conversation.

"I doubt that. The Romans let little stand in their way when after new land," Androvic replied.

"But we will still kill them, won't we?" Ludovic asked in a child-like manner.

"Of course, but we know little about their intentions. First of all, we don't even know if they *are* going to land."

Suddenly it hit Ludovic—maybe the Romans wouldn't even land at all until the main invasion.

"We will go back out with some men, and if the Romans set just one toe on our soil, we will crush them," Androvic said, crushing a brittle, imaginary skull in the palm of his hand.

"How many do you think will land?" Ludovic asked inquisitively.

"I'm not sure, but we better be prepared for the worst, just in case."

Ludovic nodded as Androvic stood up. The hunter moved out of the way as his chief grabbed his spear and shield and began to walk toward the door. Ludovic followed Androvic, and they both set off in different directions to find volunteers willing to accompany them.

IX

"We must have gone at least thirty miles by now," Volusenus said with a tinge of anger as the unchanging cliffs failed to reveal a beach suitable for landing.

They had in fact sailed over twenty-five miles since they had first reached the coast of Britannia and were now on their return trip. They had departed from Portius Itius three days ago, and still they had found only three beaches suiting their needs. Their options were dangerously limited. The first beach they had found was flanked on both sides by towering cliffs, which could expose the Legions to murderous arrow-fire from above during the first stages of the landing. The second beach was large, the best beach of all, but the cliffs didn't allow any access to the top apart from scaling the jagged slope. To storm that beach would be a tactical nightmare and undoubtedly result in the needless massacre of Caesar's men. The third beach, at almost the farthest point they had traveled, was very similar to the first beach, with more towering cliffs.

Volusenus looked down at his crudely sketched map, the arrow pointing to the beaches he had discovered. Such a long coastline and yet he hadn't located anything promising apart from the two beaches almost thirty miles apart. Now on his return trip, Volusenus waited for the first beach to show itself again. According to his drawing it was still several miles further. But that was not the only problem he had to deal with; he still had not established contact with the local people during this entire voyage.

Volusenus noticed the weather had gotten significantly colder in the last twenty-four hours too. He stood wrapped in a blanket, his cold hands and head now the only limbs exposed to the merciless lashing of the wind and sea spray. Commius stood by him, less affected by the cold than his Roman friend. The Gaul's slow, clumsy actions led Volusenus to believe that he was exceedingly bored. The Gaul was looking at his dirty teeth in the reflection of his cruddy, sea-sprayed helmet when Volusenus spoke to him.

"It seems you may have come along for nothing, I'm afraid."

The large man looked left toward the covered man.

"Do not be sorry. It is not your fault the shoreline is so unfavorable."

Volusenus nodded as he turned to look back toward the coast. Over an hour passed, and soon the Roman vessel and its occupants had made it around most of the peninsula; the beach was just beginning to edge into view. With the end of his voyage in sight, Volusenus decided he had to attempt to make contact with the local people. It was about the last thing he wanted to do, but Rome depended on him, and he didn't plan on letting her down. He watched as the familiar cliffs moved past him slowly, this time in the opposite direction. He was looking uninterestedly toward the tree line when suddenly he saw movement. *People.* The first time he had seen any on this voyage. He did not know whether they were hostile or not, but he knew he had to give it a chance. Jogging quickly to the captain, he motioned to the beach and spoke, his eyes resting on the approaching beach.

"There ... Can you drop me off there?" he asked hurriedly.

The captain looked at him skeptically. "There? Did you see someone?"

"I believe I saw movement up on the ledge."

"On the ledge," Crassius repeated, looking up at the ledge three hundred feet away from him and fifty feet above the main deck.

"I'm positive; besides, it may be our only chance to establish contact."

"It may be dangerous," he said, visibly concerned for his newfound friend's safety.

"It's a risk I must take. I have little to bring back to Caesar otherwise."

"Is your pulse not enough?"

"Trust me my friend, I will be fine. Besides, I haven't been in imminent danger the entire voyage, and I'm afraid I might get soft if I don't see any action soon," Volusenus said with a laugh.

Crassius was in no position to argue, his ship was at Volusenus' command. He nodded and, turning to his helmsmen, cried out to maneuver for the beach. The oarsmen turned for the beach and dipped their oars regularly into the frigid waters below to ebb the forward momentum while the sail was slacked above them.

As the vessel approached, Volusenus began to make out smaller details on the beach. He noticed the bushes that lined the bases of the trees, which would provide effective concealment to anyone wishing to hide there. Volusenus also studied the peculiar shape of the beach. The beach was flat which would provide ample maneuvering ground for enemy cavalry, but the land around it was all uphill. The sides were particularly high, which could provide enemy archers with unparalleled fields of fire down the length of the beach. This was a good beach to land men on, but it would be a delicate operation. The Romans, to have any chance of success, would need the element of surprise. Men would need to disembark rapidly and be ready to fend off a counterattack while others continued to reinforce the landing party. If the enemy awaited them when they prepared to land, the landing would be in significant jeopardy. The landing party could easily be overwhelmed by larger numbers in an early stage of an amphibious landing.

Abandoning his thoughts for a minute, Volusenus returned to searching for any signs of life amidst the hostile shrubbery. What Volusenus, Commius, and the rest of the crew did not notice was the presence of twelve British warriors hidden behind the bushes, who awaited their foreign victims with great impatience.

The large vessel came to a halt a mere twenty feet from the beach, its low keel allowing it to maneuver easily into shallower waters than other boats its size.

Volusenus removed his blanket from around his shoulders, repositioned his sword and belt around his waist, and headed for the small rowboat. Commius placed his helmet atop his head and followed the Roman closely. The pair stepped into the boat, and four oarsmen were ordered to accompany them. The oarsmen approached from a staircase that led to the lower deck. They stepped into the boat heavily, the small rowboat swaying dangerously as it was lowered into the turbulent waters.

The four rowers seemed like mirror images. All were missing teeth, smelled foul, and wore dirty garments that hung limply around their greasy bodies. The men were bald and had leathery skin, evidence of long hours spent rowing in the sun. As the ropes were first released and the rowboat touched the water, the smaller vessel heaved up and down sickeningly, hitting the *Fidelis* several times, causing the passengers to rapidly become sick from the motion. But gradually the rowboat began to edge away, the gap between them and shore closing slowly. As the waves carried them the boat almost overturned several times, causing both Volusenus and Commius who were unaccustomed to the ways of the ocean, to become even more seasick than before.

As the men approached shore, the waves broke brutally, pushing the small boat on a jarring ride up the beach a short distance, until the water receded and the boat was left behind, its small keel forcing it to lean to the right. The four oarsmen leaped out, their feet sinking slightly into the saturated sand, and ensured the boat would not get washed back out to sea. Crassius watched nervously from the deck of his ship, his hands clasped across his large gut, his thumbs rolling swiftly around one another.

As Volusenus stepped off, loosely followed by Commius, Crassius let out a sigh of relief, happy to have his friends on dry land rather than the upset sea. Volusenus tugged on the belt straps hanging down in front of his groin as he began his walk up the beach, apparently nervous as well. Each step he took away felt like he was walking to his execution. He listened to the surrounding wilderness, but only the dull thumping of his heartbeat resonated through his skull. He turned around roughly four-fifths the way up the beach, waiting for Commius, who was fifteen feet behind him.

While waiting for his friend, Volusenus looked at the *Fidelis*. It was truly a beautiful sight: the gray sand, the white cliffs on both sides, the turbulent blue waters topped with white froth, and in the center, the trireme floating in the waves. He tried imagining the sight of a hundred ships lining the coast, his fellow legionnaires disembarking, the Britons holding their ground ... He listened to the waves, the wind, the birds, and to another particular sound.

He recognized it, but it did not register until too late. Lost in his thoughts, he did not hear the shouts of warning from the *Fidelis*, nor the shouting of the British soldiers as the men came running out of the bushes toward the intruders. Only the sight of Commius unsheathing his sword brought him back to reality. He turned around in a flash, unsheathing his own short sword, the red crest on his helmet pointing directly at his assailants. There were twelve, he unconsciously counted. After long years in the army, he could estimate how many people were in a group with great precision with a mere glance.

The assailants were all dressed in a similar fashion. They were shirtless and intricately painted in blue, and each gripped a long spear or sword and carried a variety of differently shaped shields.

Androvic had changed plans at the last moment, but Ludovic's hotheadedness didn't allow time for the chief to explain the new plans. Androvic had decided to play nicely, rusing the Romans into a false sense of security before attacking and butchering them to the last man when they least expected it. When the Volusenus stopped to turn around, Ludovic had instead leaped out of the bushes in a flash and started running toward the intruders on their sacred land, spear and shield in hand. The rest had followed suit and quickly caught up with him.

Volusenus watched as two men ran directly past him and headed for the Gaul. The first man reached Commius and attempted to plunge his spear's tip into the Gaul. Commius sidestepped him and cut the Briton in two at the waist. Commius swiftly regained his posture and turned to face the other man, who had run behind him. The man carried a sword instead of a spear, Commius noticed. The Gaul kicked at the second man's shield powerfully, knocking him down and, quickly seizing the opportunity, he plunged his sword into the man's unprotected gut. Volusenus watched, astounded; everything seemed to be happening at unimaginably slow speed. Volusenus knew they would not be able to kill them all, and he quickly opted for returning to the relative safety of the *Fidelis* as the ten other men got within dangerously close distance. Volusenus shouted for his friend but was not heard above Commius' grunts as he slashed at his enemies.

Suddenly, Volusenus saw a spear being thrust at his face from the side and, quickly ducking, he allowed the spear to pass mere inches over his head, the point sliding through the crest and shaving many of the red-dyed hairs, leaving a sheared gap in his helmet's crest. Volusenus swiftly stood back up and slashed at the man repeatedly. The agile Briton evaded the repeated attempts and finally launched an attack of his own. Volusenus parried the sword strikes, sparks erupting between the contact points of the two blades. The two men fought fiercely. Suddenly Volusenus felt the Briton's sword hit him in the helmet above his right temple. Volusenus felt the metal helmet bend under the onslaught and suddenly became more infuriated. Launching another attack, the Briton spun Volusenus' sword from his hands and left the Roman temporarily dazed and defenseless. But Volusenus wasn't out of the fight yet. He swiftly unsheathed his pugio, a thick-bladed knife that caused wide, deep wounds, and attacked his assailant viciously. The Briton was caught off-guard by the Roman's counterattack and stumbled backward. Volusenus then jumped on the man and stuck his knife into the blood-thirsty Briton, killing him instantly.

Meanwhile, two other men had surrounded him and were now between him and the sea. Volusenus stood up quickly and was convinced he was going to die soon when suddenly he saw Commius running for the small paddleboat.

"Volusenus," Commius shouted as he waved for his Roman friend to follow, "let's go!"

Quickly retrieving his sword and spinning to face his most immediate threat, Volusenus slashed at both faces and caught one of them right above the nose. The Briton cried out as the blade sliced through his flesh and eyes, and he quickly fell to the ground in a puddle of blood. Volusenus then charged toward the second man and threw all his weight against the man's shield. The Briton, caught off guard, was knocked over. Volusenus, more interested in getting away with his life than defeating his assailants, opted to leave the man and run for his life instead. The Roman officer, dismissing the rest of his assailants, began to run toward the small boat, which the four sailors had already begun pushing back into the thrashing sea in anticipation of the Roman's retreat.

It seemed to Volusenus that he would actually regain the comparative safety of the boat. He quickly caught up with his bear-like Gallic friend and ran alongside him. Volusenus had nearly reached the boat when he heard Commius shout.

"The Britons are throwing spears!"

As if by divine intervention, Volusenus tripped and fell head-first into the sand as two spears flew two feet above him, slicing through the air where his back had been seconds before. The Roman shook off the sand, spat out the grit from his mouth, and stumbled to the boat. After what seemed an eternity, Volusenus entered the frigid waters. He stopped to wait for Commius and suddenly realized the Gaul was no longer at his side. He spun around to look for his friend and watched as the Britons rapidly closed the gap. He spotted a body lying on the ground between him and them, roughly twenty feet away. It was Commius. He was still alive, but the Gaul had been nicked by a spear in the leg and knocked out when he fell.

Volusenus resolved to save his friend in peril, but the oarsmen grabbed him under the arms and began to pull him onto the boat before he had even taken his first step toward Commius. He tried to worm his way out of their grasp but to no avail; their muscled arms easily dominated him. He was tugged against his will into the boat, and the men quickly began to paddle away from shore, leaving the Gaul to the mercy of the Britons.

Volusenus observed sadly as the warriors gathered around Commius and lifted him onto his feet. Androvic then examined and spoke to his new prisoner. Volusenus remembered watching his friend kill two within the first twenty seconds of fighting, and he himself had gotten one other, which meant that there should have been nine left. He watched as the men moved around on the beach and cursed at Volusenus and his compatriots. Suddenly two men, one of them Ludovic, broke apart from the group and ran toward the cold sea with two spears in hand. Volusenus watched as the men ran toward them and threw the first of their spears at the small boat, which was already half-way back to the *Fidelis*. Within three seconds of throwing their first spears, the men had already prepped the next two spears and threw them too.

Volusenus watched morbidly as the spears arced in the sky and fell toward him at an alarming rate. Although there were only four, he now knew what it felt like to be on the receiving end of his own army when they threw their numerous pila. It had to be terrifying, he realized.

The first spear landed two feet away in the water to the right; the second hit its target, impaling one of the oarsmen and nailing him to the boat's wooden hull. The third and fourth missed the survivors by mere inches. Volusenus quickly grabbed the oar from the dying man's hands and began paddling as strongly and quickly as he could, working his way toward the *Fidelis* with great, deep strokes. Approaching the *Fidelis*, he stole a glance behind him; seven men had dragged Commius up to the forest and were waiting for the last man, who was still halfway up the beach, watching the Romans escape with their lives.

Androvic was angry, but at least all had not been lost. He had lost three good friends and nearly died himself, but at least he had gotten a prisoner. He looked at the Gaul, who was beginning to regain consciousness, momentarily unaware of his helpless condition. Now, the Britons would learn what was going on, thanks to the Gaul.

Back on the *Fidelis*, Volusenus was lifted aboard while others helped haul the small rowboat out of the turbulent waters.

Volusenus, once aboard, quickly ran for the starboard side and watched helplessly as his friend was dragged into the forest. He began to despair. Several men behind him gathered around the dead man and tried to separate the spear and man from the hull of the rowboat. Volusenus fell to the deck; his back pressed against the railing, and stared into the void of space, realizing that for the first time in a month, he had just lost another friend.

X

Caesar had expected the prisoners to be delivered within a two-week period, but five days after accepting the Gallic surrender he watched the malnourished Roman prisoners regain their camp. He sat atop his horse on a slight mound a short distance in front of the port gates, staring into the solemn column. The forest began a hundred feet from where he was, and the prisoner line stretched far into it. Caesar watched the Gauls, who lined the sides of the road, urge their former captives along coldly. His eyes then followed the line of men down the trail, and suddenly he noticed Androvates, the Gaul who had come to surrender less than a week ago.

"I can't help but say that I am impressed with the speed at which you returned them to me," Caesar said, his eyes shifting back toward his returning soldiers.

"I worked hard to get them all back to you as fast as I could," the Gaul lied.

"Well, you would not have had many to return had you kept them any longer. I would not have accepted corpses in place of live men," replied Caesar, visibly disgusted at the Gauls' treatment of their prisoners.

Androvates felt like saying something back, but he bit his tongue instead, his rage fulminating within him.

"Now if I remember correctly, there was a second part to our agreement," Caesar said, finally looking down at the Gaul.

The Roman noticed that the man was still dressed in the same clothes as the other day. However, they were significantly dirtier than the previous time they had met.

"The swords," Androvates repeated with a nervous chuckle.

"Yes."

"They will be delivered to you later today."

"Perfect."

Caesar began to turn his horse around toward the gates.

"I am having my men count the prisoners that are returning," Caesar said, nudging his horse along.

"Yes?" The man replied from beneath him, trying his best to conceal his nervousness.

"One thousand is a lot. I can't wait until they are done. I need them for other tasks."

"I agree. I can assure you there are one thousand there," he said, pointing behind him at the former captives.

"I trust you," the Roman lied. "But I have to record their return. Their names, their rank, their legion numbers. I'm sure you understand."

"Of course," Androvates replied, jogging lightly to the horse's left.

"All of the prisoners were returned from this region, is that correct?" Caesar asked.

"Yes. Yes, indeed," Androvates replied with a fervent nod.

"And all tribes participated, did they not?"

"Yes, sir."

"Which tribes have sent their share of prisoners?" Caesar asked Androvates, as nonchalant as if he were asking how the man found the weather.

"Well, all of this region's tribes—the Nerves, Ambiani, Atrebates, Bellovaci, and Suessiones," the dirty Gaul replied.

"That excludes the Morini and Menapii, if I remember this region's tribes correctly," Caesar said, trapping the Gaul.

Androvates had not expected the Roman to be so proficient in local tribes. He attempted to conceal his surprise but knew Caesar had surely sensed his brief hesitancy.

"Ahem ... Yes, in fact. But there is a reason for this ..."

Caesar wanted none of it, and he nudged his horse into a trot, causing the Gaul to begin to jog at his side.

"I am afraid I will have to leave you here," Caesar said, passing through the gate that led into fort. "I have other matters to attend to."

Androvates nodded and slowed down.

"Besides, I'm sure we will see each other again," Caesar said, knowing full well he would.

Something was wrong; he could feel it deep inside of him; something wasn't right with the prisoners. He knew the Gauls would try to bluff him. Following the busy streets, he finally reached the principia several minutes later, dismounted, and entered the tent. Inside was Volusenus, sitting on a wooden bench to the side. He quickly rose when Caesar entered the room.

Caesar had learned that his ship was in sight when he had been called out for the returning prisoners. Apparently Volusenus had docked and reached the principia quicker than Caesar had planned.

"Volusenus!" he exclaimed, giving him a warm pat on the back. "How was the voyage? Sit, sit."

Caesar went to a small table and began to pour himself a glass of wine; Volusenus sat on a chair by the table.

"Awful, to be honest. I am afraid I have much bad news for you."

Caesar frowned and stopped pouring his drink; he knew the man was not easily upset. Something terribly wrong must have happened.

"Speak, my friend. Tell me of your misadventure," Caesar urged, still holding the half-filled goblet in one hand and the small amphora in the other.

"First, I am afraid I must report of Commius' abduction by the Britons."

Caesar slowly opened his mouth, awed at the news.

"Dead?" he asked, as his eyes suddenly spotted the dented helmet with its shaved crest on Volusenus' lap.

"It's uncertain at this point. He was either so or unconscious when they pulled him off of the beach. I tried to save him but was held back by the crew."

"A good thing—you would certainly have died yourself. How many were there?"

Volusenus said the number as he looked down at his helmet that lay on his knees in embarrassment. The man looking back at him in the reflection was not the man he had once known. His face was different. He wondered how all those good years had passed by so quickly.

"We had been scouting the shoreline for four days and found nowhere to land but one beach, so we decided to test the natives there. I had seen movement on the crest and tried to establish contact but was fiercely attacked instead."

Caesar nodded. He fully accepted the information Volusenus had just shared. There was only one beach, and it was obviously owned by hostile natives. He would have to land his troops straight into a clash they were not prepared to fight.

"And you sailed a good distance?" Caesar asked, although he knew his officer had surely done everything he could. Volusenus was not the kind to drag his feet.

"We will have to play on the enemy's terms; I don't like that at all," Caesar said, pensively.

Volusenus sat still, quiet as a rock.

"I have drawn a map for you," Volusenus said, suddenly remembering that he held it in his hand.

Volusenus handed the damp parchment to Caesar, who unrolled it and examined it before rolling it back up and informing his friend of his decision.

"Volusenus, I find that it would be better for you to accompany me to Britannia and show me the way in person," Caesar continued.

Volusenus smiled and saluted Caesar. With a grin, he placed his helmet back onto his head and exited the tent. Caesar realized he still held the amphora and a half-filled glass of wine, and he quickly rectified that little dilemma and downed his drink hastily. His agenda was extremely full and allowed for little more than a brief intermission, but he deserved it, he thought.

Caesar was in the process of pouring himself another glass when one of his aides-de-camp entered the tent and approached the great general.

"We have just finished counting the prisoners, sir."

"Ah. Perfect."

Caesar stopped pouring the red liquid and downed the little in his glass in a straight shot; he then laid the amphora and goblet on the table nearest him. After a long, deep breath, Caesar followed the man outside, placed his helmet back on his head, and began to walk toward the Porta Praetoria.

"How many are missing?" Caesar asked, surprising the aide.

"We counted roughly nine hundred men, sir," the aide replied, visibly nervous about the bad news he carried.

"Roughly nine hundred? I want a precise number. How many are there exactly?"

"Eight hundred and seventy two," the aide answered, happy to get the burden off of his shoulders.

Caesar mumbled something to himself and, despite the aide's request, refused to repeat what he had said. They reached the fort's gates two minutes later. Three officers and several other legionnaires were already waiting for him, several of the former captives gathered behind them. Androvates was arguing with a centurion off to the left of the officers. Caesar, obviously infuriated by the Gauls' attempt to bluff him, stepped up to the officers and cut straight to the chase.

"This is unacceptable," Caesar said slowly.

Androvates flinched lightly, not knowing what to expect.

One of the officers present, Q. Titurius Sabinus, stepped forward to reply. Sabinus was tall, with graying hair and dull eyes, the physical toll of time visible on his wrinkled skin. But the officer's mind was still as sharp as the sword he wielded and his reflexes as acute as they were thirty years ago.

"Absolutely. This Gaul here," Sabinus said, pointing to Androvates, "Claims he tried to convince the other tribes to submit some prisoners, but they all refused to cooperate."

"I expected this to happen, but I thought it would be a quarter to a fifth of what is in fact missing," Caesar said as he walked over to the centurion who was arguing with the Androvates.

They were still in the heat of an argument when Caesar arrived; the centurion stopped to salute him.

"You are in no position to be shouting and arguing, Gaul," Caesar said after returning the officer's salute.

"This man claims he tried to persuade two other tribes to send prisoners, but they refused each time, even threatening to kill him after negotiations went sour."

Caesar nodded and looked his fellow soldier in the eyes.

"I find his story hard to believe. What is your name, centurion?"

"Sextus Publius, sir, first cohort of the Seventh Legion."

"Sextus, I need you to bring all these men inside the fort walls and begin to rehabilitate them. I want them fed, given drink, and placed comfortably in any barrack that has room available. I will take care of this problem in the meanwhile."

"Yes, sir. Right away," Publius replied with a quick salute. Then he quickly marched toward the fort gate, urging the ex-captives to follow him, helping to carry the wounded.

Caesar turned his attention back toward the Gaul in front of him.

"You ..." Caesar growled, pointing his index finger as menacingly as if it were a sword. "I should have you killed for your incompetence and your sick belief that you could deceive me. Your lack of respect for Rome and inability to uphold your end of this deal has convinced me that you are pathetic and not truly seeking a friendship with Rome. You are my enemy, but even worse, you are an enemy to your own country. Because you tried to cheat me from recovering my men, I will instill another fine of two hundred men on you. Because of this pathetic incompetency of yours, your tribesmen will now have to release a larger number of captives than they would have in the first place. I imagine they will not be pleased with your lack of effort. In fact, I might be doing them a favor by slaying you right here, you spineless piece of trash."

"I can explain!" The man said, taking a step back.

"How do you explain over a hundred men missing?" Caesar asked, unsheathing his sword slowly as he walked forward.

"The two tribes you know of refused to submit to your will," Androvates said, cowering backward and stumbling repeatedly on the uneven dirt path.

"They surrendered and agreed to the terms," Caesar said, placing the tip of his gladius under Androvates' chin and looking down his sword into the Gaul's face.

"I tried to convince them, but after my urging they threatened to kill me. I had no choice but to let them do as they wish," the native lied.

"They *threatened* to kill you?" Caesar asked, catching the bait. "They should have actually done so. It would have spared me this talk with you."

"Yes, Caesar, they accused me of being a traitor," Androvates lied.

"Now, what am I supposed to do?" Caesar asked, tilting his head backward as if he were looking for an answer in the heavens.

The Gaul did not answer.

"What about the swords?"

"This afternoon," the Gaul replied without hesitation.

"They better all be there," Caesar said menacingly, "or else ..."

With a new campaign against rebels in sight, he turned around and walked toward his three senior officers, who stood talking to each other about the events that had transpired. He recognized Sextus, standing with his back turned to him, and then he recognized the other two men standing nearby. There was L. Aurunculeius Cotta, a short man with brown hair and eyes of the same color, and P. Sulpicius Rufus, a shorter man with black hair and green eyes. Cotta and Rufus, he knew, were the commanding officers of the Eighth Legion and Ninth Legion, respectively.

"Men," he said, getting their attention, "if you would please follow me to the principia, we have urgent matters to discuss."

XI

Commius' feet were being dragged harshly against the hard ground, his feet snagging fallen branches and upturned roots as his captors dragged him mercilessly toward their village. He was in a state of semi-consciousness, his eyes fluttering every so often as he struggled to stave off death. The last thing he remembered was running alongside Volusenus toward the boat. The last thing he actually remembered was that awful pain in his leg as the tip of the spear cut through the side of his calf. After that, everything converged in a sea of partially constructed memories.

As he stared through glassy eyes, sweat dripping cruelly into the corners, he could just make out the faint outline of the British village across the flat, open, grassy expanse. He wanted to wipe off the sand that covered his face, courtesy of the fall on the beach, but his arms dangled helplessly at his sides, too fatigued to even contract as blood struggled to reach the deprived limbs.

He was being held upright under the arms by two burly men; two more walked a short distance ahead, their blurry forms vaguely discernable. The other men must have either left or were walking behind him. He tried to move his feet, to walk, but his numb legs were unresponsive. At first he seemed like a baby taking his first steps, but soon enough, everything began to come back to him.

His vision began to clear, and his feet began to move in the forced direction. He tried to straighten up enough to alleviate the pressure under his arms. Once his porters noticed he had regained sufficient consciousness, they dropped their grasp and stopped to watch the man stagger. Commius' first steps were like a drunkard's.

They laughed wickedly as Commius tried to balance himself, the world spinning uncontrollably around him. Commius felt light-headed from the exertion but forced himself not to pass out again. He stole a glance at his leg, the pain leading his eyes to the wound, and he grimaced at the gash. It felt deep, but sand covered the wound too much to be able to adequately assess the damage.

He tried to straighten himself as the two men left their smiles behind and began approaching him menacingly. He tried to step backward but soon found himself pressed against Androvic, who stood motionless, the corpse of one of his fallen comrades slung over his shoulders like a dead deer. Commius spun to meet his new threat and found himself enclosed on all sides by three Britons. Apparently, the remainder of the men he had fought on the beach had left sooner and only three had stayed behind with him.

Ludovic, who had been carrying Commius, stood next to him with another dead comrade slung over his shoulder. Commius glanced at all of the dead being carried and smiled internally at the thought that at least Volusenus was not among them. But the thought that he might still be on the beach crossed his mind. He hoped feverishly that his friend had saved himself and was not lying lifeless on the sand but rather with the crew onboard the *Fidelis* trying to come up with a plan to save him.

The two men who had been holding him approached and began to bully him. Commius struggled to remain on his feet as they pushed him in the direction of their home. Commius decided that fighting back would be in vain. They had removed his sword, dagger, helmet, and anything else that could be used against them. They had even removed his sandals to make escape harder. He began to walk determinedly toward the village, their home, his future prison. As they entered the gates, crowds began to form around them, some cheering their return, others booing and spitting at the prisoner.

Commius tried dodging the phlegmatic missiles but was struck by several.

Ludovic and Androvic set the dead men down on the ground and began to explain their story in their native tongue. It was shameful for them, three of theirs had been killed by two of the enemy, but they smiled at the thought that they now had a prisoner in their possession. Commius, reading their thoughts, tensed at the thought of what they might do to him. If death would come quickly, he thought, he would be fine with it; but he doubted they would grant him such an easy way out. Realizing that the village was listening to the story, Commius glanced around, looking for an escape. Even if he couldn't escape at this very moment, he could memorize details that could help him escape from wherever they might hold him. He did not understand what they said, but his shoulders grew heavier and heavier as Androvic ended his speech and slowly turned to face him.

The big man took a step in Commius' direction and shouted something in his native tongue. Suddenly, the two other soldiers who had carried him came up from behind him and began to drag him, once again, to the top of the hill, where the town square was situated. Androvic followed and smiled viciously as the villagers scurried up the hill. Ludovic stayed behind to tend to his dead friends as the angry procession moved away. Commius felt a knot form in his stomach, along with another that formed in his throat. A part of him wished that he had actually died on that beach from that spear; at least it would have been over quickly.

As they reached the center of the square, the two men shoved him to the ground and stood, waiting for the crowd to gather around the defenseless man. Ludovic appeared suddenly and approached the kneeling man. Without saying anything, he suddenly punched his fist into Commius' face and knocked him onto his back. The two men wasted no time lifting the stunned Gaul off the ground, and they quickly lifted him to his feet, where they held him as Ludovic sent another punch deep into Commius' gut.

The prisoner gasped as the air was forcefully expelled from his lungs with acute pain. He coughed and gagged as the bile reached his throat. He was thirsty, he realized, really thirsty. Ludovic massaged his knuckles as he spoke to the Gaul.

"You are a traitor, you coward!" he spat in his face.

Commius' head hung limply, his battered body supported by the two human pillars at his sides. He sputtered, "You are very brave, Briton, to beat an unarmed man restrained by others."

Ludovic approached Commius slowly, lifted his chin, and looked deep into the Gaul's bloodshot eyes. "You are very stupid to be speaking in such a way."

"How have you come to speak my words?" Commius continued through gritted teeth.

"I fought in Gaul against the Romans three times," Ludovic yelled. "You are despicable, allying yourself with those untrustworthy demons!"

Ludovic dropped Commius' chin and began to pace menacingly around his captive. The onlookers watched perplexedly as their chief communicated in an incomprehensible dialect with the prisoner.

"I expected better from your kind," Ludovic said, stopping behind Commius.

Commius knew another punch was soon to follow but couldn't do anything to block it. His right eye was already starting to swell from an earlier hit, his gut was on fire, and his leg felt like it would fall off at any time.

"I was forced to come here," Commius lied, hoping to gain a few more seconds of life.

"You lie," the Briton said from behind.

Commius gritted his teeth while awaiting a blow to the back of the head, but none came. *The Briton must have bought my bluff*, he thought.

"They threatened my village if I did not comply with their request," Commius continued.

Ludovic walked around Commius and faced his prisoner once again.

"I don't seek war with you. I hate the Romans as well." Commius continued to lie through bleeding gums.

Ludovic thought it over for a second but remembered the two men Commius had killed.

"You hate the Romans, yet you killed two of my men on the beach," Ludovic said, lifting Commius' head by his hair.

"I had no choice," Commius groaned.

"You should have told us," Ludovic told his captive as he let go of his head and took a step backward.

Commius snickered.

"Told you? I had no time to tell you! Your men were on us before we could blink," Commius said, provoked by the man's absurdity.

Ludovic didn't like the tone in Commius' voice and lashed out at him with a fierce uppercut that once again left Commius gasping for air.

"You should have turned on that Roman, then," Ludovic said, calming down slightly.

He waited patiently for Commius to catch his breath again.

"If I had killed him, they would have returned to my village and massacred the entire population. You forget that there were still Romans watching us on the boat," Commius lied again.

Commius could feel the anger in his tormentor dissipating. Bringing Volusenus into the conversation reminded him that he was still unsure of his friend's state. He wanted to ask, but wording was crucial to maintain his professed feeling of hatred toward the Romans.

"Did you at least kill the Roman?" Commius asked, trying his hardest to sound hateful.

Ludovic paced a few feet away from him, his hands clasped behind his back. Commius dreaded the words that would emanate from the man's mouth.

The large man stopped a short distance to Commius' left and, looking in the direction of the hidden sea, spoke through gritted teeth.

"No ... The bastard got away."

Commius let out a sigh of relief as he thanked his gods. Ludovic heard the sound and, turning to face the disheveled man, realized he had just been misled.

He moved in until he was several inches away from Commius and looked into the man's eyes with a gaze that could have cut stone.

"You ... you vermin," the British chief said. He realized the insult was not nearly as profane, violent, or hateful as what he really wanted to say.

Commius feared what was to follow; surely he would be stabbed and killed before night. He found breathing difficult as he pondered his future. He feared death, and this antagonizing wait only helped to tighten that internal noose that crushed his air-pipe and made breathing hard. If the Britons didn't stab and kill him soon, Commius was sure he would suffocate before then.

Ludovic groped for the sword that hung at his waist and finally unsheathed it with a malicious smile. He was eager to see how the Gaul would face his death. Would he smile in his death, or would he shriek as he lay dying? Ludovic brought the tip of his sword to the base of Commius' sternum and was about to thrust when a hand suddenly grabbed his arm and stopped him from delivering the coup de grace. His head snapped to the right to face the man who was stopping him.

"Enough. I want this man to live. He has displayed remarkable courage in the face of danger, and it would not be honorable for us to kill him in this way," Androvic said.

"But he killed the others!"

"We can use him as a bargaining chip when the Romans land. He will do more for us in life than in death. Put down your sword, Ludovic, and lock him up."

Ludovic stared unbelievingly at his chief. His desire to kill the captive was overwhelming, but he knew his own death would ensue if he didn't obey. Slowly he lowered his sword and sheathed it. Looking down at the Gaul in pure hatred, he punched him one final time before turning around and walking away.

Caesar and his group reached the principia uninterrupted and gathered around a large rectangular table within. Caesar walked over to one of the cabinets lining the far wall of the principia and pulled out a long tube containing a detailed map of the region of Belgica. He moved back to the table, unfurled it, and placed two rocks on each end to keep it from rolling back upon itself.

"The tribes of the Morini, here, and Menapii, here, have yet to return their share of prisoners. We have no other choice but to proceed against them," Caesar said pointing to the two points on the map where the tribes lived.

The generals nodded in unison.

"As you know, I am heading for Britannia with the Seventh and Tenth tomorrow night and therefore won't be able to carry out this expedition myself. However much I would like to personally collect their share of prisoners, I am pleased to announce that you men will have the honor of doing so this time," Caesar continued.

Caesar took a step back from the table to better see his officers and then crossed his arms.

"Cotta," he said, and the man straightened at the sound of his name. "I want you to lead the Eighth up to the tribe of the Morini and impose upon them the return of all of their prisoners."

Cotta nodded, and Caesar quickly turned his attention to the commander of the Ninth Legion, Rufus.

"Rufus, I need you to carry out the same task with the Ninth on the tribe of the Menapii. I need both of you to be as harsh as necessary."

He looked at both men, waiting for questions, but none came. These men could be fully trusted to carry out his orders, he knew, and Caesar was glad they had no issues.

Caesar dismissed his Legion commanders, and both men swiftly exited the tent, leaving Sabinus and him alone.

"I have good news for you, Sabinus. I am sending Cyriacus back to Rome. I cannot trust him as fully as I would expect. I expect full obedience and confidence from my troops and exponentially more from my officers. Alas for Cyriacus, he has found the pleasure of drink far more important than his military career."

Sabinus remained silent.

"That is why I have decided to place you in command of Portius Itius," Caesar finally said, approaching Sabinus and placing a hand on his shoulder.

Sabinus tried to conceal his excitement, but Caesar could see right through the man.

"You are going to remain here, with over one thousand sick men unsuitable for any combat and a fort garrisoned by that same amount. Normally, the Gauls should not bother you. We are at peace with them for now, except for the two tribes that will be taken care of by Rufus and Cotta, *but* ... remain on your guard. The Gauls are fickle and can turn on you faster than wind in a storm."

Caesar looked at the man, scrutinizing him for the smallest sign of uncertainty but found none.

"Do you have any concerns or questions?" Caesar asked.

"None," the newly promoted officer answered unhesitatingly.

"Good. I trust you will take good care of the wounded."

"Yes, sir."

Caesar smiled and dismissed the man, and Sabinus quickly exited the tent in quiet jubilation. Caesar, meanwhile, returned to his table, slid the map back into the sash, and was just placing it back into his cabinet when Publius, the centurion he had seen earlier, entered.

"The Gauls, sir—they've just brought the swords."

Caesar looked at the man with a smirk.

"Let's see how many of them are missing."

He walked past Publius, who followed closely in his steps.

"Dealing with the Gauls is like dealing with children. They are so naïve it is, in truth, quite astonishing that they have managed to survive this long on their own," Caesar said sarcastically to his officer, eliciting a laugh.

Publius quickly caught up to Caesar and motioned for the latter to follow him. He led Caesar to the fort gates, where there were about a half dozen large, four-wheel wagons filled to the brim with Gallic swords. Caesar approached and began to inspect random weapons, more out of curiosity than anything else.

Caesar would surely have noticed the mud that had caked the swords had the Gauls not washed them first, but the swords he handled were clean and polished. Caesar pulled random swords, most of which were unsheathed, from the piles and noted that all were relatively heavy compared to his gladius. One sword in particular pleased him, and Caesar tossed the sword back and forth from one hand to another and made several, slow stabbing movements to get a feel for the weapon. He enjoyed the feel of the weight in his hand but realized that in a fight, he would still choose his gladius over any other sword any day.

Caesar set the sword back where he had found it and turned to walk toward the head of the column. He had debated what he was going to do with the swords upon obtaining them and had come to the decision to have them melted in Rome and cast into a gigantic statue of the god of war, Mars, in tribute to his Gallic conquest. Caesar smiled at this idea as he stopped at the lead wagon. Sitting on the side of the wagon was a skinny Gaul who had not shaved since the last blue moon and who stared dumbly toward Caesar.

Caesar asked the man to dismount, but the Gaul, who spoke in broken Latin, refused. Caesar explained that his Legionnaires were going to drive the wagons inside, remove the swords, and bring the wagons right back, but the Gaul was skeptical about surrendering his cart to the Romans. Caesar told the Gaul slowly that he gave the man his word the wagons would be returned within the hour, and finally, after a lot of convincing, the man agreed.

The Gaul dismounted, and Caesar called the Legionnaires who were standing on the side, ordering them to drive the wagons down to the dock. As the wagons began to move, Caesar climbed atop the lead wagon.

As Caesar passed through the gates, he halted his wagon briefly to order a dozen soldiers to wait alongside Publius and keep watch on the Gauls. When the men were on their way, Caesar ordered his driver to resume the journey to the dock. Once there, he dismounted and quickly began to look for a certain bireme, a boat with only two banks of oars and a sail, essentially a smaller version of the trireme. He jogged down the dock and quickly saw the ship he was looking for, the *Vita*. Motioning the wagons over, he climbed aboard and found the ship's commander under his tent at the back of the vessel, eating from a tray on a shaky three-legged table.

"Spurius," Caesar exclaimed jovially, "my red-bearded friend!"

The man was large and tall but fit for his middle age; he was dressed in his naval tunic and had removed his sandals for comfort. He sat on a collapsible short stool, with his feet propped up on another.

"Julius, you lucky dog, you're still alive," the man laughed as he stood to hug his long-time friend.

"The gods must have further use for me down here," Caesar replied.

"Same here; I see the cargo has made it in."

"Indeed it has. Are your men ready to transfer them aboard?"

"Of course," Spurius said, standing up and placing his chicken leg on the tray. He wiped his hands on a towel that hung limply from a nail on a small post to his side and exited out onto the deck.

The stairway that led down to the oar benches was right in front of him, roughly six feet away. He walked to the top and called down to his oarsmen to come up and help with the loading of cargo. Caesar and Spurius moved aside as the men stepped up two at a time and began to walk down the ramp to the dock. Caesar watched as the legionnaires handed out the swords to the men, several at a time. The latter returned to the ship with the swords and dumped them insensitively into the cargo hold before returning for more. Caesar and Spurius conversed near the railing as they watched the men transfer the swords from cart to ship.

"I have worked hard to obtain these swords, Spurius. I don't want them back in enemy hands," Caesar said with a smile, his arms crossed over his chest and his eyes drifting over the men carrying the swords.

"I understand. You have my word no one will get them."

"The nearest port would be in Aquitania. Head for Southern Gaul and land at Portius Mergus. From there you will drop them off to be carted to Rome, where they will be melted and turned into a statue of Mars in honor of this great victory," Caesar said, looking at his friend. "I do not want them to fall back into Gallic hands, so if there is any trouble ahead, do not hesitate to send the swords to the bottom."

Spurius nodded, and Caesar looked back at the men fumbling with the razor-sharp blades.

"Is that for your political career?" the sailor asked with a grin.

"People love victories, my friend. A statue devoted to the gods made from enemy weapons is better than anything else I can think of," Caesar answered with a wink.

Spurius smiled and returned to watching the working men.

"Well, best of luck with that," Spurius said with a pat on Caesar's back.

Caesar smiled and slapped the man on the shoulder.

"I am afraid I am going to have to leave you. I have much to do before I depart for Britannia, and time is running short," Caesar said. "Be careful and good luck."

"You too, my friend, you too," Spurius said as he watched Caesar climb down the ramp onto the dock.

A day had passed since Caesar appointed Sabinus port commander. Caesar planned to sail that night for the British coast, but something was wrong. Caesar sensed it the moment Sabinus walked in with a somber look on his face. Eighty vessels were gathered in and around the port of Portius Itius, among them a variety of smaller biremes, larger triremes, and swift men-of-war—eighty vessels of the expected ninety-eight Caesar had planned on. The missing eighteen vessels were in fact eight miles away but due to bad weather were not expected before Caesar wanted to set sail at midnight. Sabinus sat on a stool, his back resting against the large rectangular table, while Caesar paced back and forth a couple feet away from him.

"I was afraid of this," Caesar said, his hands clasped behind his back.

"You might have to postpone your departure. The weather around the fleet has not been very cooperative," Sabinus said as he watched Caesar pace nonchalantly in an oval.

Sabinus knew Caesar was not the easily discouraged type; in fact he liked a challenge. Life was nothing without one, Caesar always boasted. But Caesar was not in the mood for one now; he had too much on his plate.

"Perhaps the best thing would be to postpone for a couple of days, wait for the remainder of the fleet to arrive, and then cross over in unison," Sabinus suggested.

"No. The weather will only get worse. A vicious storm is in the making. We must either cross over now or wait until spring."

"But with a fifth of our army missing ..."

"Not missing, simply delayed," Caesar said, stopping to look at Sabinus.

"But I thought ..." Sabinus started, shifting to a more comfortable position on the stool.

"The majority of the infantry can cross over now on the ships. We leave the cavalry and whatever number of infantry that cannot be brought over here, with orders to move up to the fleet. They will embark and cross toward Britannia from there," Caesar said, finally finding the answer to the problem.

"You would like to cross over without any cavalry?" Sabinus asked, not sure he had actually understood.

"For the time being, yes," Caesar answered.

"Our armies will be completely unprotected on the flanks!" Sabinus realized.

"It's a risk I must take if I want to get to Britannia before the nastiest of the storm arrives. The storm will hit in two or three days at the most. I can afford several tardy ships, but I need all my infantry there before the storm hits or I might lose half of them in the crossing,"

"But what of the ships—will they be unprotected?"

Caesar nodded.

"Let us hope Neptune is not angry at us. I'm hoping we will be able to find a cove or such to help shield our navy from the nastiest of the storm," Caesar stated calmly.

Sabinus let out a quick exhale, ran a hand through his damp hair, and stood up, as Caesar gazed vacantly toward the flickering light of the candles on the table.

"Sabinus, tonight we sail for Britannia. Give the order for the Legions to begin to break camp and move aboard the ships."

"Yes, sir."

Sabinus saluted Caesar and exited the tent into the sunset.

XII

Complete darkness fell on the camp. Torches were lit and placed throughout the streets, providing small circles of refuge from the enveloping shadows. The camp was fairly still and quiet, as opposed to the dock, which bustled with life. All the Legionnaires from the Seventh and Tenth Legions marched to the dock from their tents, carrying all of the equipment they would need for the crossing. Each man brought two pila of different weights, a short sword, and a distinct rectangular shield covered in a removable leather sheath. In addition to their main battle gear, they wore helmets with the cheek guards folded down but not tied at the chin, a pugio, or knife, which hung from a sheath on the left side of the belt, and heavy sandals with nail-studded soles that helped provide traction, as well as inflict extra damage if used to kick an enemy. Each also carried a marching pack, or sarcina, to which had been attached one week's worth of food, a canteen, an axe or shovel, a satchel, one cooking pot, and one mess tin.

From within the legions, the troops were broken down into cohorts of four hundred and eighty men; cohorts were further broken down into six centuries of eighty men. Each century was then further broken down into contuberniums of eight men. These eight men did everything together, ranging from cooking and sleeping to patrolling and fighting. Each of the eight men would carry parts of the tent they would sleep in; in addition to the equipment they already carried. To Marcus' dismay, it was his turn to lug the tent on his back. It was large and heavy, but Marcus found that by placing it under his sarcina, the weight of the pack itself would hold it.

As Marcus walked down the street toward the dock, thousands of other legionnaires in line ahead of him, he thought of the new adventure at hand. At least, if nothing else, the change in scenery would be welcome. Suddenly he wondered as he walked down the triple-file line down to the port how many of the men he was with would not return from this expedition. It was a morbid thought, he knew, but in the army one always had to question how long he had left to live.

The path down to the dock was lit at irregular intervals by torches, the flickering light reflecting off the moving mass of armor in a seemingly magical way. The moon had risen, Marcus noticed. He could see the bright, waxing gibbous shining brightly in the star-studded sky. With a sigh, Marcus looked down from the heavens and toward his destination, the helmets of the men in front of him creating a metallic road which led Marcus' eyes straight to the docked ships.

As the most senior among his colleagues, Marcus was the first of his contubernium in line; the seven other men of his squad single file behind him. The mass of men walked slowly, their eyes straining to see the ground at their feet. In times like this, they were thankful for that little bit of extra work involved in making the streets straight and impeccably smooth.

From what Marcus could see through the men in front of him, he and his men were nearly at the port now. He noticed about a dozen centurions giving orders to the legionnaires as they approached the docks. He knew what it was before they gave him any orders. His contubernium was next in line; the eight men in front of him were already being assigned a ship.

Marcus heard the contubernium leader ahead of him claim he was in the Seventh Legion, and the officer assigned him a ship. The eight men immediately began to move to the right, down the north side of the dock, toward a trireme docked behind yet another. The men in front of him now gone, Marcus stepped up to the officer whose red helmet crest was vividly illuminated by the torch behind him.

"Legion?" asked the man, his face hidden in shallow darkness.

Marcus recognized the voice as his cohort's centurion, Severus Atticus.

"Tenth Legion, sir," replied Marcus; his face illuminated by the torch's dancing flames.

"To your left. You may board the first boat here," Severus said, pointing toward the bireme.

"Yes, sir," Marcus nodded.

Marcus saluted the centurion, who returned it, and began to head for the bireme. Marcus' expression turned to disgust as he first set eyes upon the tiny vessel, the two rows of oars protruding from its eighty-foot long body. He stole a glance at the trireme that was docked next to it.

The trireme was forty meters long and over six meters wide and therefore exponentially more stable in the open channel waters. With an exasperated sigh, he began to climb up the wooden walkway to the bireme's deck. The ship could carry over one hundred and fifty men, but only five dozen or so legionaries were already sitting or standing on the semi-crowded deck. They had all removed their packs and were huddled in groups playing dice or simply conversing.

Marcus began to walk down the deck, stepping over men and their equipment, and found an open corner at the front end of the vessel. He reached the bow and began to remove his marching pack as the others followed closely behind him. Marcus sat down and repositioned his pack to his side so that he could lean on it. He looked up to check on his men and noticed they had not wasted any time in removing their packs as well. He let out a great sigh, leaned backward, and looked up at the night sky. Putting all of his worries aside, he closed his eyes and drifted off to sleep.

Five hours passed after the Roman legionnaires began boarding the vessels; six nights and seven hours had gone by since Androvates had first begun spying on Portius Itius. Each night for the past week, Androvates had sat in the bushes on the outskirts of the fort, observing and studying his enemies. Androvates had been assigned to watch the port and had done so for two hours before he spotted a sudden increase in activity within the port. The sudden burst of activity was his cue to return to his village and inform Ambiorix that the Romans were probably embarking the vessels in the port.

Ambiorix and the rest of his villagers had long debated what the Romans were planning and had ultimately hypothesized correctly. Their cues came from the many detachments of Roman legionnaires that had come to question them about Britannia and the massive armada of vessels anchored in and around the port. Since the only remaining unconquered land nearby was their island across the channel, they anticipated an invasion.

After long hours spent watching the Romans, the Gauls stood and watched impatiently as the Roman vessels began to file out of the congested port, bows pointed toward Britain. It was at this point that Ambiorix set out for the fort to study the situation himself.

The fort now seemed quiet, Ambiorix noticed. With two legions fighting elsewhere in Gaul and the remaining two legions now on their way to Britannia, Ambiorix estimated the Roman defenders of the fort numbered around five hundred battle-worthy men, plus the several hundred wounded and emaciated former prisoners who had just returned.

Ambiorix leaned behind a tree, his eyes scanning the top of the walls rapidly in search of the posted sentries. He spotted several sentinels standing guard at regular intervals along the wall, and he quickly began to think up a way through them. The sky was cloudless, and apart from the torches placed at regular intervals along the rampart walls, the scenery seemed to have been plunged into a bucket of black paint. The only contrast came from the silver lunar light above. Ambiorix knew he had the element of surprise and would be concealed until they were a mere twenty-five yards from the walls, maybe even closer if they moved slowly, leaving little time for the alarm to be sounded and the Roman archers to get to the walls. The Gallic chief shifted his balance and waved his son over. Algodorix quickly shuffled over to his father and waited.

"See the sentries?" Ambiorix asked.

"Yes, father."

"We need to get to the walls and over them before the alarm is sounded."

"Shall I try to kill them silently?"

"No. Their walls are too high and too sharp—you will never be able to climb over the wall without help. We will need to use our ladders for that," Ambiorix replied with a shake of his head.

"I have some men with ladders and ten men with a severed log to break down the gate on your order."

"Perfect," he whispered back.

They knelt there another fifteen minutes, forming a plan of attack while monitoring the Roman sentries. Ambiorix also took into account the vessels' time of departure and their probable distance. There was only a light breeze on shore, but Ambiorix knew that the Roman ships were being pushed by the stronger winds out at sea. If they had not lost sight of the port yet, they were surely soon about to. Ambiorix feared that the port's garrison would light a fire as a signal they were being attacked but was confident there was little the vessels could do at this point. Either they would not spot the distress signals if there were any, or they would spot them, turn around, and land in a port held by

Gallic enemy forces. Algodorix had tried to convince his father to attack the port on a later date, but Ambiorix feared the early return of the two legions that had left several nights before; if he wanted to strike he had to do so now.

After deliberating about his plan of attack for several moments more, Ambiorix stood and unsheathed his sword. Lifting it over his head, he began to speak quietly.

"Men, ever since that last battle where we were slaughtered like cattle, we have been seeking revenge. This is our chance," Ambiorix said with zeal.

Some men knelt while others stood watching him; it was true, they had been dreaming of this day for several weeks.

"I have not taken the precaution of consulting the omens before this battle because I am certain that your unfaltering courage along with the pitiful state of our Roman counterparts will surely produce nothing less than victory. We outnumber them about two to one and we are not as crippled as they are. We cannot lose—our victory is assured. The gods have already weakened the enemy for us, and now it is but for us to seize the opportunity. Brave men, let's retake our homeland!"

With a quiet cheer, the men began to unsheathe their swords one after the other, the clanging of the metal blades breaking the silence of the night by just a fraction of a decibel. Ambiorix turned around and walked proudly to the edge of the forest, where he stopped and waited for the one thousand men to form at his sides. Once he was satisfied they were prepared to fight, Ambiorix swirled his sword over his head in a final rallying act and began to advance upon the wooden walls.

Ambiorix knew that the better tactical decision was to advance quietly, but the prospect of victory was too great for him to keep from yelling as he attacked his sleeping enemies. He began to bellow at the top of his lungs, and a cheer erupted among the men. Instantly, the mass of Gauls erupted from the woods like animals fleeing from a wildfire. The stretch before the fort was crossed in a matter of seconds, and the ladders were already being raised before the official alarm was sounded within the fort. The yells of attacking infantry served as an alarm for many of the sleeping soldiers. The dazed legionnaires began to throw off their blankets. While some bothered to put on their armor, others simply picked up their sword and shield and ran to the walls.

The invaders' ladders were shoved against the walls forcefully, and immediately the Gallic soldiers began to climb them two rungs at a time. As the first Gauls began to jump over the walls, the men carrying the battering log were just reaching the front gate. The Romans were thrown into a temporary state of confusion at the realization that the peaceful fall night had turned into an unanticipated fight for life.

Ambiorix was one of the first over the wall, and he quickly overpowered the enemy sentries while countless more Romans ran up the stairs and ladders to help repel the attack. The Romans fell by the heap; the Gauls stepped over them and fought the next wave of Romans who arrived at the walls.

Several of the Romans shoved their shields into the Gauls and, upon pushing them back a couple of feet, were themselves mercilessly slain. The din of battle severed the night's peace and quiet much as the blades severed men. Orders and screams filled the air yet somehow muted each other out, as the men engaged in lethal combat. It was clear to the Romans that the Gauls were striving to capture the port. Far from just another vain attempt to disrupt their sleep; this was an actual assault intended to slay each and every last Roman present. The Romans were only five hundred strong, and it was still unclear how many Gauls were participating in the attack. This ratio didn't guarantee defeat, but it definitely made the Romans realize the slim margin of error they could allow themselves. The Romans didn't have much maneuvering room within the camp, and as outnumbered as they were, they had to make every blow count.

As sections of the wall were lost, recaptured, and lost again, the death toll began to rise on both sides. The Romans were able to compensate for their lack of men by fighting close together on the thin ramparts, just like at Thermopylae, where the outnumbered Greeks had held off the significantly larger Persian forces by fighting in a narrow gorge where numbers didn't matter as much. Here, the gorge was the rampart. Protected by their large shields, and in some cases armor, the Romans were able to create a resilient barrier that inhibited the Gallic advance. Although the Gauls were unable to move down the ramparts any further, many opted to slide down the ladders and charge into the streets below.

On the ramparts, with no room to breathe let alone fight, both cultures clashed fiercely. As the mass of men were crushed tighter and tighter, they slipped on the blood-lubricated wooden floors. With little room to maneuver the Gauls, who were trapped on both sides by the defending Romans, began to lose their footing and slide off the ramparts onto the street below. Realizing this, the Romans began to push harder into the mass of men with their shields, not bothering to slay the enemy with their swords but trying to knock them to their deaths. Like an overstuffed bag, the contents began to overflow, and Gauls fell over the sides onto the ground fifteen feet below.

Dull thuds resounded as the men fell to their deaths in screams of fear. It was one thing to die fighting gloriously but another to slip and plummet helplessly. The Gauls realized their predicament and the Romans' intentions and fought back as hard as they could despite their cramped state. Their salvation came from the sudden crash of the main gates below them which gave way to five hundred of their bloodthirsty friends.

Sabinus, who had been one of the first to respond to the attack, struggled in the fight alongside his men. Believing in leadership from the front, he showed no regard for his own safety and led the wedge into the enemy formation that had broken through the main gate. Sabinus and his men fought savagely, knowing that they could not afford to retreat; they didn't have anywhere to retreat to.

With the Roman defenders thinning out, the Gauls quickly began to gain the upper hand. The Romans' only bet for survival lay in regrouping and holding the enemy at bay with their swords and pila. One centurion called out for them to do exactly that but was slain mid-sentence by a Gaul behind him. The Romans realized their only chance for survival lay in utilizing the same cohesion they employed on the battlefield. One after the other, the Romans began to group together, all the while moving to a more defensive position near the wall. Hacking and stabbing their way to the wall, the various groups began to converge and grow in size. Forming a half-circle with their backs to the wall, the Romans could fight without worry about protecting their rear. On solid footing, the Romans began using their deadly tactics with terrifying effectiveness.

Calidro, on the rampart, looked down at the huddled Romans and spoke to Androvates.

"Look at them! They think themselves so strong, but they are, in reality, so weak. They are not real men!"

Androvates watched alongside his friend as his fellow men attacked the Roman soldiers relentlessly but to little avail.

"I fear we may not win as easily as previously thought," Androvates said, a tinge of fear in his voice.

Calidro looked down at the Romans and spat onto the group huddled directly below him.

"Hah! You expect this mass of frightened cowards to fight? They are not going to win. Look at them! They are huddled like frightened puppies."

"Or like famished dogs waiting to be released," Androvates compared.

Calidro glared at his friend and said, "You can continue to support our enemies, but I for one will slay them like the vermin they are."

Androvates watched as his hot-tempered friend ran down the steps and into the fray. He lost track of him for a brief instant when the motion of the men covered his advance. Suddenly he saw him again at the head of the rank, wielding his sword like a demon. He watched as Calidro drew a large circle in the air and brought the sword crashing down on a Roman's head. The man began to fall, and Calidro immediately thrust his sword into the man behind the one he had just killed. That man fell as well.

Androvates had always been impressed by the seeming ease with which Calidro took another's life. Androvates feared someone would take Calidro's just as he took theirs. As more and more Gauls succumbed to mortal wounds and fatigue, the gusto with which they had initially attacked began to wear off. Swords arced heavily and slowly as arms tired and blocking reflexes came more slowly.

Androvates watched as his prediction began to come true. The Romans, seeking revenge, began to slash at their attackers mercilessly. The Gauls fell over each other as the Romans broke their ranks and charged at those fleeing. Androvates watched in awe as his fellow Gallic friends were stabbed and killed. The operation had been an awful disaster. If they had succeeded, the Romans would not have had a port to return to in this region, and many more Romans would have been slain.

Unfortunately, it was the other way around. Now, the Gauls had lost their own battle. Calidro fought fiercely as he was pushed back by the assailing Romans. Soon he found himself with his back pressed to the inner side of the wall and, realizing his fate, charged mindlessly and brutally into the waiting Romans. He thrust his sword toward one of the men but was blocked and stabbed in return. Androvates watched in pain as his friend was slain before him. With his mind still on what had just happened, he ignored the fact that two Romans were coming up from the length of the rampart. The two men made their presence known by asking him to surrender, but Androvates merely began to run. Without thinking, Androvates leaped below onto the Roman soldiers. With a great crash, he picked himself back up and quickly began to limp away. Shielded by the few Gauls who had opted to fight to the death, Androvates escaped through the battered gateway and into the night.

Ambiorix and his son were among the last survivors, stranded near the gate. The Romans had entirely encircled Ambiorix, his son, and seven others standing by their sides. And then there were six ... And then only five ... The men began to panic at the realization that their lives were closing to an end. Chills ran down their backs; they heard the pounding of their heartbeats in their ears and felt their hair rise on end. The Romans slaughtered Ambiorix's men as they fought to protect him, and soon Algodorix and his father were the last two men left standing. The Romans closed in menacingly around them like a noose around a neck.

In a last act of defiance, Ambiorix blocked a sword thrust, told his son he loved him with a brief hug, then took the sword out of his son's hand and told him to run. Algodorix watched tearfully as his father kept the Romans from maneuvering to get him before turning to run toward the gate. The Romans tried to get through Ambiorix to reach the fleeing Algodorix but the Gaul ran too fast for them.

"Continue the fight, my son!" Ambiorix shouted as he swirled his swords with ease and prepared to die.

Building up momentum, he threw one sword at his enemies in vain and prepared to cleave through the man directly in front of him when he suddenly felt a searing pain in his side. He had just been stabbed. Pain raced through his body and he immediately crumpled to the ground. The Romans then battered the dying man into a bloody pulp with their shields. They showed no mercy to the man who had plotted their death.

Ambiorix watched the Romans around him as he lay on the cold dirt. His sword lay just out of his reach to his right; he wondered if he could take another man with him to the afterlife. He was extremely disappointed that his attack had failed, yet he knew that his son would continue the struggle against the Roman invaders for him. Slowly and painfully, he crawled toward his sword that had fallen several inches away from his outstretched hand. As he grasped the handle, Sabinus walked up and placed his foot on the blade and shook his head slowly. With all hopes of killing a few more Romans now gone, Ambiorix let go of the handle and collapsed dead at the feet of the Roman officer.

The adrenaline began to diminish and soon the Romans were busy repairing the gate and tending to the wounded. They had repulsed the attack but didn't know if any more would be launched. Rapidly assessing the extent of the damage, Sabinus set about deploying repair teams to work on the most damaged parts of the wall first. He then returned to the principia to write his report.

XIII

Had it not been for the sickening motion of the ship as it plowed through the six-foot swells or the grim possibility of this being his last voyage, Marcus might have slept soundly. However, his body ached all over from lying on the cold, wooden floor. His clothes were wet and he felt like regurgitating from the nauseating motion. He closed his eyes and tried to imagine he was walking on land, but it didn't help. *That Greek "mind over matter" junk is all a lie*, he thought.

He gagged as the bow of the ship suddenly fell into a wave; the sea-spray doused him. He cursed at the voyage and leaned back against his pack. Marcus closed his eyes again, trying to go to sleep. He knew fatigue was a soldier's death warrant. How was a man supposed to fight and think soundly if he struggled simply to keep his eyes open? Trying to think of a peaceful image, he imagined himself walking through the countryside with no threat of being slain. He began to succumb to the tug of sleep, his eyelids fluttering as he began to fade away. But another wave hit, and the salty water rained onto the ship sadistically. He immediately awoke and again cursed the sea, cursed the voyage, cursed the army. He was an infantryman, not a sailor.

Marcus looked at his men, asleep on the cold deck. The boat was covered with so many men he was amazed it could remain afloat. Though it did sit lower in the water, it still navigated faithfully, ferrying the men to their next campaign. His men were all asleep, wrapped in blankets, when he suddenly felt a nudge in his side and looked over, finding himself starring into the eyes of a young man.

"You can't sleep either, huh?"

Marcus didn't respond immediately; the bow plunged downward, and he braced for the coming shower.

"No, the sea is not my element," Marcus replied jokingly.

"Me neither," the man replied, and he turned to look down the length of the boat. There was little light besides that of the moon and stars, and even those shone weakly through the increasing cloud cover. Marcus could barely make out the facial features of the man next to him through the darkness, but Marcus recognized his voice as that of his youngest recruit, Cnaeus Junius. The boy was slim and of average height, and his eyes recessed far into his head. The soldier sported no facial hair, and his head was shaved nearly bald.

"The swells have gotten larger since we left Portius Itius," Marcus stated.

"The open channel waves are bigger than those by shore," Cnaeus replied, turning to face Marcus again. "Plus there's the effect of the coming storm."

Marcus nodded. He had estimated that the worst of it would strike sometime soon. He hoped it would happen after the landing had taken place and not during. Anchored and delivering men, the frail man-made boats would be no match for the full onslaught of the sea and winds.

"This is awful," Marcus said while his stomach traveled to his throat as the vessel plunged downward over the crest of a wave.

"We should have gone to the back of the boat. It moves less there," Cnaeus said, seeing Marcus in visible agony at the motion of the swell.

"You do not seem bothered by it, although you claim the contrary," Marcus stated.

"Ah, yes. I do not like the water, but the motion does not affect me."

Marcus nodded, struggling not to vomit on the man. Cnaeus smiled back and offered his friend some advice.

"Sometimes it is best to just let it out. You'll feel better afterwards, trust me."

Marcus nodded again.

The boat plunged, and a large spray of water fell onto them. Marcus had pushed the limits as far as he could. He struggled to his feet against the rocking of the small vessel. He stepped over the sleeping, water-soaked men and threw himself against the railing as the ship began to rise over a swell. He held on for dear life as the boat plummeted again.

This is getting monotonous, he thought.

Marcus couldn't wait to be back on dry land. Clutching the rail, he tried to keep from throwing up. Even the cool wind that blew in his face did little to ebb the nauseating feeling. He closed his eyes and tried to concentrate on his stomach. Suddenly another wave hit, and he threw up over the side. He wiped his mouth with the back of his hand and began to make his way back to his spot. He sat heavily on the drenched deck. Cnaeus looked at him expectantly.

"So?" Cnaeus asked.

Marcus remained silent as he analyzed himself.

"Better," he finally said, nodding at his friend.

Cnaeus nodded and smiled.

"Glad I could help," he said, leaning back against his pack. He closed his eyes and leaned his head back as if to fall asleep.

Marcus repositioned himself and closed his eyes as well. The motion of the ship began to fade away. He felt a lot better, and thanks to his friend, he was asleep before the next set of waves slammed into the ship.

Morning did not come early enough for many of the men onboard the ships. They had spent a miserable night onboard the saturated decks and were eating the now-soggy food they had brought with them. Most of them thought that facing the Britons had to be better than spending another gut-wrenching minute onboard the cramped vessels. The few who had managed to fall asleep had been awoken once land was in sight, the landscape reminding them of Gaul. Marcus leaned against the railing, eating his meal. Fortunately, he had wrapped it tightly in cloth so it had escaped the torrential downpours from the brutal waves during the stomach-wrenching crossing. The waves were still large, but the men had at last grown accustomed to them.

Marcus took a look around him, drawing in the incredible sight. The vessels were spread out over a mile, the waves having broadened the ships' formation. He noticed he was in one of the lead ships, the third in fact. Ahead of him was Caesar's trireme, he knew, which followed loosely behind a smaller bireme. The weather had settled for the moment, the sky unchanging from its current overcast state; the sun had risen just an hour ago and was only a faded orange glow behind the thick, light-diffusing clouds.

Despite the rough crossing, the convoy had not been delayed significantly. The land ahead grew at a rapid rate, the trees becoming individually discernable. The tall cliff stood proudly, as if ready to defend itself from the Roman invaders. It all seemed foreboding. Marcus shook off his thoughts and returned to where his men were seated. He found his spot at the tip of the ship and sat down.

"How's your food?" one of his men asked, looking up from his meal.

"Soaked," Marcus replied.

"Same here," the mumbled, "Just like everything else onboard this damned boat."

Marcus nodded and looked down the length of the vessel. The men were scattered all over deck, eating, sharpening their swords, or repacking their packs. None were idle. He finished off his bread and dusted his hands. Then he pulled his pack over toward him and quickly refastened his food sack to the pack. He pushed it back against the rail at his side. One of his men stood up and unsheathed his sword and pulled out a sharpener and repeatedly ran the block down the length of the short sword. As they finished their meals, others began to follow suit. Marcus stood up to unsheathe his sword while watching the approaching shoreline.

The vessels sailed for twenty minutes more before the men realized something was wrong. The two vessels ahead of theirs had suddenly stopped. A man stood on the stern of Caesar's ship waving a large, red flag. Slowly the vessels came to within five hundred yards of the shore, the terrain clearly discernible. As the men searched the top of the cliff, enemy soldiers became discernable against the landscape. Caesar, standing in the bow, rapidly scanned the cliff top. He had hoped to avoid this. His plan had been to land some of his troops before the enemy spotted the ships and had time to react. Upon seeing the enemy, he had quickly ordered for the captain to stop the boat and wait for the remainder of the fleet to pull alongside. A sailor warned the approaching vessels by semaphore.

Caesar quickly assessed the dangers that could cause him to fail and narrowed them down to two: the sea and enemy archers. The waves posed no problem this far from shore; however, archers were known to be able to reach a distance of one hundred and fifty yards, albeit not with accuracy. Caesar then roughly calculated the height advantage the Britons had and reduced their potential range according to the strong winds coming in from the sea. Caesar ordered his vessels to sail closer to shore and halted them at a distance two hundred yards from the base of the cliff for safety.

Caesar walked to the aft section of his large trireme, where the Legion commanders, Lucius and Claudius, spoke of various landing possibilities.

"The enemy is already poised to receive our landing," Caesar said, stating the obvious.

"How did they know?" Claudius asked, already knowing the answer.

"They knew we were coming because of Volusenus," Caesar replied.

"They must have been keeping watch since their encounter with him," Lucius added.

"Most likely," Caesar said. "We need to wait for the others and then move out to find the beach Volusenus found on his reconnaissance. Could one of you go summon him?"

Claudius nodded and left to go find Volusenus among the many men who crowded the deck. Meanwhile, Caesar walked past Lucius and leaned against the railing, looking for the remainder of the fleet. They were all in sight and rapidly heading toward his position.

Within thirty minutes, the entire fleet was grouped offshore, waiting for the command to move. Meanwhile, Volusenus had been located and approached Caesar to guide him to the beach he had found. Immediately the order to follow was transmitted to the other ships via semaphore and the ships began to row in the direction Volusenus commanded. At first the enemy atop the cliff didn't react. The men stood as still as the trees around them. Then, rather abruptly, the mass of men began to jog along the length of the precipice. Caesar knew they would keep up alongside his ships and fight him wherever he would land. He watched as the British cavalry and chariots quickly passed the foot soldiers in pursuit of the Roman vessels.

Before the Roman vessels had navigated the mile to the only beach that could support a massive landing, the Britons knew where to go. The chariots and cavalry were waiting patiently at the tree line when the first of the Roman vessels came around the rocky point; the British infantry came up a short distance behind. The Roman ships were coming to a halt when Caesar summoned his two Legion commanders at the bow of the ship.

"Men, the time has come," Caesar said, his gaze moving fluidly from one man to the other.

"My men are prepared to land at your order," said Lucius, gesturing toward the fleet around him with his arms.

Claudius nodded. "The seas are still rough. It is going to be dangerous for the men," he said.

"I realize that, but we must attack now," Caesar replied.

"Yes, but the swells are tall, the enemy occupies a position of superiority, and due to the uncooperative seas, our ships will be forced to remain farther from shore to avoid being beached," Claudius said, bringing all of his fears to light.

Caesar nodded but remained silent and looked at the beach.

"Incoming," suddenly shouted a man standing at the bow.

The four officers spun to look at the vessel's captain; a large man in his mid-forties who had a face that seemed chiseled from stone and who appeared as though he enjoyed eating rocks in place of food. His head was covered in thin, sparse hair and his face sported a boxed beard. All present noticed he was staring intently toward the shoreline.

Caesar immediately turned to face the British shoreline as the first salvo of arrows began to impale the water fifty yards in front of the boat. Caesar quickly ran to the bow and peered over the edge of the railing. The captain had given the order to move out farther from the beach, but Caesar quickly intervened.

"Save their energy. The arrows can't reach us; we are too far from shore."

The captain looked at Caesar and then quickly cancelled the order.

The wind suddenly died down, and Lucius made Caesar aware of it.

"Caesar, if you want to land, we must do so now."

"Indeed," Caesar said, moving toward the port side of the ship. "Signal the order to land."

One of the sailors quickly ran to the stern and began to wave a large blue flag with a yellow diagonal stripe down the center; the signal to commence the landing. The vessels quickly began to reposition themselves in preparation to swoop by the beach and disembark the legionnaires. Debarkation required that the vessels move in as close to shore as possible whereupon the legionnaires would jump overboard into the rough surf and fight their way through the waters to the beach. However, chariots now paraded down the length of the beach, their riders screaming and shaking their heavy swords angrily at the Romans. The landing was going to be bloody and the battle hard fought, but every legionnaire knew what was expected of him and they would be damned if Rome's finest was kept at bay by mere unshaven barbarians.

XIV

The legionnaires were under attack by British archers from the moment they came within range. The Roman soldiers aboard the vessels adopted defensive formations with their shields as each jumped over the side in turn. Before leaping overboard, the men had been ordered to remove their packs and carry only their battle accessories. Still the men landed with big splashes, weighed down by their heavy armor and multiple weapons. The men cursed their gear during the swim to shore but knew their very lives would depend on it from the moment they touched shore. To the legionnaires, drowning was an acceptable risk in exchange for some measure of security against the thousands of enemies waiting ashore.

Scores of men were hit and killed by enemy archers as they floundered in the water, slowed by their heavy gear. The first ashore knelt and hid behind their shields as salvos of arrows thudded into them. Both men and vessels were dangerously exposed, and the Romans were thankful the Britons were not firing flaming arrows at their wooden ships. From the sea, the Roman men-of-war retaliated with their own salvos of arrow fire. However, the friendly fire was neither concentrated nor accurate, and the legionnaires were all too conscious of the fact it would take time for all the proper adjustments to be made before the heavy weapons would begin to wreak havoc on the enemy.

The majority of the enemy arrow fire was concentrated on the landing party, and those debarking were anxious to help those exposed on the beach. In less than five minutes, the beach was littered with arrow-riddled and maimed bodies, while others struggled out of the water only to meet the same fate. Not daring to venture out alone, the surviving Romans remained huddled on the beach as they waited for additional reinforcements from the ships. The legionnaires formed groups and arranged their shields in such a way as to provide an impenetrable wall against the enemy archers.

All along the beach, British cavalry and infantry charged into the frigid waters and engaged their enemies where they were weakest. Romans who were struggling out of the water were slain by the Britons, who fought on dry land. Some of the more determined natives ventured out into the frigid waters to fight but quickly opted to leave that miserable experience for their Roman counterparts.

The Roman vessels continued to disembark masses of legionnaires, but the outnumbered men were rapidly slain on the beach. Here and there, small groups of legionnaires were able to hold their own, but for the most part, the beach remained in enemy hands. The Romans, cold and struggling in the surf with their large shields and pila, were cut down by the enemy before they were able to throw their javelins at the charging soldiers.

The British cavalry ran up and down the length of the beach, slaying every Roman unlucky enough to be cut off from the remainder of the army or struggling in the surf. This infuriated the legionnaires both ashore and aboard ship, who thought the Britons were too cowardly to engage the pockets of resistance like real men. To further complicate the landings, three dozen chariots suddenly came rolling out of the forest down the length of the beach, their scythed wheels severing men in half.

Marcus watched his fellow soldiers being massacred from where he waited impatiently for his turn to jump. He saw some men who, upon reaching the beach, lost their footing when waves broke over their backs and knocked them down, only to be attacked by multiple enemies waiting for precisely that situation. Others below him were struck by arrows as they swam and sank to the bottom of the frigid waters, never to be seen again. Marcus felt a profound sense of gloom as he watched his fellow brothers-in-arms die before his eyes. From the railing of his ship, he waited impatiently for the order to jump in and help his comrades in peril.

The seawater was already pink from blood. The Romans ashore, who had formed into makeshift centuries, ignored their legion affiliations and fought merely for their lives. They arranged their shields to form a wall to the front and sides, leaving the rear open to others who were running to them for protection. Too great a number of soldiers were being killed early in the battle, and Caesar was aware that the landing was turning into a bloodbath. As vessels unloaded the last of the troops, they lifted anchor and rowed out to a safe distance from shore, allowing other ships to discharge their human cargo. Marcus was now poised to be in the next wave. His boat began to row toward shore, and he lifted his shield to protect himself from any stray arrows.

Soon his vessel came to a halt a short distance offshore. Marcus scanned the beach to see where they were needed most and suddenly noticed a small detachment of men huddled together near the base of the cliff on the right side of the beach.

"Sir, those men seem to be in desperate straits over there. We should land in that area to lend them a hand," Marcus said, pointing toward the trapped legionnaires. Other vessels were clearly refusing to land men there due to the abundant enemy forces and archers, but Severus knew Marcus was right. Those men were holding their ground valiantly in desperate hope that some of their fellow comrades would come to their aid. Both men knew they had to land there. Severus, the top-ranking officer on board, ordered the ship's captain to land them on the far right side of the beach.

"It's too dangerous! Are you crazy? My ship is going to receive those archers' full attention," the captain replied.

"*Too dangerous?*" Severus repeated. "Those men are stranded and about to be overrun on the beach and you're worried about a couple arrows denting your ship?"

"I will drop you off there," the captain replied, pointing to a stretch of ground too far away for Severus and his soldiers to reach the trapped men in time.

Severus' blood was boiling and he unsheathed his sword.

"As centurion of the First Cohort of the Tenth Legion, I command you to navigate your vessel to the precise point I order you."

"You could be Caesar himself. I couldn't care less about your desire. You're on my ship, you go where I say," the pompous captain replied.

Infuriated, Marcus deliberately unsheathed his sword as well and began to walk quickly and menacingly toward the captain. The latter saw Marcus and his undaunted stare and smirked at the approaching soldier, not fully certain how serious the man was.

Marcus made a show of twirling his gladius in his hand before he pulled his arm back, preparing to stab.

Suddenly the fat man realized Marcus was not kidding and thrust out his hand, "Alright! Alright!"

Marcus stopped and looked at Severus as if seeking approval.

"You know where I want to go," Severus said before turning to face Marcus. "It was about time."

The men turned their attention back toward the men they were going to try to save as they sheathed their swords. Archers lined the top of the cliff on that side, but due to the fragility of the cliff's edge and the height, the British archers remained several feet behind the edge to avoid slipping and becoming casualties themselves. The brittle nature of the cliff's edge turned out to be favorable for the Romans below, as it allowed those Romans nearest the base of the cliff a protected spot against the incessant arrow fire from above.

The stranded Romans were bogged down dangerously close to the water and in grave danger of being pushed back into the sea if not rescued or reinforced in time. They had formed a long line with their backs to the water, and those farther from the base of the cliff presented a large target to the archers above. From aboard the vessel, Marcus was trying to develop a plan that could save them. He would have to find a way to move the legionnaires nearer to the cliff to escape the archers and somehow rapidly kill many enemy soldiers or risk ending up in the same predicament.

With their numbers dwindling, the trapped Romans watched the approaching vessel with hope, but the elation quickly wore off as they saw British cavalry advancing from their left, seeking to flank them and put an end to the trapped men's lives. The legionnaires aboard Marcus' vessel saw this too and realized it was only a matter of minutes before the trapped Romans succumbed to the British cavalry. Before the captain had even stopped the vessel, Severus gave the order for his men to jump overboard in a desperate attempt to replenish their lines before the Britons punched through.

The waves the Romans jumped into were rough and high, and their heavy gear added to the danger of crossing, but the determined soldiers made their way to the beach one by one. Marcus fought his way out of the sea's grasp and breathed a sigh of relief as he felt his sandaled feet touch the sand underneath him. The archers immediately began to focus their attention on the fresher soldiers as they struggled from the water. Marcus quickly raised his shield as arrows began to strike the water around him. Without bothering to catch his breath, Marcus sprinted out of the water and crossed the dozen feet of sand, reaching the trapped Romans just as the British cavalry hit their left flank.

Immediately, the Roman lines buckled as the exhausted legionnaires were trampled by the charging beasts. To some of the Romans, it seemed these would be their last moments, until suddenly Severus and his men reinforced their collapsed flank and began to attack the fatigued British cavalrymen. The British cavalry, so obsessed with driving deep into the Roman flank, had not realized how tired they were themselves until they met the heavy blows delivered by the fresh Roman reinforcements. Surrounded in turn and with their steeds exhausted, it didn't take long before the Britons realized what would become of them. Presenting large, immobile targets to the heavily clad enemy, the British cavalry opted to flee rather than fight, but they were cut down mercilessly by the avenging Romans.

Before long, the last of the horsemen succumbed to fatal wounds, and the Roman lines reformed, ready to wipe out the enemy infantry in much the same way. The annihilation of the enemy cavalry spurred their spirits, but their arms were still heavy and their breathing still rapid and shallow. Although a much-needed second vessel was approaching behind Severus', the Romans on shore were still gravely outnumbered and in direct line of sight of the archers on the cliff.

"Who's your commanding officer?" Severus shouted to one of the soldiers as he reached the mass of men.

"He was hit early in the battle by an arrow, sir, as were three other centurions. I'm afraid we haven't had the benefit of any senior leadership for the past half hour," the man replied as he wiped the sweat off his face.

Severus nodded and pondered what to do. He realized he had to stop the archers somehow. The men-of-war fired occasional salvos toward the archers but were concentrating mostly on the infantry that littered the beach. Suddenly, he heard one of the legionnaires shouting orders from within the ranks.

"Rotate to the right! We need to get to the base of that cliff!" Marcus shouted with all his strength. Marcus' arms felt like lead weight, and he knew that if he and his fellow soldiers didn't find a more suitable position to fight from, they wouldn't last another ten minutes.

Severus was awed by Marcus' initiative and realized that was the best maneuver. Without further delay, he joined Marcus in shouting the order. Any who had been reluctant to follow Marcus' order now obeyed Severus, and the Roman formation began to pivot nearer the base of the cliff. Wounded Romans were pulled backward out of harm's way while the dead were left to be trampled by the mass of men.

Slowly, the exhausted legionnaires began to maneuver and rotate their flank as they crept toward the base of the cliff. As they neared the cliff's base, the archers began to lose sight of them, and the arrow-fire steadily slowed until it finally stopped completely. The exhausted legionnaires breathed a sigh of relief as the archers ceased to rain death from above. They could now concentrate the last of their energy against the enemy infantry. As the Roman flank continued to rotate closer to the cliff, the enemy infantry rotated accordingly, not realizing that Marcus was exposing them perfectly for fire from the men-of-war.

Caesar watched the slaughter unfold from his ship. He felt sick at the thought of his helpless men being slain. Nearly two thousand men were on shore and another four hundred floated or lay lifeless in the breaking surf and on the sand. The legionnaires on shore were moving toward each other slowly, forming one large group that offered more protection. British chariots, however, continued to rampage murderously through the legionnaires.

Chariots had gone out of favor in the Roman provinces, and now the legionnaires were being given a painful lesson about their true value in warfare. The scythed wheels slashed through the legs of legionnaires who ran from the terrifying vehicles, while galloping horses stampeded others. And the hellish rattle the wheels made as they spun further unnerved the Romans.

The chariots provided transportation to and from the battlefield as well. Each one, led by a highly trained charioteer, carried a nobleman to the fray. The chariots wreaked havoc and put fear into the hearts of enemy and then dropped off their nobles to fight. If the situation got harsh for their masters, the charioteers would swoop in like eagles and pick them up without even slowing down. This made it extremely difficult to kill the charioteers, and the Romans made it a point to stab the passing horses as best they could out of sheer rage at their apparent invulnerability. Many legionnaires had lost their pila during the landing. Surprisingly few had lost their shields—finding them too valuable a possession to relinquish before a battle. With their few remaining pila protruding through gaps in their shields, the Romans speared at the wheels and horses of the passing chariots. Eventually one of the Romans was able to spear a horse and watched as it crashed to the ground, pulling the other horses down with it. The charioteer was flung from his chariot and hit the ground with a rolling thud two dozen feet farther down the beach. Not one of the legionnaires moved up to finish off the incapacitated driver.

Caesar continued to scan the battlefield. He spotted Marcus' position on the far right side of the beach and thought he could see archers on the edge of the cliff firing downwards. Immediately, he realized that although the men were in jeopardy, they had managed to expose the Britons' unprotected flank. Without wasting any precious time, he called one of the officers over.

"Give the order for the men-of-war to reposition themselves on the right flank and begin their attack," Caesar ordered. "We're going to nail those sons of bitches hard and fast before it is too late."

The officer nodded and quickly jogged away. Caesar's last chance for success lay in providing covering fire for his landing party. Although the men-of-war had been firing their ballistae and catapults at the British defenders, the vessels were spread out and not firing concentrated salvoes.

Caesar couldn't stop smiling; the exposed Britons were in desperate straits. Although they hadn't realized it yet, the full might of Caesar's navy was about to concentrate their fire on that select group of enemy soldiers. If they held their ground they would be decimated within minutes, and if they fell back, his army would have the first true opportunity to gain some ground and regroup. Finally his luck was beginning to return. Caesar noticed that his soldiers, who were scattered across the beach's expanse, were starting to regroup and fight their way toward the right flank. They must have seen the warships being repositioned and understood that they needed to solidify their ranks before being able to attack farther up the beach.

The men-of-war captains had received the order via semaphore and began to move their ships to the far right side of the armada. They began firing their catapults and ballistae while archers fired their arrows from the top of the towers.

The ballista was a terrifying weapon that resembled a large bow placed on its side. The weapon was powered by coiled sinews; long bolts were fired at frightening velocities. The bolts were so powerful they were able to pass through several men before losing their inertia. The sight of several men skewered together was a frightening sight to Romans and Britons alike.

As flaming arrows and canisters of burning oil were fired from the nearby ships, the British resolve began to weaken. Burning jars of oil exploded into fiery infernos, igniting dead and live men alike, while the ballista bolts punched through the smoke and fire into the men huddled behind them.

Along the beach, the smoke from earlier salvoes helped cloak the Romans from the British leaders who stood at the edge of the forest, watching the battle unfold. Receiving the order to attack again, the British soldiers who had retreated partway up the beach peered through the waves of heat and the thick, pungent smoke toward the Roman legions. The desperate natives charged down the beach once more but within minutes were pushed back by the tremendous volume of fire coming from the Roman ballistae and catapults.

The Britons, who continued to suffer casualties, began to pull back up the beach for the second time. The Romans did not dare to venture out and remained kneeling in the moist, crimson sand, protected by their shields.

As time passed, the men-of-war began to take their toll on the British forces. The number of Roman soldiers landing on the beach began to increase, and the last of the British line began to crumble. Both sides knew the beach would be in Roman hands within minutes.

As the Britons began to flee, those closer to the Romans were killed immediately while those in the center of the formation were trampled by those Britons who struggled in vain to pass the slower men. Many Britons tripped and fell prey to the horde of Roman legionnaires, who devoured the gap between them and the forest's edge like famished wolves. As the Romans mercilessly overwhelmed the fleeing enemy, British chariots and the cavalry made a futile attempt to aid their fleeing friends but were quickly slain and fought off by the unforgiving legionnaires.

Ludovic, among those nearest to the forest's edge, was surprised he had not been killed during the battle. He had taken many unnecessary risks and killed many Romans as a result, yet he felt he still had not killed enough to avenge his friends who had perished during previous engagements. He heard several of his compatriots plotting to ambush the passing Romans from within the forest but knew the odds of success were slim. It would be far wiser to regroup and fight another day.

Those Britons who were bent on fighting to the death took swords from the routers and, shielded by the mass movement, began to climb low trees in anticipation of Roman pursuit. Concealed, they watched the fleeing men run for their lives, closely pursued by the Romans. The last of their tribesman swiftly passed beneath them, and the ambushers were stranded above the pursuing legionnaires. Quietly, they remained concealed until the majority of the Roman pursuers had passed along the trail; they waited patiently to ambush unsuspecting stragglers. Five minutes passed before a small detachment of Romans came jogging in their direction. One Briton waited impatiently as the men began to run past and then leaped from his tree onto a Roman soldier with a blood-curdling cry.

Marcus picked himself up from the ground and collected his sword from the dirty sand. The beach was littered with dead men and horses as well as battered chariots; navigating the beach was a chore. Many men had tripped on debris during the pursuit, and Marcus was embarrassed to have been one of them. He watched the legionnaires ahead of him race toward the forest as he wiped the sand off his tunic and armor.

Legionnaires poured onto the beach at increasing rates once the enemy had been overrun, and Marcus knew the battle was just about over. He desperately wanted to pursue the Britons and finish what they had started but realized that it was too late. The Britons would have vanished into the forest, and pursuit would yield very few enemy casualties.

"Do you think we're still in the fight?" Vibius asked as he peered toward the forest.

Marcus squinted toward the tree line. "There's only one way to find out."

The men set off toward the dark forest, loosely followed by two dozen others. Marcus and the others reached the forest's edge in little time and began to head down the trail. They could hear but not see the legionnaires ahead of them as they jogged the serpentine path. Suddenly Marcus heard a crash behind him, closely followed by a shout of pain. He spun on his heels and quickly realized he had walked his men into an ambush. Several more Britons leaped from trees and into the Roman formation without warning. Quickly, the Britons wreaked havoc among the legionnaires.

"Regroup!" Marcus yelled as he sprinted back toward where the heaviest fighting was taking place.

One Briton had singlehandedly killed two Romans and Marcus rapidly singled him out as his target and charged him with his shield.

The Briton was back on his feet, his bloody sword slashing, within seconds. The other concealed Britons then leaped from their trees and engaged the Romans as well. Although still slightly outnumbered, the Britons had begun with the upper hand by surprising the enemy.

The first Briton to leap had already fought and killed two men and was engaging with a third when he noticed a shield being thrust toward him from his side. Instinctively, he sidestepped the wooden shield and slashed at the man's back, angry when he felt his sword clatter against the legionnaire's armor. The top of the shield nicked his mouth and shattered several teeth along with bone, sending a burst of pain through his head. Fresh anger jolted through him as he regarded what he considered a coward; any man who did not fight shirtless did not deserve respect or honor. The Roman soldier was plated in armor and wore a large helmet of Gallic design, and he cowered behind a large shield that was too cumbersome for one-on-one combat. How was this method of fighting supposed to display the valor and bravery one was supposed to boast about in combat?

The Briton tightened his grip on his sword and spat pieces of teeth to the ground, more infuriated than ever. Marcus had just been another enemy, but now it was personal. He bellowed deeply before charging headlong toward the Roman, his sword stretched out far to his side. His tactic was not to place a well-delivered stab but to use his brute force to cleave through the shield and armor straight into the man behind. A foolish move, he realized too late. Parried by the large shield, he fell victim to Marcus' sword and collapsed, unblinking, to the ground.

A second Briton appeared, and Marcus quickly realized that his large shield was cumbersome and too difficult to reposition to parry blows from his agile nemesis. Instead of dropping it, he threw it to the best of his ability toward his opponent. He heard the handle crack as he heaved it and watched as the large shield flew oddly through the air.

The man easily sidestepped the odd projectile and suddenly came running back toward Marcus. Marcus got into position with his sword, the blade circling slowly, menacingly, over his head. He blocked a shot to his groin, quickly hooked the Briton behind the knee, and shoved him away with his hand. The man crumpled and swiftly rolled away from Marcus' follow-up downward blow. The infuriated Briton rose to his feet and charged toward Marcus. The Briton slashed toward Marcus' gut but missed, the sword hissing through empty space. Marcus took a step backward as the Briton charged him and tripped on an upturned root just as his enemy dove onto him. Marcus fell hard on his back, but was able to toss the medium-sized man over with his feet as the latter dove onto Marcus. The barbarian spun threw the air and fell heavily onto his shoulder at the base of a tree, snapping the bone forcefully.

The man shouted in pain and rolled to his side, his eyes fluttering.

Marcus shook off the pain in his back and walked toward the injured man. The native stood slowly and defiantly, his body trembling from a broken shoulder, a broken ankle, and several broken ribs. Marcus was not one to kill viciously for no reason, and he decided he would give the barbarian a final chance to live, although he was certain he already knew the answer. He placed his sword gently under the man's chin and asked the dying man to surrender. Vibius approached silently behind the injured Briton, his sword at the ready.

"I will accept your surrender if you wish to do so," Marcus told the native.

The man grinned and answered in fluent Latin.

"I would rather die on my feet than live at yours," he replied, spitting on Marcus.

Marcus didn't move. He had expected that answer, knowing that surrender was too cowardly in their eyes. "As you wish."

The men stood painfully for a few seconds before his knees buckled and he fell at Marcus' feet, gasping for air. Suddenly his eyelids closed, and he passed.

Marcus turned and focused his attention back on the others. All fights had been settled. Several Romans lay dead, but then again only Romans were left standing. He counted eighteen dead Britons who had leaped from the trees. He regained his composure and caught his breath. All that was left to do was return to the ships, beach them, gather their equipment, and erect the fortifications before night fell. Marcus thought that was not too much to ask from men who had just survived freezing waters, a sprint up an arrow-riddled beach, and two consecutive encounters with the enemy.

XV

Marcus was appalled at the speed with which fog appeared in this strange new land. Five minutes earlier the smell of freshly felled timber and moist dirt filled the crystal clear air as they worked. Now, he strained to see his feet through the dense fog. To avoid accidently reshaping his foot, he stood with his feet spread far apart as he axed the cold, hard-packed ground. Relentlessly, Marcus raised his ax and brought it down into the cold dirt. Vibius then scooped the loosened soil with his shovel and tossed it over the top of the five-foot-deep ditch. All around them the remaining soldiers dug the trench, raised the palisade, or marked out the streets, which they had been working at for over three hours now. The principia had been set up, as well as the hospital, where the wounded were currently being tended to. Down on the beach, others were in the process of beaching the ships.

Marcus felt the weight of the cold fog on his body and on his senses. He didn't like the reduced visibility, despite knowing that numerous squads were patrolling the surrounding wilderness. Marcus still felt uneasy. He, probably along with the entire group of men, couldn't wait for the fort to be erected and then to be nestled comfortably within its protective womb.

Marcus and Vibius had been working jointly since the erection of the fort had begun. Not much conversation had taken place in that time. In fact, the entire fort area was eerily quiet, as if the fog deprived the men of their ability to speak in addition to their sight. Only the clanging of pikes and axes impacting their targets or the occasional order were audible. Marcus stopped for a moment as he waited for the man to finish scooping out the loose dirt at the bottom of the ditch. He stuck his ax into the dirt and leaned backward, stretching his back for the first time in several hours. Then he began to rub his hands, trying to get the feelings back into his palms and wrists. The life of an infantryman was never easy and, although his wrists had grown accustomed to the shock and trauma of sword fighting, hacking dirt with a pickax took a toll on his forearms.

The circular ditch he and his fellow comrades had been digging reached its prescribed depth, and Marcus let out a big sigh of relief, realizing that today's work was almost done. Inside the fort, the engineers were placing the finishing touches on the streets and interior layout of the camp. As the drifting fog thinned in transient patches, Marcus could temporarily see down the length of the ditch. It was V-shaped, ensuring little shift in the dirt and thus the least amount of maintenance. Every aspect of the fort's layout had been designed for greatest ease of maintenance for the troops garrisoned within its confines; without slacking on defensive capacity.

Suddenly a voice spoke out from behind Marcus and shook him out of his trance.

"There we go. The ditch is done," said Vibius as he slung the last mound of dirt over the top and stuck the shovel into the ground with a sharp breath.

"Perfect," Marcus replied, eager to get out of what he thought resembled a grave.

Marcus climbed out of the ditch with relative ease and stopped at the top to help his partner out. As Vibius climbed with Marcus' help, the dirt at the top crumbled slightly beneath his weight but retained enough structural integrity to keep the pair from sliding back down. Looking at the bear of a man climb out, Marcus was always amazed at the imposing figure Vibius presented. The man, Marcus swore, could probably crush a tree to pulp with his bare hands or even grapple with a bear in his sleep and still manage to win. Vibius' forearms were the size of a horse's neck, streaked with large veins that scaled the sides like vines on a house and throbbed in rhythm with the man's powerful heartbeat. Nearly shaven curly hair covered his head and dark stubble covered his lower face, causing the man to resemble one of the many street thugs that plagued the nocturnal streets of Rome.

"The weather here is worse than in any other place I've been to," he muttered in his deep voice.

"I couldn't agree more. In fact if I had been born superstitious, I'd say this is an awful omen about this voyage's outcome," Marcus replied, half-joking.

It seemed that the moment the gates were closed and the fort was deemed secure, the fog enveloping them lifted. Visibility grew to several feet and finally to several miles. From the top of the wall, Marcus and Vibius could see the reflection of the setting sun beam down toward the horizon from behind them. Toward the east, just over the horizon, was Gaul, while to the west, just past the fortification, was the unwelcoming British wilderness. The wounded had all been carried in from the beach and there had been no sign of the enemy since that morning. Marcus turned to face the countryside and began to consider the day's events. It was strange, Marcus thought, how in the morning the territory had seemed extremely hostile and nearly unconquerable, yet now, as he peered through the ramparts toward the country, it didn't seem much different from Gaul.

Below him, his fellow legion comrades were rummaging around the fort and carrying out various orders. Marcus was happy he had been assigned vigil duty at this hour. He loathed standing watch at night. It wasn't the fear of the dark that got to him but rather the threat that if he fell asleep and was caught, he would be forced to camp outside the fort walls or even be beaten to death in front of the entire legion as an example. At least now, his chore would be over and he could sleep restfully tonight. Vibius stood next to him, his eyes scanning the agitated seas.

"Somewhere over there," he said, his chin pointing in the direction of Gaul, "is our cavalry."

Marcus nodded and stole a glance at the waves. To claim the waters were turbulent would be an understatement. They were that and worse. He wondered how the cavalry would come ashore. They were surely planning on crossing the channel tonight, and he wondered if the waves were as bad across the channel. The sea conditions had been deteriorating exponentially since they had landed.

"Do you think they're going to make it?" Marcus asked as a trio of seagulls flew a dozen feet above them, their squawks muting his voice for several seconds.

"It is hard to tell. If the waves keep up, then surely no," Vibius replied, slowly shaking his head in disgust.

"We're probably going to be left here alone," Marcus said slowly, "without any cavalry for reinforcement."

Vibius nodded and looked back out toward Gaul.

Suddenly, Cnaeus approached them from the right.

"It seems that those hairy barbarians have learned who's in charge around here now," Cnaeus said, pointing his pilum in the direction of the main gates, which faced away from the beach.

Marcus looked toward where the pilum seemed to be pointing and spotted two British messengers being led to the principia. Marcus smiled as he looked over to Vibius.

"Why can't they do that *before* the fighting?" he laughed.

"Beats me," Vibius answered with a shrug.

"What are we going to do," Cnaeus asked, "now that they've surrendered?"

Marcus and Vibius looked at each other with simultaneous smiles. Cnaeus had only joined Marcus' contubernium a month ago and was still relatively naive. A fresh supply of men had arrived from Rome then, with men ready to be assigned positions in the legion, and the contuberniums had been rearranged to allow one or two new recruits into the battle-hardened squads. Previously, new recruits had been formed into their own contuberniums. Yet at the outbreak of battle, as a result of lack of experience, many had often been killed. By mixing new recruits in with those who had already seen combat, the death toll had fallen significantly.

"They'll change their minds soon enough, kid. Those people are too erratic to be trusted for long," Marcus replied.

"So ... now do we just wait around?" Cnaeus asked, far too innocently.

"You haven't learned yet, have you?" Vibius asked, with a small grin on his face.

Cnaeus looked at Vibius but didn't answer.

"My friend," Marcus said, putting his hand on Cnaeus' shoulder, "Caesar is down there with two legions and unconquered lands in front of him. What do you think is going to happen?"

"And don't forget the fact that we are without cavalry," Vibius added.

"What? But the Britons don't know that," Cnaeus replied, his gaze shifting back and forth between Marcus and Vibius.

"Kid, they may be uneducated barbarians, but they know what a horse looks like. They've surely been scouting us since the end of the battle."

Cnaeus didn't believe it at first. "The cavalry is on its way though, *right?*"

Vibius shook his head slowly. "Not for a while."

"What? Why?"

Marcus pointed toward the large whitecaps out at sea. "That's why."

Vibius smiled and punched Cnaeus in the shoulder gently.

"Son, the day the army gets paid to do nothing will be the day cows rain down from heaven."

"So, this peace ..." Cnaeus began.

"Temporary," Vibius replied.

"Why?"

"Just to give them time to find our weaknesses and to give us time to plan our attack without interference," Marcus replied. "Better get back to your patrol, kid. I don't want you getting flogged for failing in your duties."

Marcus and Vibius pressed themselves to the side to let Cnaeus pass through the narrow causeway. Cnaeus began to walk forward, his mind still racing over the fact that they were in a perilous situation and the two men were laughing about it.

"I'll see you later," Marcus said over Vibius' shoulder, and then he returned his attention to the horizon and his search for approaching vessels.

XVI

Caesar was leaning over his table talking to his two legion commanders when suddenly his aide walked into the tent unexpectedly.

"Enemy envoys have arrived, sir," the skinny man said.

Caesar looked between his generals' heads in front of him and thought for a second before nodding and telling the man to let them in. Quickly finishing his talk with his generals, he dismissed them and prepared for the envoys. Caesar began to light candles throughout the dimming room as the two native envoys walked in. Ignoring their presence, he continued to light candles on several tables around the tent. The British envoys stayed still as they watched the general walk around, apparently oblivious to their presence. As Caesar lit the final candle, he spoke.

"Let me guess ..." Caesar said sarcastically.

"We have come to surrender," the first man replied. He was tall and skinny, his dirty hair pulled back in a ponytail that fell slightly past his shoulders. His nose was contorted, his eyes bulged, and his large eyebrows gave the man the appearance of a carnival freak. His colleague was short, fat, and baby-faced.

"Yes, I know. But why so soon?" Caesar asked. He moved to a chair to their right, sat down, and crossed his legs. The natives turned to face him.

"Why so soon?" the man repeated slightly appalled. "Why, because we do not wish to make the same mistake the Gauls did. We seek peace, not war. We tried to resist you, but we are clearly no match for you. It was agreed among us that a symbiotic relationship would be more beneficial for the both of us."

Caesar knew the men were lying. It was evident in their mannerisms. Clearly they had not practiced surrendering many times.

"How do you know about the Gauls?" Caesar asked, intrigued.

The two men looked at each other before the second, fatter man answered.

"A man named Commius ..." the short man began.

Caesar cut him off mid-sentence. "Commius! What have you done to him?" the Roman asked, suddenly angry. Caesar stood and walked across the rug toward the two men.

"What have you done to him?" he asked again, grabbing the short man by the collar. "If he has been hurt, I swear I will make life so miserable for you and your tribe that you will lament being alive."

Caesar spoke through gritted teeth, his voice colder than ice. He squinted as he looked deep into the man's eyes. The man's jaw dropped and he began to sweat despite the cold. The Briton feared the Roman would have him killed.

"Answer me!" Caesar yelled into the man's face with a brutal shake of his collar.

The man stuttered as he tried to form a complete sentence.

"Commius is still alive, Caesar, I assure you of this. He has not been harmed," the first man said, speaking on behalf of his friend.

Caesar looked at him and released the terrified man with a shove.

"He is unharmed?" Caesar asked again.

"Yes."

Caesar calmed down at the thought that his friend was okay, but then his temper grew again as he remembered that Commius was still their prisoner.

"I want him back immediately, along with two hundred of my men you have managed to acquire," Caesar stated.

The short, spineless man was still too frightened to talk and simply looked at his friend, waiting for him to speak.

"Caesar, we do not have any prisoners," the man said slowly.

"You expect me to believe such nonsense? Of course you have prisoners. Upon being captured, my soldiers in Gaul are being sent here as slaves."

The man hesitated momentarily before answering.

"I will see what I can do. Perhaps you will be lucky, and we will have that number."

"Perhaps *I* will be lucky?" Caesar repeated, incredulous at the man's insolence. "*You* should consider yourself lucky to even be allowed to beg for quarter. I want one hundred men that I *know* you have. If Commius has a single mark on his body upon his return, I will annihilate your village and all of the poor bastards that call it home. Have I made myself clear?"

The man didn't budge or even reply.

Caesar, aggravated by the man's impudence, simply told him that he accepted their surrender under the terms he had stated. After the British envoys agreed, Caesar sent them on their way.

With the enemy now semi-compliant, Caesar began to formulate plans to explore the surrounding countryside with his men.

XVII

Four days had passed since the Roman legions had landed in Britannia. The natives, knowing full well they were in no condition to attempt another strike against the Roman invaders yet had, at least temporarily, resorted to acting civilized. Men and women throughout the camp provided their services to the Roman legionnaires. Ironically local blacksmiths repaired and crafted new swords for the Roman soldiers, while others repaired shields or fabricated new sandals. The women traded and provided fresh produce, which the legionnaires were too reluctant to forgo. Stale bread and diluted wine were replaced with eggs, fruit, and other local produce. Tender pieces of meat were also sold to the legionnaires, who voraciously devoured their meals.

The wind had picked up significantly since the beginning of the day, and the dark sky was ominous, an omen of events to come. Leaves and pieces of trash were blown down the streets as a light drizzle fell. Nature was not at peace with the men. However, a bizarre stillness had settled over the Romans and the natives, a peace none of the Romans would have expected from their barbarian counterparts.

"I don't trust 'em," Marcus said grimly as he stopped next to Vibius, who stood vigil near the front gate.

"This shouldn't be allowed," Vibius agreed with a shake of his head.

"Look at that. Here they are, wandering freely within our camp, and here we stand, letting them scrutinize our fort."

"You know it's all just a ruse—they'll turn on us soon enough. Those slimy cowards are quite the backstabbers."

Marcus nodded to his friend before resuming his patrol down the western wall. Marcus did not dare loiter too long in fear of being spotted by a keen-eyed centurion. Besides, he would be back within minutes to continue his interrupted conversation with his friend. The rampart Marcus followed was narrow and slick; the near-constant rain had encouraged moss to grow on parts of the wall, which made even the simple task of walking a bit treacherous. He walked slowly, not out of fear but out of boredom, having gone around this path countless times in the past four hours. The lack of variety was beginning to take its toll. Rather than watch where he walked, he began to succumb to temporary bouts of day-dreaming, his feet doing the walking for him. Suddenly, he slipped on a small patch of moss and nearly fell over the edge onto the people gathered below. At the last minute, a hand reached out and grabbed him by the collar of his chest armor and pulled him back from the edge of the precipice. Marcus, jolted from his reverie, turned to look at the man who had saved his life.

"That was a close one," said Cnaeus, letting go of Marcus.

"Tell me about it," Marcus replied, realizing what had almost happened.

He approached the edge cautiously and peered down. It was roughly a twenty-foot drop to the crowded street below.

"It seems that moss is a more dangerous adversary than the enemy," Cnaeus joked.

Marcus laughed. "It would be a shame to have made it this far and then die from a slip."

Cnaeus nodded. "So do you still think they're plotting against us?"

"I can guarantee it. There is no reason for the natives to give up yet. They still outnumber us. We are alone in their territory. They have lost one battle against us. It is only a matter of time before they mount another strike."

"So we wait ..."

Marcus pursed his lips and nodded slowly, "Why are we here, anyway? We're not even done in Gaul, and we're already sticking our necks out even farther."

Marcus watched the locals walking throughout the streets below.

Cnaeus shrugged and looked down at the people below. "For the glory of Rome."

By the time the sun was sinking over the top of the trees in the west, many of the locals had left for their village. Very few remained, attempting to sell the last of their goods. Money was easier to carry home than merchandise. Several women and children from surrounding villages were still walking the streets, talking to various legionnaires, while the husbands were engaged in the trading of goods.

Marcus didn't like it at all. If all his years in the army had taught him anything, it was to never underestimate your opponent, a fatal mistake far too many generals and soldiers alike made. He, Vibius, and Cnaeus stood by their tent on the Via Principales. The others from Marcus' contubernium had left, despite Marcus' warnings to refrain from engaging with the locals. Marcus was convinced there was a sinister plan behind this façade of peace. He even thought the local foods they traded were poisoned and that the women and children were brought solely to appeal to the Roman soldiers' emotions. When the time came for the battles to renew, the Romans would be reluctant to attack villages in fear of harming the seemingly innocent women and children they had befriended days before.

Perhaps it was not true. Maybe he was just being overly cautious. But in a situation where there are no second chances,

Marcus opted to be safe now rather than sorry later. Even if that meant depriving himself of that mouth-watering beef he had seen Cnaeus devour earlier.

"Maybe it isn't all part of a sinister scheme," Cnaeus said.

"I told you before, Cnaeus. If the enemy comes within ten miles of you, be prepared for the unexpected. Here they are all around us. If we drop our guard for a second, they will be all on us like ants on honey. This is solely to find our weaknesses."

"They get acquainted with our fort, and when the moment comes," Vibius smashed his fist into his palm and ground it, "they'll know just what to do, just where to go."

From the right, a small five- or six-year-old boy and his mother approached them slowly, and the boy began to pull on Marcus' belt, his legionary belt, the honored symbol that one belonged to the military. It was regulation that even when in civilian attire, the soldiers were required to wear their belt to signify who they were. To have this young boy try to pull it off, strip him of his status, was too much. Marcus slowly pushed the young boy aside, not caring for the scowl the mother gave him.

The mother was a pretty woman with long brown hair that cascaded softly over her small shoulders and came to a stop down the middle of her back. She was dark-skinned, with an aquiline nose and deep blue eyes that seemed to penetrate straight through his very soul. Her jaw was soft, and her figure would have made any man turn his head in her wake. If she had not been the enemy, he surely would have initiated a conversation. But since that was not the case, she ranked just as high a menace as the men he actually fought hand to hand. She was the eyes, the men were the brawn.

She gently scooped the boy and approached Cnaeus, who undoubtedly seemed the most amicable, with his large smile and innocent look. The mother spoke to the boy, who managed to cease sniveling, and looked at Cnaeus with newfound curiosity. She approached the young man and placed her hand gently on his chest armor and commented to her son how solid it felt. The boy reached out and began to tap the armor with his small fist, a dull, metallic ring accompanying the child's weak taps. The mother quickly stopped him and began to point to the helmet Cnaeus wore. Cnaeus interpreted the various motions and grunts the woman made as a sign that she wanted to put the helmet on her son. Cnaeus looked over toward Marcus, who returned his look with slight disgust.

"Should I?" he asked.

"Do as you desire, but know that he is going to grow up wanting to separate the head your helmet is on from the rest of your body someday," Marcus answered.

Cnaeus looked back at the innocent woman and gently lifted his helmet off of his head and placed it onto the boy's. A woman like her could not possibly be a menace.

The helmet was extremely large and the boy's head disappeared inside the metallic pot. He tried turning his head, but the weight pinned it, and the boy began to whimper for his mother to take it off. Cnaeus quickly lifted the helmet and moved to place it back on his head when the woman motioned for him to put it on her head. Marcus watched as the innocent legionnaire flirted with the attractive woman. Both began to laugh when he placed the helmet on her head.

"Where's the husband?" Vibius asked aloud what the men had been thinking to themselves.

"Either we've killed him already or he is somewhere planning our demise," Marcus replied.

Marcus watched the woman again and immediately noticed she was looking around while Cnaeus played with the small boy. Vibius was looking the other way when a jab to his ribs hinted for him to look at the woman.

"See what I mean?"

The woman had handed the little boy to Cnaeus and was peering cautiously around the inside of the fort. He watched as her eyes examined the interior layout of the fort and followed the ramparts, counting the guards positioned around the walls, the archers in the towers.

"Cnaeus," Marcus said sharply.

Cnaeus turned his head in Marcus' direction and raised his brow inquisitively.

"Let's go."

Cnaeus smiled to the woman and handed the boy back to her. Cnaeus caught up with his comrades and asked what the matter was. He was told what had been going on behind his back.

"Maybe she was just intrigued by our design. What could she possibly learn from looking around that they don't already know?"

They spent the rest of the hour walking around camp, noting all of the flirting and bargaining between the legionnaires and the locals. Suddenly a shout came from the rampart that the Roman vessels were in sight. Cheers rose from the legionnaires at the news that they were no longer alone in this hostile territory. Within hours, two thousand cavalrymen would disembark and allow Caesar to initiate explorations of the surrounding countryside. Caesar had ordered preliminary forays into the wilderness, but without cavalry to provide security, Caesar had been reluctant to send his men any farther than the nearest village, a mere mile and a half inland.

Immediately upon hearing the cheers, centurions stepped out of their conversations and donned their helmets. One centurion approached Marcus' position and was heard giving the order to escort the natives out.

"My pleasure," Marcus replied.

The order spread through the camp like wildfire and less than fifteen minutes later, the last of the locals marched out through the gates. From the moment the ships had been spotted, additional men had been positioned on the ramparts to monitor the ships' approach, while countless others marched down to the beach to provide assistance to the landing parties. Marcus' cohort had been selected to march down to the beach along with two others to provide security along the top perimeter of the beach. The Roman legionnaires lined the edge of the forest, their red shields facing inwards, their backs facing the sea. If the natives decided to attack the landing cavalrymen, they would have to fight through the fifteen hundred men first.

Meanwhile, another two cohorts were assembled on the beach, excited by the sight of the approaching vessels. The assembled men were lightly armed, having left their shields and pila behind in order to be freer when wading through the waters to help those who would land. Marcus had protested, claiming he would rather his men carry all their equipment in light of a possible attack, but the centurion had denied his request.

Marcus and his men stood at ease several feet from the crashing waves, the froth slithering nearer and nearer to their cold feet. He shuffled his feet in anticipation and to ward off the cold. The temperature had dropped significantly after the arrival of the storm, and the air, already chilly, had dropped to a nippy forty-five degrees. The wind chill did nothing to abate the biting cold that ran across each man's flesh. Fortunately, fires had been started down the length of beach to warm the cold men.

Above, the clouds had coagulated to form an impenetrable blanket of gray that deprived the anxious men of the sight of the full moon. The storm was only partly responsible for the thrashing waves; the full moon amplified the magnitude of the waves. The usual high-water mark was currently ten feet into the ocean. These channel waters were much more volatile than the calmer Mediterranean seas the Romans were used to sailing. Marcus' eyes continued to scan the heavens. It wouldn't be long before the skies would open up and release a torrential downpour, which would only further hamper the debarkation in the already choppy seas. The ships were only one hundred yards offshore; for the first time since the vessels had been spotted, Marcus realized how pitiful the odds were for a successful landing.

Marcus saw the boats they had crossed the channel in and beached after their landing now only a short distance away from the cold froth churned by the thrashing waves. The tides had come in and the waves were slowly pulling them out to sea. Upon seeing this, the senior centurion ordered some men to return to camp to fetch reinforcements and supplies for the anchoring of the ships.

Immediately, two men broke rank and dashed hurriedly in the direction of the fort while the rest stood in distress and watched hopelessly as their ships awaited their somber fate. Their ships were about to be carried out to sea, and there was nothing they could do about it. Marcus debated whether a detachment of men could be sent to sail the vessels a good distance from shore where the waves were significantly less and ride out the storm but opted against it. There were too many variables that could go wrong and lead to unnecessary loss of life.

He searched the far recesses of his mind for other solutions to the predicament. But there were none. The incoming ships were roughly seventy-five yards offshore when a lightning bolt tore open the skies. The air turned gray, with drastically diminished visibility, as the men peered through the falling sheets of rain at the vessels. The crafts, their bows still plowing relentlessly through the beating waves, emerged slowly through the gloom. The Romans on shore had observed men scurrying about on the decks, working the sails and manning the rudders, but now the rain-shrouded silhouettes of the men aboard the vessels resembled ghosts.

Aboard the vessels, the terrified men continued to work, their hands working with lightning speed as they brought down the sails to keep the ships from capsizing. Below decks, the oarsmen coughed up mouthfuls of water as the waves poured into the vessel through the oar holes carved into the side of the ship. The vessels were dangerously near to floundering.

The captains barked orders to their men as the waves thrashed the vessels about, knocking the occasional man overboard and into the frigid, merciless water below. Many could not grasp how the sea had turned so swiftly. There was more to this than just nature having its way. The gods must be furious. For carnage like this, they had to be seething with anger.

Unsure of the men's condition at sea, yet suspecting the worse, the Romans on the beach continued their own struggle with the elements as they fought to keep their boats from being carried out to sea. The men on the beach struggled to find a way to secure their boats from the current and waves. Unfortunately, nature beat man, and the vessels continued to be dragged out to sea. Marcus's eyes were locked on the slowly receding vessels and he did not see Vibius coming. Vibius knelt by Marcus, squinting under the onslaught of the rain.

"I don't think we can do anything," Vibius shouted over the sound of falling rain and the shouts of other men.

"No... And you don't see our native friends coming out of their warm huts to help us, either," Marcus said, throwing a glance to Cnaeus, who stood several feet away.

Cnaeus heard him and thought about responding but reconsidered and looked away. The vessels were presently thirty yards out, apparently stopped, except for one ship, which was sailing ever closer as if determined to beach no matter the outcome. The trireme made it to within eight yards before the waves became so large and relentless that the lower decks were flooded, and the ship began to flounder. The men on the beach watched helplessly as men and supplies rolled overboard into the turbulent waters. Three men ran out to save the drowning but were quickly beaten back by the waves. After the vessel sank with many who were onboard, the other ships sailed out farther into the channel waters, leaving the men on the beach more anxious than ever. Alas, few of those who had been on the now-capsized vessel managed to reach the safety of land. Severus approached the huddled mass of men and ordered them back to the fort. There was nothing they could do. They would have to wait for the storm to abide. The posts that had been placed along the edge of the forest broke rank and escorted the unarmed soldiers back. Within minutes, the men had returned up the hill, and they watched helplessly from the ramparts as the ships continued to struggle in Neptune's domain.

XVIII

By the following morning, the rain had stopped. Although the dark sky still threatened, a single drop of rain had yet to fall. The wind blew strongly, and the waves continued to assault the shore relentlessly. To no one's surprise, the waves were still too large to allow vessels to land safely. As the first of the sun's rays began to reach the sleeping fort, the buccinators sounded throughout the fort, waking all of its occupants. Quickly remembering the vessels in peril, talk about the latter bloomed, and many ran to the ramparts to see for themselves. Looking over the wall, the legionnaires peered toward where the vessels had been the previous night; but there were none visible that seemed unscathed. The onlookers concluded that many of the vessels had floundered and broken apart in the storm the previous night and the remaining ships had turned and taken up position farther out at sea. In danger of being swept away, many of those vessels had opted to return to the safety of Gaul. There was no telling how many of those who had attempted the return had floundered in the channel, never to be found.

The shore was covered in flotsam and pieces of broken ships that had broken off during the tempest the previous night. Larger sections of the wooden vessels floated in from the sea while actual vessels themselves lay half-sunk a short distance off the beach, their bows jutting from the frothy water. Some of the luckier vessels had managed to beach and now lay on their keels.

Caesar, who had woke shortly before sunrise, stood in one of the guard towers on the northern wall and looked to the beach. The sand was strewn with wreckage, equipment, and the corpses of dead men and horses. Few of those who had tried to ride out the storm had survived the onslaught. He watched somberly as the birds above circled and landed on the beach to feast on the corpses of the dead, a grisly sight to even the most seasoned of soldiers. Without turning, Caesar ordered his officers to send men down to recover the dead and search for wounded. Immediately the order was relayed to the troops, and centuries were marched to the beach. As the men approached they were overcome by the ghastly sight of the drowned. The gruesome carcasses of bloating bodies of men and beasts littered the otherwise tranquil beach.

Having reached the beach, the men broke rank and advanced through the wreckage at their own pace. Marcus walked solemnly through the debris, searching in vain for any man fortunate—or unfortunate—enough to have survived. He approached a man that had been speared by an oar and lay dying. Marcus wanted to help but knew he couldn't spend his time with a man beyond help; he had to move away. It was a hard thing to do, and Marcus felt sick knowing he would not keep the dying man company in his final moments. Marcus gagged and turned away to spit out the bile that formed in his throat.

Not far away was a dead horse with a large gash in its side and whose intestines had slithered out and come to rest on the bloody sand. Quickly looking away, Marcus stared back at the others who were also scouting for survivors. But death was everywhere.

Without warning, an icy-cold hand grasped Marcus by his ankle, causing him to yank his foot from the dying man's grasp before realizing there was nothing to fear. Marcus knelt down and stared blankly at the injured man, his mind not processing the grisly sight at his feet. The man gasped for air, and his cold, shaking hand reached for something more than just empty space. His other hand was squeezed against his stomach, trying in vain to stop the bleeding.

"Medic," Marcus shouted in vain.

The unit capsarius ran over, his capsa slung over his shoulder, two stretcher bearers following closely. The capsa contained basics: bandages, stitches, and several vials of vinegar as a disinfectant. The capsarius knelt and pulled the man's hand away from his neck, revealing a deep gash. The medic shook his head and looked at Marcus solemnly.

"It's too late."

Marcus stared down at the wounded man; his eyelids were beginning to sag. Marcus felt sick at the realization that it was indeed too late. Soon, the groping hand fell slowly to the sand, and the man's head rolled to the side. He was dead. Marcus stared unbelievingly at the man and forced himself to look away. Others who were less severely injured and could be saved before hypothermia set in needed him. Marcus stood and walked across the beach, taking care to step over wreckage and walk around corpses. Marcus reached one man who was still alive and whose leg had been crushed. Without waiting this time, Marcus called out for a medic once more.

Long seconds passed as he waited for one of the capsarius to reach him. Upon arrival, the medic began to work on the injured soldier. From around him, Marcus could hear others shouting for medics as well and he watched in mild horror as the doctors ran from one man to the next, assessing whether they were even worth trying to save before running off to the next injured person. Marcus was jolted from his trance by a shout from a wounded man next to him. Marcus turned to face him. The dying man's face was white, his eyes wide with fear, and his shaky finger pointed at the tree line behind Marcus. Although guards had been placed there, the locals had come to witness the carnage for themselves.

Vibius ran to Marcus from across the beach and stopped to catch his breath.

"They're watching us."

"I'm surprised it took them this long," Marcus replied slowly.

"What do we do?"

"Get the hell off the beach—they must be itching to attack us. I wouldn't be surprised if the news has already reached their village and they're getting all geared up for battle," Marcus replied.

Vibius nodded and heard Severus shout out to his men behind him.

"Men," Severus said walking down the line. "Let's get the hell out of here. Things are going to get hot here shortly, and I don't want to be here when it does. Let's go, let's go!"

"What about the wounded?" one of the men asked.

"What about the wounded?" Severus repeated in stupefaction. "Take them with you!"

Marcus grabbed the man at his feet; other legionnaires wasted no time hoisting the remaining wounded, and they moved toward the fort at a fast jog. The wounded moaned in pain from the brutal motion, but their porters didn't slow down. They couldn't slow down. The natives were already energized by the thought that the Romans were now stranded on their island. With nowhere to go, the Romans were now at the mercy of the British natives. It was evident they were aching for revenge, thirsty for blood. Roman blood.

The front gates opened as the legionnaires approached, and the soldiers ran through quickly, dropping off the wounded at the entrance. They then sprinted off to their tents to gather their weapons and shields. As the legionnaires poured in from the beach, Roman archers already lined the ramparts, while those legionnaires who had remained within the fort fell into formation on the wide streets.

Although there was not much distance between the forest and the fort, the fifty yards would allow the archers clear view of their enemies. Because many more wounded would be returning to camp shortly, the wounded from the beach were quickly shuttled to the hospital and tended to.

Still at attention near the front gate, the legionnaires awaited the order to advance and take position along the edge of the forest. There was not enough maneuverability to fight from the confines of the fort. And although the Roman legionnaires excelled at fighting hand-to-hand, their main strength came from taking the offensive. Cowering behind walls waiting for the enemy was not what they were trained and bred to do.

"Our little vacation's over," Marcus said as he formed up next to Vibius at the main gate.

"They always end too soon, don't they?" Vibius smiled.

The rest of the cohort formed up behind them. Soon the gates opened, and the men marched out. While some remained inside and on the ramparts to defend against a possible attack to the legions' rear, over two-thirds of the combined legions were marched out. The two legions, after suffering staggering casualties during the debarkation, now numbered about eight thousand five hundred. Their numbers had been slashed, but their fervor and morale remained strong.

The legions were marched out about thirty yards from the fort, the effective range of a pilum, and halted abruptly. Twenty yards separated the Roman infantry and the forest. The stretch of open ground also offered the Roman archers the ability to fire unobstructed on emerging Britons. As the enemy approached menacingly, the centurions went about giving the orders.

"Ready, pila," the centurions shouted loudly, their cold eyes in hard-set faces watching the enemy.

The entire legion in one uniform motion suddenly prepared to discharge their lethal projectiles as the Britons emerged from the forest gloom and approached. The newer recruits ached to throw their pila as the white of the enemy's eyes grew discernable.

But their long hours of training and self-control kept the men from succumbing to their temptation—that and the whip that awaited anyone who disobeyed an order.

Once the enemy had crossed the first five yards, the order was given for the two front ranks to discharge their pila. The men obeyed immediately and heaved their pila into the approaching men. Accompanied by loud yells and curses, the missiles flew toward the assailants and impacted viciously into human flesh. Marcus, who was in the front row, watched as the pila crashed into the British lines with spine-chilling cracks as men were forcefully skewered. At this short range, the Romans were sure each pilum had hit home.

The British ranks collapsed under the onslaught but were replaced by men who continued to emerge from the foliage like ghouls. The third and fourth ranks threw their pila in turn. The order was repeated, and again the pila arced through the sky and into the British ranks, impaling the enemy on the same stretch of ground as before. Yet again, soft flesh gave way to pointed iron, and the ranks crumbled to the bloody ground, the mutilated bodies quickly trampled by the advancing mass of men. Out of pila, the Romans resorted to tightening their ranks and bracing themselves for the oncoming human wave. Seconds passed like minutes as the figures grew ever larger. After what seemed an eternity; the men collided in an ear-splitting cacophony of screams, shouts, and frenzied fighting.

As trained, each Roman held onto the man in front of him to prevent men in the front ranks from being carried away by the thrill of the fight and advancing alone into the enemy formation. The strategy also allowed the man behind to pull him back into safety at the end of the minute of fighting.

The centurions watched as the men tussled ruthlessly, and blood and screams spattered into the air as swords cut flesh and shields cracked bones. The Roman archers fired relentlessly into the enemy below. Arrows cut through the air and struck men dully; arrow shafts protruded from men's bodies like pins in a cushion. Some were killed instantly and fell heavily; others were wounded and fell slowly and loudly, their screams muted by the crash and ringing of metal on metal as the fight continued around them. To their great despair, the wounded were ignored and trampled underfoot as others fought and died above them.

Meanwhile, those Britons who remained unscathed or who were wounded but were still fit enough to stay in the fight continued to struggle with the Roman soldiers. Some men tried to tug the Romans' shields to no avail, while others tried to worm their way through the Roman ranks, only to be cut down on the spot. The Roman ranks remained impenetrable, the result of countless hours of training and the strong bond between the soldiers. The Roman legionnaires all fought to protect the man to their left, meaning each soldier had to trust the man to his right without the least doubt for sixty seconds at a time.

Around campfires at night and during the first days of training, each man had been told by his seniors that one minute in combat felt like eternity. A single minute, measured by itself, never felt very long, but when fighting, wondering whether each second would be your last, the seconds seemed eternal.

The trumpeters sounded a long, deep note, the order to switch positions, and the front ranks melted into the mass of men behind them and wormed their way back through the lines while the second row moved up and covered the retreat by slamming their shields into the enemy formation and continuing the fight. To the rampart sentries, the tactic was impressive to watch. It allowed no time for the enemy to move up and gain terrain lost by the front row of the Romans and also provided no time for a parting shot as the men retreated between the columns of men behind them.

It was now the second row's turn to fight, and Cnaeus held the man in front of him to prevent him from being sucked into the enemy formation. He felt the man wrestle brutally, stabbing and blocking with an unsettling grace. Over half a dozen men succumbed to the man's agile thrusts and the Britons were infuriated to see him retreat unscathed when the order to switch sounded again. The legionnaires switched positions with ease, and the archers watched the second row become the first, the third became the second and so on down the remainder of the columns.

Now his turn to fight, Cnaeus moved up. Seeing those repugnant men try to stick their swords into his neck put fear into his heart, and he felt his knees shake. He had fought in only three battles before, including the debarkation days before, and his nerves had not yet hardened to steel. Unlike those who were battle-hardened and had seen more than one friend die in the thick of battle, the concept of death still seemed terrifying to him. He had never understood how some talked of death as nonchalantly as if they spoke of the weather. He believed in the gods, but now that Elysium was closer than ever, he wondered whether he would really wake up there upon dying or whether everything would just go black and simply cease to exist. But that seemed so odd; would he even know he was dead? If he ceased to exist, would he know it? But then again, how *could* he know it if he didn't exist?

His mind was racing when suddenly his shield was tugged down, and he saw the tip of a sword line up with his face. He was seconds away from eternalizing himself if he didn't act fast. Seconds felt like hours as he debated what to do. He quickly brought his sword up through the gap in the shields and felt the resistance of the man's flesh and organs as the gladius cut into the man and killed him. He immediately raised his shield and placed it between him and the Briton on the other side in fear. He was too panic-stricken to do anything but cower behind his shield. He was overcome by a desire to push the enemy back as far as he could, and he immediately began to shove his shield against the Briton on the other side.

The man holding Cnaeus struggled to hold him back from being absorbed by the enemy and was beginning to be pulled forward himself. The strap he was holding onto was threatening to snap under Cnaeus' jerking and lunging. Cnaeus kept trying to enter the enemy formation to push them farther away, the exact thing *not* to do in combat. Many Romans had succumbed to fear and lost their lives in just that way. Suddenly the order to switch echoed out again, and the winded front ranks gave way to fresh troops. All switched, except for Cnaeus, who feared turning his back on the enemy. His arms grew tired, and he was pulled back from the fight by the man behind him just as the Briton's sword collided into the advancing Roman's shield as he covered Cnaeus' retreat.

"Follow the damn orders, you idiot! You're going to get yourself killed and me with you," the man said as he jerked him back and took his place. Cnaeus looked at the man blankly before continuing down between the columns of men.

Without cavalry to flank the enemy, the battle was lasting longer than usual, but due to their superior tactics, the Romans were killing the enemy while suffering few casualties themselves. While the legionnaires didn't fight to the point of exhaustion, the Britons were growing more and more fatigued by the minute. The order to switch came again and the legionnaires obeyed, revealing yet another layer of fresh men ready for combat.

As losses mounted and fatigue gave way to despair, the British lines began to waver. The enemy's front ranks splintered, and exhausted men began to flee, sealing the fate of the battle. As the fleeing Britons were followed and cut down mercilessly, the Roman dead and wounded were carried back into the fort. At the back of the formation, Marcus was ordered to tend to the wounded rather than pursue the enemy. With the help of Vibius, he bent down and took hold of a man whose arm had been severed at the elbow. He quickly tied a tourniquet around the stump and lifted him onto a stretcher, which Cnaeus had already called over. The Roman medics quickly approached and placed the wounded man on the stretcher. Leaving the wounded man in the capsarius' care, Marcus continued down the line and tended to other wounded. Shouts for help reverberated ceaselessly across the stretch of bloodied ground.

XIX

The following days passed without enemy attack. The Romans were confined to their fort with no means of escape; it was evident the Britons were planning on starving them out. Several scouting parties had been sent to collect cattle for slaughter and wheat from surrounding fields, and the occasional skirmish had been reported, but few Romans had been wounded and even fewer had been killed.

The legionnaires were divided into four groups: those that repaired the various half-sunken ships, those that protected the beached vessels, those charged with collecting food from the surrounding countryside, and those left to garrison the fort. Each group rotated on a daily basis at noon to keep the men from growing bored or envious of each other's duties.

Today, Marcus had been assigned to the ship-reparation team. Down on the beach the crews switched twice daily due to the frigidity of the waters and the turbulent conditions in which they worked. Marcus, who had been assigned the early morning guard duty, was not pleased when the order came for him to enter the water. He set his shield down on the sand, curved side up, set his sword and pilum down on the shield, and then removed his chest-armor and set it gently down. Ready to enter the frigid water before him, he advanced slowly to the edge of the water and waited momentarily, despairing of the temperature of the water he was about to be working in. Around him were forty other men who were just as reluctant to enter the water. Those who were exiting the water grinned sarcastically and teased those who were to take their places.

Roughly one thousand men participated in the reconstruction of the fleet. Despite their relentless efforts to salvage every piece of flotsam, much had been carried back out to sea, and they were forced to sacrifice some damaged vessels for wood in order to save some of the less damaged ones. Efforts had been undertaken to beach the ships that lay half-sunk to render the reparation crew's work somewhat easier. A total of five boats had already been beached, and many more remained in the waters just off shore, their keels resting in the mud several feet underwater.

The storm had passed, and the waves were smaller and the boats less prone to being swamped and carried out to sea. The centurion standing beside Marcus finally gave a tap on his shoulder and gave the order to swim out to the trireme ten yards away. The ship listed heavily, the port side of the vessel just grazing the top of the water. All they had to do, the centurion said, was swim out, climb aboard the ship, tie the rope to the vessel somehow, and then swim back to the beach and help pull the ship to shore. Child's play.

Three eighty foot ropes curled at their feet, and Marcus bent down, grabbed the end of one, and tied it around his waist, leaving his hands free for swimming. Satisfied with the knot, he entered the frigid waters, the first to do so. His legs tingled immediately as the cold enveloped his body, and Marcus gasped repeatedly as he lowered his shoulders under the water and began to swim. His head throbbed slightly as he swam the thirty feet to the vessel. The tide was high and, although difficult, Marcus was able to climb onto the deck of the trireme. His fingers were numb so he tucked his hands under his armpits to get the blood circulating again while he waited for the others. The cold had inspired him to swim quickly and he watched as the other men made their way through the cold water as well. Within short minutes all were aboard.

Vibius approached Marcus from the side and slapped his friend on the back.

"Refreshing, wasn't it?"

Marcus was in no mood for jokes; he hated cold water more than anything in the world. Rubbing his hands together one final time, Marcus untied the rope from his waist and began to walk awkwardly toward the mast near the center of the ship.

"This good, you think?"

"I don't see why not. The mast doesn't seem damaged anywhere," Vibius said, scanning the mast from top to bottom.

Vibius took the rope from Marcus' hands and began to wrap the saturated rope around the mast. The pair knotted the thick rope by lapping the coils around and under each other and, satisfied it would not come undone, walked back to the bow. It wasn't the most beautiful knot, but it would hold. The last thing any man wanted was to have to swim back out to the ship because the rope had come untied.

The others attached the other ropes to two different parts of the vessels and approached Marcus when they were done.

"All set on this end," one man said, pulling none too gently on the rope to confirm he wouldn't have to swim back out a second time.

"Same here," a second man said, tucking his hands under his arms.

"Everything's secure on the mast. We can head back to shore," Marcus replied.

Sliding down the slanted deck into the bitterly cold waters, the men half-pulled, half-swam their way back to shore, their numb fingers towing their numb bodies along the wet rope.

As their feet touched bottom, the men stood and pushed their way through the waist-deep water before emerging completely from the sea like creatures of the deep. Several legionnaires quickly placed blankets around the men's shoulders and the drenched men sat down around the multiple fires that had been started on the beach. Marcus, shaking from the chill, watched as three hundred men split equally into groups and prepared to pull on each of the three ropes that had been attached to the ship.

"Ready!" The lead men in each group shouted after ensuring each man was holding onto his rope.

Soon the battle began between man and sea. The men pulled on the ropes with all their might, but the water and mud kept the ship locked in place. Pulling ever more fiercely, the legionnaires grimaced as they continued to fight against the enveloping waters and viscous mud that held the ship down. To some, it seemed the boat would never move.

Like everything else however, even the sea could not stop the legionnaires and soon enough the bond between the keel and mud gave way and the boat began to slip closer to shore at a snail's pace. It was an awful strain on the men yet they continued to pull on the rope relentlessly. With time, additional men joined the tug-of-war as well as the boat inched closer and more rope was available. Within fifteen minutes, the boat reached the sand the men stood on. With cheers, the boat was pulled and pushed a short distance toward a large trench that had been dug into the sand from the sea. As the waves ran into the trench, the bow of the vessel was pulled ever closer and finally came to rest in the trench. The men's hard work had been worth it; now they would be able to repair the ship and make it seaworthy once again. The repairs would not be to the same degree of craftsmanship as the dock workers in Ostia, Rome's harbor city, could achieve, but the work would surely hold until they had regained Gaul. Each and every soldier would undoubtedly prefer to take their chances with the sea than remain huddled in hostile country waiting for a rescue fleet.

"I wouldn't mind getting picket duty," Vibius said after rubbing his aching biceps.

"Or getting food," Marcus added, stretching.

Both men, although cold and dripping, had abandoned their places around the fire in order to help pull the heavy ship.

Suddenly a centurion began to issue orders to the men. There was no respite in the Roman army.

"I want those ropes off now! All of you standing around doing nothing, there's wood in that pile waiting to be nailed to the ships," he said, pointing to a large pile of broken pieces of wood of all sizes that had been collected from the beach and sea.

"That guy clearly has not been participating in today's fun-filled activities," Marcus said with disgust.

"Let's go! I've got dead ancestors that work faster than you little girls," the uncouth centurion said, clapping his hands in time with his voice.

Marcus and Vibius walked toward the pile of wood, grabbed several large pieces, and returned to the boat they had just salvaged before setting the wood down next to several large cracks on the starboard side of the vessel. Another man handed them nails, a saw and a hammer and then proceeded down the length of the ship. As the legionnaires worked in unison, some spoke about their fate and debated on the outcome of this expedition.

"I'm not sure this is going to turn out as well as Caesar planned," Vibius said as he sawed a fractured piece of wood, the sound of saws blending with the hammering of nails and breaking of boards.

"Honestly, I am not sure what the hell he was thinking, coming out here ..."

"Yeah, you'd think he'd take care of securing Gaul before sticking his neck out across the channel," Vibius agreed.

The duo stopped speaking when the order was given for them to stop working. The pair looked at each other in surprise; they hadn't even been working for five minutes. They turned, to find themselves facing the angry centurion, Brutus.

Brutus was rather tall. He had emerald eyes and a prominent chin. He was the kind of man who seemed like a natural leader, a man who would keep cool-headed in the thick of battle, a man meant to do great things; but he clearly was not. Brutus had been responsible for the near massacre of his cohort in Gaul the year before. Failing to judge the enemy's forces accurately, he had opted to leave his men in the kill-zone of an ambush until a timely rescue had saved the few survivors from death's grasp.

"You have twenty minutes to eat," he said curtly in a deep, nasal voice.

Brutus stood watching the two men as they turned and began walking back toward their equipment laid out on the beach. Marcus hoisted his armor back on and waited for Vibius to tie his on as well. Once they were all reequipped, they were assembled and marched up to the fort.

"Did you hear about those guys from the Seventh who got ambushed?" Marcus asked as he climbed the sandy slope.

"No! Where?" There was worry in Vibius' voice.

"Out there gathering wheat from a farmer's field somewhere," Marcus replied with a vague motion of his hand toward the hostile forest.

"How bad?"

"Fifteen dead. Fortunately the enemy were neither well prepared nor numerous. The thing is, there aren't many fields left for us to forage. The Britons are bound to get wise and begin attacking us more often and more brutally. With only a few fields left to harvest, it isn't too hard to guess where we'll be going next and set up ambushes."

"Are we bringing much food back?" Vibius asked.

"Not sure. We've been going out for a couple of days now, but the locals are taking everything they can before we get to the fields, and what little is left is being dearly guarded."

"When are we slated to go?"

"We haven't gone in two days, so I'm guessing we're probably going this evening sometime."

Vibius glanced skyward. The sun, a blinding orange globe on a canvas of cloud-speckled blue, was at its zenith. "Two days ago already?" he asked, incredulously.

"Time flies when you're having fun," Marcus quipped.

"You know it."

"With so much routine work, the individual days don't stand out much anymore," Marcus laughed.

They reached the fort along with the three hundred other men who were slated to eat as well. A reserve corps of roughly that same number was standing at attention inside the fort walls on the main avenue, waiting to be marched down to the beach to replace those coming in. Marcus's group was ordered to halt. After a brief salute between the centurions, the three hundred fresh men were marched to the beach.

"You have twenty minutes to eat. We've been ordered to go out and gather anything that is left from the countryside," Brutus shouted.

Brutus saluted them, and the men were dismissed. Each contubernium began to walk to their tents, including Marcus and his men. After a quick meal of stale bread, flavorless soup, and much needed water, the men began to make their way back toward the front gates. The centurion was already there, waiting for his men.

"Come on! We don't have all day!" he shouted aggressively.

"This guy's a real pleasure to serve under," Marcus commented coldly.

The men had barely entered the fort when the group was suddenly called to attention. The centurion began parading in front of his men. Marcus glanced around and estimated the men around him to number around two hundred and forty— most likely three centuries.

"Men," the centurion roared, taking obvious pleasure in being in charge. "A-tten-tion!"

The legionnaires clicked their heels together and looked upward at a slight angle, their chins extending proudly. Brutus took several well-calculated steps to the front of the men and stopped near the farthest end of the ranks.

"It is our turn to go out and scavenge the countryside for food. However, the previous patrol has reported that only one field is left to forage. A certain wheat field on the other side of the forest," the man shouted to his subordinates, scanning for the slightest irregularity so that he could once again assert who was in command. But he found none.

The cold, sleep-deprived men were first-rate, a crack squadron of men led by an egotistical commander with poor leadership. The men missed Severus, their previous centurion. He had been cut by a sword in a battle days ago, however the wound on his arm was healing quickly and it was expected he would resume command of his men within a week. It would be a great relief to all of the men to be under the command of one who cared and was close to them. Many of the men under Brutus' command joked sardonically that he cared more about his sandals than he did about the lives of his men.

Brutus stopped speaking, crossed his arms, and scanned the men before him one final time. Believing he was responsible for these men's perfect appearance, he grinned and spoke to himself softly.

"Splendid, splendid," he said with a subtle nod of his head. Satisfied and ready to march, he bellowed, "Men, about face!" The veins in his neck bulged as he enunciated each syllable.

As one, the men turned to face the opening doors of the Porta Praetoria. In time with the thudding of the doors against the side walls of the gatehouse, Brutus shouted the order to advance. Quickly the men began to file out four abreast. Marcus had the privilege of being at the head of the procession on the right flank. Ahead of them, the forest stood, uninviting. The trees towered over their insignificant bodies. As the men marched deeper into the forest, a profound sense of gloom and apprehension overcame them. The sun had been shining brightly, yet within the forest only small beams of light filtered down in cones through the dense foliage. A small layer of fog covered the ground and shrouded the men's lower legs midway up their calves.

The tense men advanced slowly, using their pila as hiking sticks over the uneven terrain. The centurion lead them from the side; too much of a coward to lead from the front. It was evident Brutus was the most apprehensive of them all, and he made no effort to conceal his dread. Marcus could not help but wonder how this man without the slightest evidence of leadership had been promoted. Brutus, who at first glance seemed like a natural leader, was now known to be a man whose mind would freeze in a stressful situation. Marcus quickly realized he and his men would have to fend for themselves if they were attacked.

The soldiers-turned-foragers penetrated far into the forest; the beach and fort now completely veiled by the trees surrounding them. Just shy of twenty minutes later, the men finally emerged from the woods and the sudden appearance of light and open terrain came as a breath of fresh air to the men.

As the legionnaires emerged from the forest in rows, a vast emptiness greeted them. Far to the left, roughly two miles away, the village that housed their enemies could be seen; the only sign of life was the smoke that swirled darkly above a handful of chimneys, carried gently along by the breeze. Below them to the front ran a creek that divided the plain. The wheat field they had come to scavenge was on their side of the stream; a vast field of wild grass that stretched as far as they could see was on the other. The forest continued in an L-shape to the right of where they emerged, flanking the wheat field along two sides. The men had left the dark, unwelcoming forest behind and emerged onto Elysium. The legionnaires were taken aback by the beauty of the countryside and even forgot they were alone in hostile territory for several liberating seconds. There were rolling hills as far as they could see, and the tall blades of grass combined with the azure skies lent a divine tranquility to the panorama. Although alone in enemy territory the men felt at peace with themselves and the cruel world. The legionnaires inhaled the fresh air while the chants of birds drifted along the drafts of air, soothing the apprehensive men with their peaceful melody.

Brutus eyed the countryside silently. Even he was awestruck by the unexpected beauty of these savage lands. His eyes quickly darted toward the village. At this distance, he would have time to see the enemy coming, take a nap, and still have moments to spare before calling his men to prepare for battle. *If* the enemy had the guts to attack him and his men …

Brutus took a cursory glance around the edge of the forest and, content that nothing seemed unusual, called for his men to disarm. Swords, shields, and pila were set down on the earth, though they kept their armor; scythes were then unsheathed, and the men descended the twenty remaining feet down the gentle slope and entered the wheat field. While the Roman army was highly disciplined and organized, the foragers progressed at their individual paces.

As the gentle wind blew, the blades of wheat bent softly in the wind, creating a beautiful display of nature at its finest. The shades of gold varied as the blades bent in the wind, and some of the men were mesmerized by the beauty of the sight. The combined melody of birdsong mixed with that of the legionnaires' whistling replaced the cacophony of clashing steel and pained groans. The scent of grass and wheat replaced the pungent stench of blood and death. And the sap-covered scythes they held replaced the blood-covered gladii they clenched in combat. Before they knew it, the men were shoulder high in wheat.

With only the birds for company, the men began to slice the wheat and placed the slivered stalks into sacks and wicker baskets on their backs.

XX

Androvic spied the Romans from the tree where he hid and silently relayed his observations to the men below via hand signals. He watched angrily as the legionnaires slowly sliced their way through the wheat field. Although this wheat field wasn't cultivated by his fellow villagers, it bothered him to see the Romans feeding off his homeland. He prayed the Romans would get sick from the crop and die, but he knew the chances of them actually dying were greater if he attacked them himself rather than pleading to the gods for their involvement.

Androvic was bent on exacting his tribe's revenge. His fingers twitched nervously as he awaited the opportune moment to strike. Meanwhile, he counted the Romans, his fingers signaling the number two hundred and fifty to the soldiers huddled below. The foreigners seemed at ease, and Androvic quickly concluded it would be an easy battle. He waited several more minutes to ensure that no additional Roman soldiers were arriving before he silently slid down the tree and landed on the muddy ground.

"I counted two-fifty, give or take," he said, speaking to his subordinates. "What did you men come up with?"

"Same."

"The bastards are more numerous this time," Androvic cursed. "I was stupid not to bring more men."

"What? We outnumber them five to one. Our archers will have taken them out and the thousand men behind me will have come for nothing," Androvic's son answered.

Androvic turned to face his son, who had still never tasted the sting of battle.

"Son, don't be fooled by sheer numbers. In war, they count for little."

Androvic's son didn't answer; although he didn't believe his father that there was a chance they could not win despite the ratio. It was absurd. *Father is a fool*, he thought.

"Shall we wait for a better time?" asked one of the two men kneeling before Androvic.

"No," Androvic said aloud, suddenly realizing he had almost compromised his men. He looked over to the Romans. Satisfied they were still oblivious to his presence, he continued to address his men.

He spoke in a whisper this time. "Are the archers in place?"

"Yes, sir. As are the infantry and cavalry," one man answered.

Androvic eyed the men kneeling behind him in the thickets. He was pleased with what he saw. Between them and the one hundred cavalrymen he had brought with him, he was fairly confident his ambush would succeed.

"All right, men. Sound the carnyx," Androvic said with a small nod.

The men nodded in unison and shuffled down both sides of the tree-line. The order for the archers to line the trees was passed along swiftly, and the impetuous men were thrilled they were finally going to have a shot at avenging their fallen comrades, all those who had died in the defense of their land. In less than a minute, the fifty archers had assembled shoulder-to-shoulder and stood partly hidden along the forest's edge. The time for revenge was upon them. The men knocked their arrows quickly and silently and waited for the final order to attack.

Behind the archers were the additional one thousand men, waiting with bated breath for the order to attack. The mass of huddled men was an impressive sight, even to Androvic. He had dispatched messengers to surrounding villages, and many men had volunteered to lend their aid to this ambush.

Many of the men present had fought the Romans before when they had first landed and now ached for the sweet nectar of revenge. Once the archers had depleted their arrows, these men would be called forward to finish off any survivors. A task all were eager to tackle.

The huddled infantrymen were concerned that no Romans would be left standing after the archers had depleted their arrows and that their thirst for blood would go unquenched. The men grew restless while Androvic took position at the archers' left flank and observed the unsuspecting Romans a final time. No Roman was closer than three dozen feet from his belongings, and no men had been left to provide security around the perimeter. Androvic thanked Brutus under his breath. He had heard the centurion dismiss all advice from his men to place a detachment of soldiers around the perimeter to keep vigil or to stay near their weapons while they harvested. The Romans wouldn't suffer a big loss with this man's death, but at least it would quench Androvic's thirst for Roman blood for several hours. Suddenly the deep, rumbling sound of the carnyx sounded the order to attack and Androvic watched the ambush unfold with great excitement.

Marcus, who was placing severed wheat in his bag, turned to walk back toward the hill. He gazed across the tree line one hundred and fifty feet to his left when he suddenly caught a glimpse of what looked like men standing side by side. Squinting, he peered more sharply and suddenly realized they had walked into a trap. Brutus had been mistaken; they would have no time to prepare for the enemy.

Without thinking he cried, "Ambu—!" as the sound of the British horn cut painfully through the air like a dull blade.

Immediately, arrows erupted from the tree-line, the whooshing of the arrows finishing his word for him.

Instinctively, the men ducked as arrows zipped murderously above them and they quickly began to crawl toward the hill where their equipment had been laid, almost forty feet away. Spilled bags of wheat fell to the ground and were disregarded as the men tried desperately to regain their weapons. Their chest armor provided a small feeling of security as they crawled blindly through the blades of wheat.

Marcus felt the wheat shake violently around him as arrows whizzed by, knocking grains loose and severing the occasional stalk of wheat. The terrifying *zip-zip-zip* of arrows mixed with the crackling of wheat created a terrifying din that unnerved many of the men. Marcus, for the moment, ignored the state of his friends and crawled blindly toward where he thought the slope was. He pushed the wheat down in front of him abruptly, striving to edge his way out of the kill zone. Suddenly the earth began to tremble, and the sound of galloping horses resonated through the deadly air. Realizing they had walked into a well-planned ambush, Marcus' hopes of survival ebbed even further. He had only two options: lie in the grass and hope for the best or sprint for the hill and try to fight his way out of the mess. With the galloping horses almost on him, he took a deep breath and flung himself forward with all his might. The wheat stalks slapped his arms and legs as he sprinted through the vegetation. Behind him, the enemy cavalry had already reached the wheat field and were engaging the Romans trapped there. Quickly dispatching the unarmed Romans, the cavalry continued moving through the legionnaires, their blades crimson with Roman blood.

Marcus sprinted as mightily as he could, ignoring the zipping arrows and painful screams as he made his way through the vegetation. Elysium had turned into hell in the blink of an eye. With his attention placed on reaching the hill, Marcus did not notice as one of the British horsemen rode up behind him. The Briton swirled his sword high above his head, preparing to slice the escaping Roman's head clean off his shoulders when suddenly Marcus was hit by an arrow in the chest and fell to the ground, leaving the barbarian with nothing to cleave but the tips of wheat. Furious that he had missed the Roman, the native slowed his horse and turned to charge the Roman once more.

Marcus recovered from the fall and clutched his chest with his hands, feeling for blood. Luckily, the armor had served its purpose and deflected the arrow. Thankful to be alive, he praised the Gods as well as the man who had crafted his armor. Marcus quickly got back onto his feet when he saw the Briton was onto him once again. He quickly unsheathed his pugio, the short, fat combat knife he had been issued years ago upon having joined the Legion and prepared himself for the worst. The Gods had spared him once but this time even they would not be able to save him. Holding the weapon firmly, he quickly planned his defense. Bizarrely, everything around Marcus seemed to come to a standstill as he awaited the charge. His attention was no longer placed on the rain of arrows or the screams of the wounded; only the charging cavalryman. The Briton could sense Marcus was preparing to die fighting, but in his blind rage he dismissed two important facts. The first was that an infantryman was exceedingly more agile than a cavalryman, and second, the horse was in full gallop. If Marcus planned his attack well, he would be able to slay the horse and send the steed and its rider crashing in a death roll.

When the horse was at the proper distance, and the Briton was still convinced he held the upper hand, Marcus leaped across the charging horse and thrust his knife into the horse's throat up to the hilt. The horse's momentum knocked Marcus' hand away and dropped him to the ground once more as the screaming steed tumbled to the ground and sent its rider careening overhead.

Marcus quickly shook off the pain in his sprained wrist and looked in the man's direction. The native was nowhere to be seen. Content he had taught the overconfident Briton a mortal lesson, Marcus quickly resumed his flight toward the hill. The archers and cavalry were still wreaking havoc among the dispersed and defenseless Romans, but Marcus could see that a small bastion of shields had been erected by survivors on the hill. Most of the cavalry now circled the trapped men as countless other Romans continued to sprint in their direction.

Marcus was only fifteen feet away from the base of the hill when two chariots picked him as a target and began to approach him at an alarming rate. With his heart racing and his luck running out, Marcus put every last bit of energy into his race and pleaded to the gods to let him live. Marcus reached the base of the hill and ran up the gentle slope hastily, darting between several of the circling horsemen and reaching the relative safety of the Roman shields. His comrades made a gap in the shields and allowed Marcus and two other survivors to dive within their protective ring. Marcus was amazed that over one hundred men were present; most of them had been bringing back their first collection of wheat when the ambush was sprung. They had quickly regained their equipment and held off the enemy cavalry.

Marcus found a shield and pilum on the ground, neither of which actually belonged to him, then quickly joined the outer ranks of men who held the enemy cavalry at bay with lowered pila. Marcus was not happy to be using someone else's equipment, but harsh times called for harsh measures, and he was certain that whoever owned this equipment would understand his motive; if they were even alive by the day's end.

Awed that the Romans were putting up such a strong fight, Androvic gave the order for the infantry to charge the Romans who were already regrouped on the hill. The cavalry had been effective in running down and nearly halving the enemy forces, but infantry would be better suited for the next step of the ambush. Their sheer numbers would overpower the remaining legionnaires. By attacking the formation, the last of the Romans who had yet to reach the formation would be cut off and be taken care of piecemeal by his archers and cavalry. *Their* fate was sealed.

The carnyx sounded once again from within the forest and the British cavalry began to peel off, leaving the Romans time to reposition themselves before the forest edge suddenly came alive with charging men. Like ants swarming from an anthill, a seemingly endless stream of soldiers gushed from the dark forest. With little time left before the two armies would collide, the legionnaires turned to Brutus, who had been standing in the center of the circle until now. Soldiers in the inner ranks saw that he had been struck by a spear in the thigh, the shaft pinning him to the ground like a bug.

"Shit! He's dead!" one man shouted.

"What do we do?" was the question heard around the circumference of the tactical circle.

In fact, Brutus was not dead but semi-conscious.

"Do we break and run?" one man asked, his voice shaking.

The others quickly identified him as a novice, green in the art of war.

"We break and we'll get cut down by the cavalry. We must stay and fight," the man beside him said calmly and sternly.

With only seconds left before the Britons were upon them, Marcus seized the initiative and shouted out for the men to form a hollow square, the optimum formation when all else had failed. At first the men looked peered around at each other, wondering who this man was who was taking command. Suddenly one of the men recognized him as the one who had saved his unit from complete annihilation on the beach during the landing.

"Form a hollow square!" The man shouted as well, trusting Marcus. Of all people present, Marcus was the one to listen to.

Before long, the soldiers were reforming their perimeter to form a hollow square. Those still with their pila formed the outer ranks, while those with only their swords left filed in the gaps.

With only seconds left to spare, the last man got into position and the formation was secure with all of the wounded huddled in the center. Then there was a loud crash as the Britons collided into the Roman soldiers' shields, spears and swords.

The Romans were pushed back slightly by the unending torrent of men but quickly gained the upper hand by delivering the first stabs with their gladii and pila. As one, the outer ranks of the Roman formation plunged forward with their weapons, and the first rank of the enemy fell lifelessly, only to be replaced by others who naively believed their outcome would be different. But as the preceding rank had discovered in their last moments, these men also learned the brute effectiveness of a stab to the gut followed by a lunge with a shield, and countless other British soldiers fell dead. This pattern went on for minutes, a mound of corpses beginning to rise around the outside of the Roman formation, whose perimeter had not buckled since the initial charge. Sensing that the men were holding firm, Marcus backed out from the front lines and slithered his way to the center of the circle where the wounded were gathered. Several had been struck by spears and were bleeding too badly to be saved, yet Marcus tried to help them.

One man in particular stood out. The unfortunate soldier had had his right forearm cut off at the elbow and was attempting to bandage up the bleeding stump with his left hand and knees. Marcus used his knife to cut a piece from his tunic and secured a tourniquet inches above the wound. In time, the bleeding stopped, and the man thanked Marcus profusely.

"Now that we've stopped the bleeding, do you mind if I borrow your sword? I'm afraid I may have dropped mine," the man said, showing his stump to Marcus with a feeble grin.

Marcus was amazed by the man's courage and desire to rejoin the fight.

"You're too wounded, you have to stay!" Marcus shouted back over the deafening clamor.

"To hell with that! Didn't you see what these sons of bitches did to me?" The man stood and pulled out his knife before staggering back to the fight.

Marcus didn't want the man to continue fighting but knew he was in no position to stop him, so he continued to move among the group of wounded men. Several others had lost significant portions of flesh and limbs and Marcus' tunic grew shorter with every tourniquet and bandage he cut from it. He came to the last man, Brutus, who was still stuck to the ground by a spear through his thigh, roughly a hand's width below the inguinal. The man's face was pale, and blood pooled all around his leg. One soldier had placed his hand around the point of entry and was trying to stem the blood flow, in vain.

The young soldier's face showed fear, and the man was on the verge of panic.

"I can't stop the bleeding!" he shouted.

"You have to tie this off several inches above the wound; the hole is too large to cover up!" Marcus shouted back, handing him the last strip of cloth he could afford to cut from his tunic. The man didn't budge, too panic stricken to tie the cloth.

Without wasting any more precious time, Marcus slid Brutus' tunic up and went about tying the tourniquet, realizing he was sealing the leg's fate but might manage to save Brutus himself.

"He's all set!" Marcus shouted before motioning the boy back to the fight. "They need us up there!"

Marcus began to rise when he felt a hand grab his armor at the neck and pull him back. He looked down at the man who held him.

"How are we doing?" Brutus asked, his feeble voice almost entirely muted out by the enveloping cacophony.

"We're completely enveloped, sir, but still holding our ground!"

Brutus nodded and let go of Marcus, lying his head back down. Seeing that Brutus had passed out once more, Marcus hurried back to the front line and replaced one of the legionnaires to give him time to rest. Since the first of the enemy cavalry had sprung from the forest, the attack had continued for about half an hour and the Britons were beginning to grow restless at the thought that they still had not managed to kill off the outnumbered Romans.

Infuriated, the Britons began to hack more carelessly than before, their angry blows doing little against the stolid wall of shields opposing them. Watching from the tree-line, Androvic could see the attack was losing momentum and that his men were not making any more progress. He cursed the Romans for the thousandth time that week and began to pace back and forth.

"Should I give the order to retreat, sir?" one man asked, sensing Androvic's unease.

"Absolutely not! In fact, give the order for the cavalry to attack. We're going to kill every last one of those little bastards! Every ... last ... one!" Androvic yelled at the man.

Within seconds, the carnyx sounded once again, and the cavalry charged the surrounded Romans alongside the infantry. The Romans immediately knew the outcome of the battle. For the enemy commander to send cavalry into a hacking contest was suicide. Cavalry was best suited for cutting down the fleeing and seizing advantages around the battlefield, but to match them up against organized infantry was a death warrant. Although the enemy ranks continued to be filled by the other men waiting to get a shot at the Romans, this was not the Romans' primary concern at the moment. In fact, the most urgent matters were fatigue and dehydration. The men were sweating profusely; their arms were growing tired from combat and although the men were switching at will, it wasn't long before it was one's turn to fight again due to the limited number of soldiers present. Minutes dragged on, and some of the legionnaires began to succumb to fatigue, their arms too heavy to stab swiftly. Enemy swords and spears quickly struck those too tired to fight any longer. Although superbly trained and astoundingly fit, even Romans could tire. The Roman ranks began to thin out, and the square began to shrink as the battle entered its fortieth minute of continuous fighting. More men began to die. Slowly, the square shrank, though the men continued to hold their ground. These men would go down fighting to the last man, their pride too great to surrender to the unshaven barbarians. Although all present knew that the Britons would never even consider taking any of them alive. If they did so, it would be only to make a public display of their death back home.

The Romans' despair grew gradually as they realized their lives were apparently coming to an end. Suddenly a muffled sound resembling the Roman order to charge was heard from the forest behind them and the men were certain their minds were playing tricks. Clearly, their fate was sealed. They would be left here to die alone.

Unbelievably however, from the forest's edge came the rumble of charging infantry, and the last of the Roman survivors turned to face the din, amazed to see legionnaires charging in their direction. The Gods had been impressed by their display of courage and bravery and would grant them mercy. With lighter hearts, the fatigued men doubled their efforts and began to slash at the surrounding enemy with renewed vigor. With a burning desire to avenge the fallen, the Romans broke rank and chased the now-fleeing natives. The fresh legionnaires quickly passed the exhausted Roman survivors who slowed to allow the fresher troops past them. Although they ached to slay the fleeing, their legs would not carry them. The survivors huddled on the bloody ground, fatigued and oblivious to the carnage around them. With their hearts still racing and their bodies sore from head to toe, the men tried catching their breath.

Eighty-nine men of the original two hundred and forty that had first set out survived. It had been a bloody battle, and many good Romans had died. More than one thousand of the enemy dead were counted, in comparison to the one hundred or so Roman casualties, and the men later rejoiced in the knowledge that the deceased had not died in vain.

Marcus rested, his hands clasped behind his head as he concentrated on his breathing, when a man came into view to his right. The man's face was smeared in blood, most of which was not his own, and his dark damp hair was plastered to his scalp with sweat. His helmet was scratched and slightly dented in various places, but the glitter in the man's eyes could not conceal his joy and wonder at being alive.

"I wanted to thank you for what you did ..." The man paused and wiped the sweat and blood from his face before continuing. "You saved us out there. We are all very grateful."

Marcus pursed his lips. "I didn't save you guys. We saved each other."

"You're the only man I heard give a single order during that entire time," the man said, looking around at the huddled men.

"I just did what any other man would have done in my place ..." Marcus said modestly.

"Well, I'm grateful for it, and I hope I can repay the favor some day," the man said, extending his hand.

Marcus smiled and both men grasped forearms; the legionnaire pulled Marcus to his feet.

"I'm afraid you've got more grateful guys coming," the man said, pointing at the approaching herd of men with his chin.

Marcus turned to face the men. Suddenly a man burst through carrying a stretcher followed by another stretcher bearer. They cut through the throng of men rudely and stopped just short of Marcus. On the stretcher was Brutus, the sawed-off spear still protruding slightly from his right thigh. The tourniquet had stopped the bleeding, but Marcus knew the man would eventually lose his leg as a result. Although Marcus hated the officer, he still felt a pang of sympathy and sorrow, knowing the man's life was wrecked forever. Marcus knelt by Brutus and looked him in the eyes. Brutus looked at Marcus dryly for a long moment, but slowly his face relaxed and he lowered his arm onto Marcus' shoulder.

"Thank you for saving my life," he whispered.

"All these men saved you, sir, not just I," Marcus answered.

"You're the one who put a tourniquet on my leg."

"This man here was trying to help you before I got to you. He deserves more credit than I do."

"Duly noted. But you're the one who led my men. You're the one who gets commended."

Marcus smiled but shook his head.

"I appreciate the honor, sir, but I must refuse."

"You refuse? You'll get the highest honor for saving an officer's life and for saving over thirty men! I could have you promoted!"

"Yes, sir," Marcus replied.

"Why?" Brutus asked, shocked by the man's response.

"I would rather be an exceptional legionnaire than just another centurion, sir,"

Brutus was appalled; he hadn't expected this response.

"Well, then ..." he grabbed Marcus by the arm and squeezed gently. "You are a brave man. None of us would be standing had it not been for you. We are all indebted to you."

With a flick of his hand, Brutus motioned for the stretcher bearers to take him away. He suddenly shouted for them to stop and turn around part-way.

"I did not get your name," Brutus said, suddenly remembering.

"Marcus Caius, sir."

Brutus smiled and nodded as the capsarius carried him away, and Marcus watched as he was absorbed into the mass of men running around and caring for the wounded. Like a statue, Marcus simply stood there and thought about what had just transpired in the last hour and half. Everything seemed different now, although nothing had truly changed, and he wondered why.

XXI

Androvic leaned on a tree at the edge of the forest, the Roman fort in front of him cloaked by falling sheets of rain. He and Ludovic were not taking any precautionary measures to shield themselves from the Roman sentries, knowing that they would never see them at this distance through the intense precipitation. Androvic thought of the failed ambush and felt powerless against the mighty Roman fort ahead of him. If he couldn't destroy a paltry two hundred and fifty men, how could he ever expect to annihilate two entire legions? The Roman fort stood defiantly, provocatively, and ever more proudly with every battle its soldiers won. The mere sight of the wooden palisade aggravated Androvic. *Something has to be done*, he thought, *but what?*

Two days had passed after the failed ambush, and rain had fallen incessantly since. Almost immediately once the British survivors had regained their village, the skies had opened, as if to wash the shame off the demoralized survivors.

"At least this rain is keeping them confined to their fort," Ludovic said as he peered through the bushes.

"For now, but once it ceases they'll start provoking us again," Androvic spat.

"We need to attack them. Kill them to the last one," Ludovic said through clenched teeth.

"They are too strong."

"Are you losing faith, Androvic?"

"I am not losing faith. I'm just being rational. We had them cornered two days ago, and yet they managed to hold their ground until the damn sentries spotted the dust and sent reserves to their aide. We were five times stronger than they, and they managed to kill over half of our troops, while they only suffered scant casualties."

"I understand. What we need is to isolate them into small groups and overwhelm them. Perhaps *then* they will question the benefit of any further expeditions here."

Androvic smiled but shook his head.

"We were over one thousand strong and they only two-fifty, yet they still managed to win. You were there, Ludovic, you saw what happened," Androvic said. "Even now, they are still over eight thousand strong, despite the dead and wounded."

"Then we will at least halve that before they leave," Ludovic interrupted him.

"We have only a couple days left before they return to Gaul. Reports have it that they are advancing rapidly with the repairs of their ships. As long as they are stranded on our island, we have a chance. But we will need thousands of men," Androvic said in despair.

"I will find the men!" Ludovic answered with fervor, "I will find the men from surrounding villages, and we will attack relentlessly until their fort lies in ashes. They will be killed like the dogs they are, and those who are unfortunate enough to survive will become our slaves and feel what others have felt in their wake."

Both men leered at the Roman fort across the plain.

Androvic hesitated before he replied. "You think surrounding villages would want to lend us their aid?"

"Sir, villages for miles around us have provided men to fight in Gaul against the Romans. I assure you, many men would want nothing less than to get another shot at the Romans." Ludovic let the words linger before looking at Androvic.

"We must act fast, then. Once the rain stops, they will resume construction of their ships and escape from our grasp only to come back stronger."

"We should raid their ships—burn them to the ground."

"No, the Romans are guarding those preciously, perhaps even more carefully than their fort. The Romans know those ships are their only means off the island, and I'm certain every Roman present would rather fight to the death than let us burn down their ships."

Ludovic grunted.

"Well if we can't destroy the ships, then we will make sure there is no one left to fill them," he said slowly, his eyes glistening with fanatical hatred.

Before the day's end, messengers had been dispatched to all corners of the British province. Every village visited by a messenger would dispatch an additional ten, and soon much of southeastern Britannia had been alerted to the need to crush the stranded Romans once and for all. Each village provided between several hundred men to over a thousand, depending on the size and history of the village. Those villages that had previously clashed with the Romans in Gaul had a tendency to provide many more men than those who had not.

Before the last village had been alerted, twelve thousand of the enemy was already waiting to fight the legionnaires. The omens were taken and upon reading great victory in the liver of a hare, the men began to prepare for battle. Swords were sharpened, shields manufactured, and arrows carved. The villages surrounding the fort soon were overcrowded, yet few lost their will to fight despite the rain and winds.

Days passed before finally the last of the volunteers arrived from the surrounding countryside. Roughly half a dozen villages encircled the Roman camp, and each was crowded with volunteers from around the province and beyond. In each village, chiefs gathered and offered uplifting stories, heralding the spoils and glory that lay ahead. Cheers filled the air as spears and swords were rattled vigorously, the natives craving Roman blood. In Androvic's village, over five thousand British volunteers stood in the field, where he paraded in front of them atop his horse, rousing the bloodlust inside each man present.

"Men, I am Androvic, chief of the Palutii. For two years I have been engaged in fighting these treacherous fools, both in Gaul and here, our very homeland. I have served in Gaul, as many of you have, and have seen many of my friends die in combat with the Romans. I have strived to keep them away from our sacred lands, but unfortunately, I did not fight hard enough. Today, we pay the price of our lack of effort."

The men were silent, listening to the large man talk.

"The Romans spread like the plague, and they must be stopped. I do not know about you, but I want my children to grow up far from their dark ways and their foolish teachings," Androvic said, shaking his head with fury.

There was a large cheer as the prospect of revenge drew ever closer.

"The Romans have come to us. We did not seek war, but they are apparently interested in our ways. So let us not be selfish—let us share our culture with them, our culture ... *and our steel!*" he shouted, unsheathing his sword and lifting the weapon high into the air, sunrays gleaming off the polished steel.

Britons began to thump on their shields with their weapons in applause; others shouted insults at the Romans.

"Fellow countrymen, you are terrifying to me, and I am one of you! Imagine what they will see as they stare at you before the battle. You men are unstoppable, and the omens are in our favor. The Romans stand no chance against us. The Romans are our guests, uninvited it is true, but our guests all the same, and it would be rude to leave them waiting. What do you say men, shall we go greet them?" he shouted even louder, bringing his motivational speech to a climax.

The men replied with their usual shield thumping and bellowing. Androvic eyed the men proudly. This day was his to seize.

"Men from adjacent villages are already advancing on the Roman fort and I do not want them to have all the fun today. We too will bathe in Roman blood tonight!"

The men cheered once more as Androvic quickly turned heel and joined his villagers, who were beginning to march away. At the front of the procession was the cavalry which consisted of mounted warriors as well as the more heavily armed charioteers. Following the cavalry was the infantry—thousands of warriors bent on the annihilation of the Roman legions nestled comfortably within their lands. The column was nearly a mile long as the men marched to the plain that separated the fort from the forest. The Romans had felled the trees surrounding the fort shortly after their arrival to have better visibility and that insensible act angered the natives even further. The gods lived in the forests: the trees, the streams, and the air. To lay waste to them was a sacrilege that could not go unpunished.

Soon, the men thought, they would exact their vengeance. Soon, they would teach those over-confident Romans a bloody lesson. Soon, the gods would be avenged. Soon ...

XXII

The Britons had gathered across the field from the Roman fort, the mass of men and horses poised for attack. The cavalry and charioteers had formed on the flanks, and both waited impatiently for the carnyx to sound the attack. Androvic sat atop his horse and watched restlessly; the urge to attack tugged at him. The Roman infantry was headed straight for him, and the British chief was itching to charge. He had had enough of these people, and the anticipation of ending it once and for all was overwhelming. Androvic nudged his horse forward several feet and rolled his head to relive the tension in his neck. He looked around him anxiously as he tried to soothe his burning neck with the squeeze of his hand.

The dirt was moist but not saturated—beneficial conditions for the heavy chariots, which were liable to get stuck in mud. Although he was counting on the chariots to lead him to victory, he knew that the mass of infantry and regular cavalry would be more than sufficient in themselves. He looked to the sides at the men who had volunteered.

The British infantry had formed a line across the field, while the cavalry had positioned themselves on the flanks. Ahead of the mass of men were the skirmishers, men armed with javelins

176

and small shields who were to probe the Roman lines in search of a possible flaw. Both sides watched as the exposed men advanced in the direction of the Roman ranks, stopping roughly forty yards from the Roman legionnaires. The javelins used by the Britons were lighter than the pila used by the Romans and, from this distance, the British skirmishers would be near enough to throw their missiles while keeping a safe distance from the Roman soldiers and their pila.

The advancing men halted and stuck their javelins into the ground in preparation for the javelin shower they were preparing to discharge. The skirmishers, instead of forming up shoulder-to-shoulder, positioned themselves loosely across the expanse. They intended to take advantage of their large numbers to probe greater swaths of the Roman ranks.

The skirmishers, armed with the first of their multiple missiles, flexed their arms and backs in preparation for hurling their javelins toward the opposing army. With the liberty to fire at will, one man after the other began to heave his missile at the Roman ranks, the long, thin javelins cutting through the air like angry wasps. Before the first of the javelins had even reached the Roman shields and men, the British skirmishers had already prepared their second salvo and flung them also.

Before the first of the skirmishers had discharged their projectiles, the Romans had already been given the order to form the testudo. Now presenting a solid wall of shields, the men were prepared to receive and parry the projectiles meant to maim and kill them. The first of the javelins hit the shields with a great hiss and thud. Many struck the tops of the raised shields and slid harmlessly down. Some Romans in the front ranks received the impact of the javelins straight on. The tips of the spears penetrated the shields but lost their momentum and left the men unharmed. Although their light javelins achieved little against the more heavily armed legionnaires, the Britons continued to discharge their salvos without respite. Realizing the futility of the engagement, it wasn't long before the skirmishers were given the order to retreat and give way to the infantry. *Hopefully they will have better luck than us*, one of the skirmishers thought as he retreated.

With a sigh, more of boredom than of relief, the Romans reformed into their proper ranks and the testudo was no more. The few wounded were pulled to the back of the formation by their fellow legionnaires, where they were then taken back to the fort on stretchers.

On the other side of the field, Androvic raised his sword high, and the soldier at his side sounded the carnyx. Immediately following the deep, beast-like blast, a loud cheer filled the ranks, and the infantry began to advance. Realizing the enemy would be on them within seconds, the centurions began to shout orders.

"Ready pila!"

The younger, more inexperienced soldiers swallowed difficultly as death charged them head-on. The older, experienced soldiers stood their ground and helped reassure the newer soldiers. They all raised their pila in preparation for the order to discharge the lethal projectiles. When the enemy was within forty yards, the order to throw was given. Within seconds, the sky was filed with pila arcing toward the charging Britons. As the Britons continued to run forward, the pila intercepted them at a distance of roughly thirty yards, the heavy javelins offering greater punch than the lighter British javelins. Men were skewered two, occasionally even three, at a time; the tightly packed mass of men offered little resistance in the face of the projectiles. The first rows of Britons melted to give way to the succeeding ranks as the human wave gained momentum.

With precious few seconds to spare before the two cultures collided, the second order to discharge was given, followed by another storm of pila. Again, Britons were maimed and killed by the javelins before having a chance to engage the Romans. Next, the distinct, metallic hissing of hundreds of swords being unsheathed resonated down the length of the ranks as the Romans prepared for the fight. The anxious men grasped their weapons tightly. Feet shuffled in search of reliable traction. Sweat was wiped from brows, and long, deep breaths drawn. The time had come for them to fight.

In a blur, the Britons crashed into the Roman ranks and the start of the carnage immediately ensued. The Britons hacked viciously at the solid mass of shields before them, frantically attempting to force their way through the obstacles to stab at the men behind. The Romans responded with precise and controlled upward jabs through the abdomen; the tips of bloody swords protruded from maimed upper backs. The grisly sight was one the men had grown accustomed to after long years in the service. The newer additions to the Roman army gagged at the sight and stench of death; several with weaker stomachs vomited onto their own cramped feet and, due to the confines of the formation, even onto the backs and legs of others. The metallic ringing of colliding swords filled the air, along with the shouts, groans, and huffs of the living and dying. Relying fully on their numbers, the Britons continued the futile attempts to force their way through the impenetrable Roman shields, only to be met with a swift stab to the belly and a punch with a shield. Roman whistles blew, signaling the front ranks to fall back and give way to fresher, somewhat anxious men who were eager to take part in the action. Bloodied swords and shields gave way to clean ones as the fresh men continued the battle.

From his horse, Androvic watched restlessly as his infantry were cut down by the dozen by the legionnaires. He was itching to send his cavalry and chariots into the melee but held back, waiting for the opportune time. It wouldn't be long before the Romans tired under the continuous mass of men at his disposal.

On the other side of the field, Caesar watched as his men exemplified the pride and honor of the Roman army. The legionnaires were fighting valiantly, killing over ten of the enemy for every one lost of theirs. He stood on the ramparts of the fort; the wind blowing his cape softly in the wind, presenting the enemy army with what he thought was a god-like stance. To his side were aides, messengers, officers and the generals in charge of the Legions fighting below.

"Their attack has lost momentum. They should be sending in their cavalry at any moment," he said, his eyes rolling over the carnage unfurling beneath him.

He was itching to ride down and be a part of the fight, but with no horse at his disposal, the great general was confined to the ramparts to get a good view of the battle.

"I want half the reserves to flank the enemy and prepare for a cavalry charge. Order the men already in the melee to give ground at a slow pace and lure the enemy deep into the center of the formation. We're going to encircle these sons of bitches and finish them off once and for all."

"Yes, sir," said one of the messengers before departing to relay the order to the officers below.

"Don't you think it may be too early to commit the reserves, Caesar?" one of the officers standing to his right asked.

"You don't win a battle, or a war, by doing what the enemy expects you to do, Marius. It is standard for the Roman army to keep its reserves out of the fight until the enemy is either fleeing or our boys are in desperate need of backup. At this point in time, I can see that the enemy forces do not have enough momentum to keep their attack going for much longer. The enemy cavalry is going to charge when the infantry begins to waiver, and at that point we will halt the cavalry charge and pursue the enemy when they turn to flee shortly afterward."

Marius nodded.

"By bringing more men to the fight, we'll speed up the process and also slay more of them as they turn to flee," Caesar said, turning to face the officer at his side.

"But what if it fails? What if our line begins to break?"

"You don't trust our boys, Marius?"

"Of course I do, but just out of precaution ..."

"Marius, there is something you must always remember: the greater the risk, the more substantial the reward."

"*If* successful," the officer replied, turning to look at the men below struggling for Rome.

After a drawn-out silence, Caesar spoke again in a hushed tone.

"If successful," Caesar murmured to himself. "*If* successful."

Shortly after the order to commit the reserves was received, half of the latter were sent around the flanks to encircle the enemy. The ranks engaged the enemy infantry, while the ranks facing the enemy cavalry poised across the field lowered their pila and hoped feverishly the enemy cavalry would not charge them yet.

But Androvic had entirely different plans. From what he could make out across the field, the Romans had sent their reserves forward into the melee, a sign of either their upcoming victory or their looming defeat. For the moment, he was still unsure, and he settled to await the arrival of a messenger who'd been sent to assess the current situation of the battlefield.

"A deserter?" asked a fellow chieftain, his paw resting on the pommel of his sword, ready to dispatch the traitor if the occasion called.

"No. A messenger," Androvic rectified before taking a step forward to meet the tired man.

The bear-sized man next to Androvic grunted with displeasure. His bushy eyebrows shielded the murderous eyes that were recessed in the man's skull; the thick facial hair covered the man's face below his helmeted cranium. His thirst for blood far from quenched, the large man would settle for killing any of his men who showed the slightest signs of wavering, merely to satisfy his twisted craving.

"What's the news, my boy?"

The messenger was a young man in his late teens, his clean shaven face smeared with blood and dirt from the front. He stopped to catch his breath before relaying the message.

"They've ... They've committed their reserves, sir. We're making headway up there, sir, but ... we're taking heavy losses," the man said, his pulse beginning to slow.

"Ha! They're committing their reserves! We're wearing them out," the large man replied excitedly.

"What about a cavalry charge?" Androvic replied with a large smile before turning to slap the man to his side on the back. "You ready, friend?"

"It's about time. I've had my heaviest sword polished in preparation for this great moment," the man replied in his deep, booming voice.

Androvic smiled again before raising his sword above his head.

"On me!" he shouted as he leaped forward on his steed, closely followed by the cavalry and chariots. The thundering sound of galloping horses accompanied the creaking of the chariot wheels as both roared toward the battle line. Androvic changed the course of his horse slightly to the right while in full charge, lining himself up to impact the Roman line that had enclosed his infantry by almost two-thirds.

The Romans, hearing the thunder of approaching cavalry, relied on those nearest the approaching wave to lower their pila and hold their ground while they continued to fight the infantrymen.

From atop the ramparts, Caesar watched as the horde of cavalry fell upon the thin line of enveloping Romans and encircled the Romans in turn.

"Shit, the Britons have attacked with their cavalry! Our soldiers are stretched too thin around the rear to hold them off for long," Marius shouted.

"Calm yourself, Marius. I had accounted for this. Give the order for the remainder of the reserves to be sent around the right flank and trap the British cavalry. The Britons have foolishly committed all of their forces, and we must seize the opportunity," Caesar said, and another messenger was again dispatched.

Within minutes, Caesar spotted the reserves moving around the right flank, arriving at their position to encircle the enemy.

Androvic had not seen this coming. He was hacking his way through the thin throng of Roman legionnaires when suddenly an additional mass of fresh men swooped around his left and came into position behind him. Androvic quickly realized what was happening and turned in their direction and called for his men to regroup.

"We're being surrounded!" the bear-sized chief shouted over the din of battle.

In a fit of anger, he slashed with his sword and butchered a legionnaire beneath him, the heavy sword slivering the man's neck with ease.

Slowly, the infantry and cavalry began to converge as the two encircled forces attempted to fight their way out of the trap. However, the Britons had now been completely surrounded by the last of the Roman reserves and found themselves in a perilous situation.

The legionnaires, remembering the near-annihilation of the famous foraging party, were keen to return the blow to the now-entrapped Britons.

From inside the maelstrom, the fatigued British soldiers were fighting with renewed spirit, realizing their only hope for survival came in fighting their way out of the envelopment. There were no reinforcements, no infantry or cavalry to come to their rescue this time. Quickly, the men realized their cavalry had been committed too early in the battle.

From atop of the ramparts, Caesar watched as the noose around the Britons closed ever so slowly. The cries and shouts were ear-splitting, yet Caesar felt no remorse at all. The bulk of the dying men were Britons, anyhow.

"Do you intend to slaughter them where they stand, Caesar?" asked Marius, intrigued by Caesar's method of warfare.

"Absolutely not. We have slain a good number of them, but they are still too strong. We will lose many more men than necessary in doing so. Surrounded men are desperate men, Marius, and they will fight to the death in lieu of surrendering. Give them a way out and ..."

"They will flee," Marius finished the sentence for him.

"The secret is to make it look accidental, though. Give them a way out, and you will notice many of the enemy will turn and rout rather than continue fighting."

"Then we pursue them," Marius continued.

"The hunt," Caesar said under his breath before turning to face one of the messengers on alert at his side. "Now, I want the far flank to begin to separate and pull around the side flanks slowly. I want the Britons to get the impression they are succeeding in their effort to break out. Let the rout gain momentum before pursuing them. Tell the men to wait for my command before pursuing them. Understood?"

"Yes, sir," the young messenger shouted before turning to climb down the ladder and relay the order to the officers below.

"Now," Caesar said calmly as he rolled his head from side to side, relieving the tension, "we wait."

"They're giving way," came the cheerful shout of a British infantryman as he yelled over his shoulder to alert his comrades. "They're giving way!"

The fatigued men peered through glassy eyes burning with sweat at the parting Romans. The far Roman flank was slowly giving way to them, and although dead-tired, the men let out relieved sighs and feeble shouts of elation. Their throats were dry and their voices hoarse, but the cries of joy still resounded from the front ranks.

"Keep it moving!" came the shouts from those stuck in the inner ranks.

With growing momentum the Britons were wedging their way through the parting Romans, the end finally in sight. Although they had not beaten the Romans, almost all were happy to merely be alive. It was better to be standing than to be among the unidentifiable mutilated corpses littering the bloody ground.

Finally, after what seemed an eternity, the first of the Britons broke free from the Roman strangulation and darted across the field, without nary a thought or concern for the well-being of their comrades. For now, returning to the relative security of their village was their primary objective. The disheveled men, a good number of whom were hunched over from fatigue and dehydration, ran as fast as they could still muster, spots flashing before their eyes. In the interim, their comrades who had not broken free were still fighting their way out of the widening gap in the Roman flank.

Within minutes, a gap almost one hundred feet wide had been left at the disposition of the Britons, allowing greater numbers of the enemy access to the wilderness lying at the edge of the field. The gap grew even wider and the rout gained momentum with every passing second. Before long the majority of the British army was fleeing, leaving only the boldest and most fervent zealots behind to fight to their death rather than retreat.

Seeing this, Caesar gave the order to hunt down the routers.

"Sound the horn. I want every man chasing those barbarians to pursue them to the gates of hell and not to stop until every last one lies dead on the ground."

The buccinators nodded and sounded the horn to pass the order to attack down to the men below.

With a great cheer, the Romans received the order to track and kill the fleeing down to the last. The nearest of the Britons along with the last of the fighting men were cut down mercilessly as the Roman legionnaires broke formation and overran the exhausted Britons. Stumbling atop one another, many Britons collapsed from fatigue and were either stabbed or trampled by the human wave.

Nearly three minutes passed before the Romans arrived at the edge of the forest, leaving heaps of scattered corpses in their wake. The legionnaires slowed at the edge of the forest but followed the deserters into the woods and watched as men vanished easily into the thick brush and undergrowth. Scanning the terrain in front of them repeatedly, the legionnaires watched helplessly as they lost the Britons to the enveloping gloom.

"Stay with them, boys! Don't lose 'em!" urged one of the centurions.

The Romans continued to hack and fight their way through the forest, striving to keep up with the fleeing enemy. Although the men were putting every ounce of effort they could muster into stalking their prey, their large shields and armor kept snagging on branches and slowed their progress in comparison to the agile deserters.

Many of the legionnaires were able to follow the small path that snaked through the forest toward the British village, and they kept close on the enemy's tail. Vibius, who was following Marcus, tracked the fleeing as best he could despite his excessive thirst. Some legionnaires were farther along the trail than the legionnaires following in the forest, and the fleeing Britons seized the opportunity to strike the pursuers once more. Those who still had their shields and weapons halted and crouched in the underbrush, waiting with bated breath for the Romans to come around the bend. They would have maybe thirty seconds to fight the Romans on the trail before the remaining army trudging through the forest would be upon them.

The Britons peered through the brush. Within seconds, the first of the enemy would be upon them. They could hear their voices, the metallic clanging of their armor, the dull thudding of their hobnailed caligae on the moist dirt. One of the men grabbed several rocks near him and noticed several others do the same. A rock wouldn't do much against a shield or armor, but it would wreak havoc on any unarmed portion of the body.

The first of the legionnaires came around the bend in the path and continued to scout the trodden path, their eyes darting back and forth, searching for Britons. Marcus, at the front once again, wiped the sweat from his face and glanced down the flanks of the path.

"We're losing them!" Marcus said in despair.

The man to the right of Marcus cursed and spoke through gritted teeth.

"Where did those hairy sons of --" The man's face suddenly burst as a rock thudded into his nose and killed him instantly. The soldier fell slowly and hit the ground with a metallic clang as dozens of rocks erupted from the brush. There were loud thuds as the rocks uselessly hit the men's shields. One Roman had been killed and two others wounded by the rocks before the Britons suddenly erupted from the forest like angry wasps.

Panting and out of breath, both sides collided yet again as the Britons fought to allow their friends more time to escape back to their village.

"You sons of whores," one legionnaire spat as he plunged his sword mercilessly into the enemy ranks. Vastly outnumbered, the Britons quickly lost ground. Upon seeing the remainder of the Roman army make their way toward them from the forest, the natives wavered. Before the legionnaires knew it, the Britons were turning tail and escaping farther down the trail yet again.

"After them! You men can rest tonight, but for now, we fight!" cried one centurion as he ran past the men, bloodied sword and shield in hand.

Marcus was out of breath, as were most of the men, but this didn't stop him. He knew that this time, they would not stop hunting the enemy. Marcus knew that Caesar would order his troops to track the enemy until every single one of the Britons lay dead on the ground.

The road meandered through the forest; on every likely occasion, the Britons tried to ambush the passing Romans, only to be repelled and then resume their flight. As the Romans fought bravely up the trail, light from an opening farther down the dark road came into view.

"Their village," one of the legionnaires shouted enthusiastically. "I can see their village!"

They cheered as the wooden walls and houses came into view. Without slowing, the Romans erupted from the forest and into the fresh, open air. There, they stopped. The last of the fleeing were already two-thirds the way back to the village, with only a dozen or so stragglers, the last of the ambushers, following farther behind.

"Halt," came the order from the centurions. From this distance, it would be futile for the men to continue their pursuit. It was time to regroup and take a quick breather. The village was roughly one thousand yards away, located on top of a small gradient. The village was impressive in size, and Marcus knew immediately it would be hard to take. The women and children, Marcus thought, had probably not evacuated because they thought they would win, and they would now crowd the streets as they ran for shelter. Some of the more fanatical might even put up a fight. Marcus shuddered at the thought. He didn't know if he would be able to kill a lady, armed or not, and feverishly hoped the situation wouldn't arise.

The Romans halted at the edge of the forest, their blood-red shields in beautiful contrast to the lush green forest behind them. Roman archers quickly ran past the halted infantrymen and unleashed their lethal projectiles at the last of the fleeing Britons, slaying only a few of them.

Marcus, who had lost track of his element during the pursuit, quickly began to search among the raised standards in search of his unit. But there was no time.

"Raise standards!" he heard the officers shout.

The golden Eagles were raised alongside the cohorts' standards with pride, their surreal glint adding to the already awesome sight of the Roman line.

Without wasting any time, the men formed up under the nearest banner, and soon the soldiers were in position to advance.

XXIII

Androvic watched from behind the protection of the surrounding wall as his followers scurried toward the village like ants. The Romans were preparing to march on his home. Fleeing crossed his mind, but he found it too cowardly, although he knew fighting would presumably result in his death and deaths of plenty others. He turned and looked at his village. All the peaceful memories came to mind. His wife and two young sons stood beneath him, looking toward him for a sign of reassurance. But he had none. He had lost all will to fight. The legions were just too smart, too tough, and too strong.

The Romans stood arrogantly across the field, and Androvic wondered where the man who would ultimately kill him stood at that moment. He thought painfully about the fate of his village, which would be pillaged, and the women raped. Hatred quickly boiled within him once more, and the desire to fight grew with every passing second. He knew he would ultimately die, but he planned on taking many of his enemy with him to the afterlife.

He peered down at the gate. His soldiers were already busy closing the massive doors, and others brought up a large log and heaved it into the brackets on both sides of the gate, effectively locking the gate.

Upon hearing the clank of the log fall into place, he began to shout out orders.

"Archers, to the walls!" he bellowed, without averting his gaze from the approaching Romans.

He heard shouts behind him as the men ran toward the ladders and took position along the walkway. The men quickly knocked their arrows and stood, eagerly waiting for the order to fire.

Across the field, the Romans had formed the testudo and were marching on his village at a slow pace.

"Damn, they've formed their wall of shields," Androvic muttered.

Although the Romans were within ample range of the archers, Androvic still held the order to attack. He was puzzled by the enemy formation. As far as he could see, they carried neither ladders nor rams to batter down his walls. Those too, he guessed, were protected under the wall of shields. With nothing more to lose, Androvic raised his sword and slashed forward, the tip pointing straight toward the Romans. In unison, the archers released their arrows and watched as the deadly rain drenched the Romans farther downfield.

Huddled beneath the shields, the Romans moved forward unimpeded by the arrows, the tips imbedding themselves into the shields harmlessly. The barrage continued. Volley after volley fell on the advancing soldiers in vain and fortunately for the Romans, very few arrows found their way through gaps in the shields and into the arm or leg of an unfortunate man.

In time, the Roman legions finally arrived at the village gates, and the order to halt was sounded. With a loud clack, the legions stopped in unison. From behind the Roman ranks, the archers began to fire at the Britons on the ramparts. Outnumbering the natives, the Roman archers quickly overpowered the Britons and drove them off the walls, leaving heaps of corpses instead of live men to defend the walls.

With the ramparts clear of archers and spear-slinging maniacs, the Romans lowered their shields and made way as ladders were carried forward and a ram was pulled to the gates. Within moments, the ladders were raised, and the ram began to batter the gates. Dust and splinters of wood flew from the gates as the heavy log pounded relentlessly against the thick wooden doors. Meanwhile, the legionnaires filed up the ladders and began to scurry along the ramparts, finishing off any unlucky enough to still be alive. With the enemy now in sight again and, protected from the enemy archers, the Britons began to fire at the Romans from within their own houses. Spears, arrows, rocks, and anything else heavy enough to inflict bodily damage was flung at the Romans as they worked their way down the ramparts and ladders into the village. The sounds of the dying mixed with the clanging of metal and the creaking of the wooden gate echoed through the narrow village streets and struck fear into the hearts of many.

Meanwhile, the soldiers at the gates continued to batter relentlessly, the ram distorting the gates more and more with every heave. Eventually, the gate cracked, and the final push flung both gates open, knocking one of the contorted doors off its hinges. The heavy gate fell to the ground and kicked up a cloud of dust. Like waters from a burst dam, the Romans poured through the two-chariot-wide entry and leaped into the fray.

However, the Romans were held at bay in the initial moments of the attack. With only so many men able to enter through the gates at once, the Britons held an initial advantage. For what the Romans lacked in front-line men, they compensated with fervor. The Romans literally cut their way into town, carving a path through the British ranks, as countless more legionnaires entered the village via the burst gateway and ladders.

Androvic watched dejectedly from the top of the street as the Romans gained ground on his unarmored men. He had relocated there shortly before the Roman archers had returned fire on his men and saturated the ramparts with arrows of their own. Now, he watched helplessly as the Romans murdered his villagers. He watched in horror as his men fought valiantly but achieved little due to the Roman soldiers' armor. The same slash that would sever the limb from one of his villagers would merely glance off the thick Roman armor. With fatigue and dehydration growing by the minute, the Britons began to lose ground faster than before. Those too weak to go on fighting collapsed and were quickly crushed by the tide of advancing men. Swords, which had grown hot and contorted from relentless use, began to break and become useless. Like every other clash, the barbarians were no match for the Roman army. The Britons were channeled into the narrow streets, and the fighting became more intense as every house became a stronghold, a bastion of defense. Roman casualties mounted as houses were cleared slowly and painfully. Everything from boiling oil and knives to stools and flower pots were used as weapons by the zealous villagers.

Marcus was at the tip of the formation, slashing his way through the enemy ranks. One man tried stabbing him, but Marcus quickly raised his shield, parried the block, and quickly stabbed his attacker in his heart. The man fell over dead, and another moved forward to take his place. But it was too late; Marcus had already moved into the gap. Again, he stabbed at the enemy, and again he moved up another foot. Behind him, the men followed.

The stink of hot metal, sweat, and blood filled the air, along with the screams and moans of the dying and fleeing. Standing shoulder to shoulder, both sides fought viciously, each vowing to kill the other to the last. Marcus understood the Britons would be disappointed. The legionnaires were still pouring reinforcements into the large village; while the Roman force grew ever larger within the village, what was left of the British force was shrinking rapidly. Fatigue was rampant, and many men were crumbling from exhaustion, ignored by their friends who continued to fight, withdrawing up the streets, alleys and houses.

With every passing minute, the damage to the settlement grew. Soon fires began to break out where the fighting was thickest. Desperate villagers set fire to their homes, allowing the flames to cover their retreat and block the advancing enemy.

Acrid black smoke billowed above the thatched roofs and merged with the gray, ominous clouds hanging menacingly above. Soon, the sound of the crackling flames could be heard above the ring of battle. Orange light from the flames lit up both the low-hanging gray clouds and silver armor of the legionnaires, lending a surreal glow to the already incredible sight.

With their homes going up in smoke and now entirely surrounded by the Romans, the last of the survivors fought bravely and with determination despite knowing they would perish soon ... maybe *because* they knew they would perish soon. There was no sense in raising your hands and letting yourself be killed or taken prisoner. There was no virtue in being nailed to a cross and left to feed the crows. Fighting to the death, defending your homeland to the last drop of blood, standing up to Rome ... therein lay the *true* honor—the ultimate, *truest*, noblest act they would ever make.

Cnaeus was afraid, and reasonably so. After charging up the hill, he had been attacked by one man who had tried to cut off his head, and he would have succeeded had it not been for the timely rescue by a fellow soldier. Losing all composure, he fled into a side street and became lost among the narrow, snaking streets. Soon he found himself alone, the noise of the battle muffled by the surrounding houses. He realized how alone he was and how vulnerable. He turned around to try to find his way back, but two British soldiers carrying spears and shields ran across the street and into a house, dissuading Cnaeus from walking down that road for fear of being spotted.

He pressed his back to the wall of a house. His knees were shaking slightly, and his throat felt like it had been knotted. What would his father think of him now? *He* had served in the legions proudly. *He* had served honorably, before being discharged and starting a family. What were his ancestors thinking of him as they looked at him from the afterlife? Those who had served and died fighting for Rome were surely mocking and loathing him at this very instant.

The young man wiped the sweat from his face with the backside of his hand and took a step forward. He took several more steps down the street, and then he suddenly heard approaching voices. He quickly turned the corner and pressed himself against the wall as five British soldiers ran across the street and down another street, eager to join the fight. Cnaeus peered around the corner and ensured that no other enemies would catch him in the open. There was very little road left before the street ended, and as he began to move out from around the corner, he heard a noise behind him from within a house. He turned and waited silently, his ears straining to hear the faintest sounds. He heard nothing but the somewhat muted sound of battle, so he approached the door to the house and raised his shield hesitantly. He opened the shutters of a window using the tip of his gladius and peered into the room. The room was dark and uninviting and Cnaeus was in no rush to clear the house.

He began to move up toward the thin wooden door when it was suddenly flung open, and a small child ran out. The small boy looked terrified and, upon seeing Cnaeus, he began to sob hysterically. Cnaeus tried to appease the frightened boy and approached him slowly, lowering his guard. Upon seeing the soldier approach him, the boy stumbled backward and feel on his bottom, crying even harder. Cnaeus quickly moved forward, sheathed his sword, and picked up the small child. The small boy hid his face. When Cnaeus gently turned the child's chin, he recognized the boy he had held back at the fort.

He was struck by the improbability of the encounter and chuckled, the child still in his arms. Cnaeus knelt down and lowered the boy to the ground.

"There you go. You can stop your crying, I won't hurt you," Cnaeus said reassuringly.

He was stopped by the sound of an object falling inside the dark house. Cnaeus quickly stood up and unsheathed his sword once again. The notion of running back to his fellow soldiers crossed his mind, but he considered what his ancestors must be thinking of him and decided to investigate the crash.

He advanced slowly into the house, squinting in the darkness. His eyes had not yet adjusted to the dark and had he been able to see, he would have noticed the figure coming at him with a knife from the side. But it was too late.

The blade sliced into his upper arm beneath his armor. He immediately cried out and dropped his shield and sword to clench his bleeding wound. Stumbling backward into the small street, he fell down the two stone steps onto his back with a loud clash. He had failed to fasten the strap on his helmet, so it rolled away several feet, leaving the wounded, young man with little means to defend himself. There was a brief moment of darkness after he hit his head on the ground, but he quickly shook off the flashes of light and tried to focus his eyes on the figure standing above of him. To his surprise it wasn't a man but a small woman. Cnaeus' eyes came into focus, and he found himself staring into the blood-shot eyes of the woman he had befriended back at camp. He was bemused but less than when he had seen the child. She had seemed so friendly, and now she had just tried to kill him-- perhaps *was* going to kill him. He tried to crawl backward toward the center of the street to get his helmet when she suddenly kicked him in the leg and spat at him.

"You killed my husband!" she screeched in her native tongue.

Cnaeus ignored what she was saying, but he could tell she was bent on destroying him. He looked fearfully at the knife. The blade was covered with some of his blood, some of his life. He tried to get back to his feet, but she jumped onto his back and drove the knife into his neck. As his head dropped to the ground for the last time, his breathing becoming difficult and shallow, he looked up at the woman, who backed slowly away. Her figure was already getting blurry and shadowed, and his head throbbed agonizingly. The last thought that crossed his mind before he died was Marcus and the warning he had given Cnaeus regarding the lady.

XXIV

Marcus was out of breath. He was exhausted and felt like lying down and sleeping but knew he couldn't. Every other man in his outfit felt like he did, yet they continued to fight. What made him so different? He had led the charge ever since the enemy had broken and fled from the field, almost two hours ago; now, he could barely lift his shield and stab any more. Realizing that if he didn't fall back soon, he would wind up no different than all the other mutilated corpses littering the bloody streets, he decided to let the anxious man behind him take his place.

"Switch?" he said more than asked.

He knew the men behind him who were not fighting were aching to get back at the remaining Britons. Finding a man to replace him would not be a hard task.

"Switch!" the legionnaire behind Marcus confirmed.

With a final heave of his shield, Marcus stunned the enemy soldier before him and made way for the Roman behind him to advance. By the time the Briton began to recover from the shield strike to his gut, the fresh legionnaire had plunged his gladius into the man's chest and let him fall like the piece of litter he thought of him as. Minutes went by, and the Romans gained several more yards. Only the town plaza and a dozen houses around the latter remained in enemy hands.

To the left, the nearest house was on fire, and smoke billowed from the thatched roof. The occasional breeze blew acrid smoke across the men fighting in the streets. Struggling through the mass of men to get to the side and rest, Marcus caught his breath and wiped the sweat, dirt and blood from his brow.

Between the heat of the fire and the exertion from the fight, Marcus was dying of thirst. Although the air reeked of death and smoke, the deep gulps of air he took helped slow his heartbeat and cool him off. From near the center of the formation, he suddenly spotted about three dozen Britons running across the intersection to his left, just fifteen meters down the alley, heading downhill. The men carried large shields and razor-sharp spears, while long swords hung proudly from their belted waists. Several of the men peered down the alley toward the legionnaires as they ran past, their eyes visibly cold and vengeful even at this distance.

The Britons were vastly outnumbered, yet they ran down the hill toward where the majority of the Roman army still poured through the battered gates and walls. Marcus immediately realized something was up. That these men were attempting to sneak down the hill and attack the legionnaires from behind was bad enough, but the fact that they wore armor signified that they were smarter than the average Briton, and wealthier. Wealth and intelligence could make a man brutally efficient with his sword. Forty such men could spell disaster for many a Roman soldier in the streets.

"Spearmen, alley to the left!" Marcus shouted as he tried to force his way through the mass of men.

Severus, who was closest to the alley, immediately parted from the fight and sprinted down the street through the smoke and sparks.

Severus covered the gap in seconds, stopping a meter short from the corner where the men had run past seconds before. A dozen legionnaires filed behind him, their shields and swords at the ready.

Suddenly, a loud crash resounded behind them, and a large cloud of dust and ash spread down the street as a house collapsed and effectively blocked the path. Fire blocked the passage across the ruins, trapping the pursuing Romans. The men realized they were cut off from the remainder of the army but knew what was expected of them.

Severus wiped the blood from his sword on his skirt and stuck the blade beyond the corner of the square house. Staring intently at the blood-smeared reflection, he immediately spotted a Briton hugging the wall, waiting to ambush an imprudent pursuer.

As his mind processed what he was seeing, Severus' sword was struck from his hand as the ambushing Briton came around the wall and swung his sword in direction of Brutus' exposed neck.

Marcus stopped just short of being flattened by the collapsing wall and shielded his face as sparks and ash were blown out in a gust of wind. Behind him, twenty more legionnaires also slowed to a halt, a few of them cursing at their luck.

"Are you kidding?" one of the men protested in anger.

"We're going to have to find another way," said another.

Without wasting precious seconds, the group turned around and ran for the packed street.

"Go, go, go!" cried one of the men as he shouldered his way through the massive group of men.

"Move it! We've got men trapped on the other side!" another shouted, pushing his way through with brute force.

Seconds seemed like minutes as the men struggled through to the next street intersection. Sensing they were wasting precious time, Marcus stopped at the door of one of the houses and called for the men to follow him. The door had already been knocked off its hinges, and he penetrated into the gloom, trusting his comrades had already cleared it of enemy soldiers.

He crossed the house and reached the back door, which he suspected led into the alley his friends had been caught in. Stepping forward, Marcus put every ounce of energy into kicking the door open. The wooden door smashed open and Marcus was out the door and charging back up the slanted road in the blink of an eye. Ahead, he could see the men struggling and felt relieved that the men had not been killed ... yet.

The sword was flung from Severus' hand with force, and he instinctively ducked as the Briton's blade cleaved the wall just above where his head had been seconds before. In a flash, the Romans charged the enemy and then poured into the streets as the remainder of the Britons joined the fray. Severus was pushed to the other side of the street by his comrades as they charged the Britons, giving him time to recover his sword. Picking up the dented and chipped weapon, Severus wasted no time leaping back into the struggle. Being unusually well-equipped, the Britons were holding their ground against the equally matched Roman legionnaires. With impressive footwork, the Romans attempted to maneuver around the Britons, who, with equally impressive ability, were able to parry the Roman envelopment with an envelopment of their own. The Romans were taking aback by the men they faced and their impressive ability.

Who are these men? The Romans thought as they fended off incessant slashes and stabs with their large shields.

It seemed as if the Roman soldiers had finally met their match. With the road now blocked, reinforcements would take a while to reach them. The Romans began to realize the peril they were in. Flashbacks of the ambush at the wheat field flashed through the minds of those who had been there.

"Hold the line!" Severus shouted as the two sides fought, shield crashing against shield.

Not much time passed before the Britons tossed their spears aside and unsheathed their swords, a much more suitable weapon to wield in the cramped street. Slowly, the superbly trained Britons began to overpower the cramped and outnumbered Romans. Those legionnaires in the front ranks received fatal stabs to their exposed necks and legs, increasing the ratio of Britons to Romans. Within several long seconds, the Romans fell back around the corner of the building, pressed dangerously close to the blazing rubble that blocked the street. The fire was intense, the flames only feet away from their skin. Those in the front ranks envied those in the rear and vice versa. Caught between sharp metal tips and searing flames, the men were in desperate straits.

Only a handful of Romans were still standing when Marcus' contingent engaged the unsuspecting Britons from behind. Still numbering in the dozens, the Britons were now caught between two Roman formations. Now outnumbered themselves, the Britons were bent on fighting to the death. Defending their rear, the Britons began to press into the fire-trapped legionnaires, pushing them closer to the fire. Severus knew that if they were pushed any farther back, their clothes would catch fire and death would be excruciating, much more painful than being stabbed. With renewed effort, Severus heaved against his shield with his men and gained an extra two feet between them and the fire, enough to provide a more comfortable buffer zone. Standing their ground, Severus and his comrades prevented the Britons from overriding them and driving them into the fire.

Before long, the Britons were reduced to a bloody trio. The three men, realizing their fate wouldn't differ from those who lay dead on the ground, opted to surrender. Severus came up from behind them however and plunged his gladius to the hilt in the first man's gut with a roar. Following his lead, two others stepped forward and killed the unarmed men, letting them fall to the ground in tattered heaps.

"The sons of bitches kill over a dozen of my men and then plead for their lives when they are in our shoes! Ha!" Severus spat on one of the corpses. "Let's get the hell out of here. We've got a village to capture."

The houses that lined the street were constructed of stone and sported thatched roofs, which would eventually succumb to the voracious flames. The crackling noise of the fire, mixed with the more distant clanging of swords, floated above the village ominously. Marcus had separated from the group and began to walk down the slope in the direction of the main gate. Alone on the rubble-strewn street, the unpleasant stench of smoke and death filling his nostrils, he wondered if he hadn't accidently stumbled into hell. He made his way across a small pile of rubble topped with small, dying flames and stopped on the other side. During the last engagement, a lucky Briton had managed to slice Marcus' upper arm below where his armor stopped. Despite Marcus repeated requests to stay and fight, Severus had ordered him back down the hill to seek attention from a doctor.

Marcus continued down the trail, peering left to right and back again inside the homes to ensure he wouldn't be attacked from behind down the trail. The path was leading him downhill, away from the fighting, and Marcus was certain the area was devoid of Britons, but still he crept along cautiously. Roughly thirty feet down the rubble-lined street, he found himself in a small plaza. Dead bodies of all sorts were strewn across the charred ground, and Marcus gagged at the stench and sight.

Crossing the grisly square, Marcus was reabsorbed into yet another rubble-strewn street. He made it twenty meters before he spotted a lone Roman lying dead in the middle of the square, his shield, sword, and helmet far from his inert body. A pool of blood had soaked into the ground around him, and Marcus found himself breathing with difficulty. Something struck him as odd; he realized there were no dead Britons near the dead Roman, and the thought that whoever killed the man was probably still hiding somewhere near crossed his mind.

He cursed himself for having only a knife. Marcus' sword had broken inside a man's chest during the extensive fighting, and his shield had finally cracked from the repetitive blows in had taken. Although he had requested another shield and sword, no man on the front could afford to give his up. Besides, his comrades had assured him that the houses had been cleared, one by one. Marcus had crossed many soldiers during his trek back down yet something told him his fellow soldiers had perhaps missed this road or someone inside one of the houses that lined it.

Marcus suddenly noticed that the houses in this part of the village had somehow escaped the voracious flames that had laid waste to the majority of the village and remained largely unscathed.

Reaching the lone Roman, Marcus discerned certain features of the fatally wounded man. His face was badly bruised and bloody, and numerous cuts covered his body. The number of slashes covering his exposed limbs revealed that whoever had done this had continued to attack the man long after he was dead.

Despite the numerous slashes, Marcus recognized the inert body as Cnaeus. Grief overcame Marcus, and he suddenly felt sick at the thought that the new recruit was lying dead at his feet. Whoever had done this unspeakable act would pay with his life, Marcus swore.

If he hadn't already.

Suddenly, movement to the right caught Marcus' eye and he looked over and saw the woman who had taken his friend's life. He turned toward her and unsheathed his knife, ready to defend himself from the deadly woman. Their stares lingered for what seemed like minutes before the two recognized each other.

The seemingly fragile woman held her son close to her with one hand, the other clenched around the handle of a long knife, Cnaeus' blood drying on its long, wicked-looking blade. She approached Marcus menacingly and Marcus had no concern that she was a lady. The woman let go of her son's hand and, blindly, she charged Marcus and slashed in vain, the tip of the knife hissing in empty air. In one quick motion, he grabbed her by her clothes and, using her momentum, flung her across the street. Stumbling, she crashed into the wall, but she surprised Marcus when she shook off her pain and charged him once again.

Marcus' arm was throbbing in pain, and he knew the playing field had been leveled, a blood-thirsty woman against a seasoned, yet injured, soldier.

Had she not raised her knife high above her head when she charged him the second time, the outcome would surely have been different. Unused to fighting hand to hand, she exposed her abdomen, and Marcus quickly seized the opportunity to bring the fight to an end.

Gender played no role in determining whether she was an enemy or not. A woman's stabs were just as deadly as a man's, and Marcus was intent on not ending up like Cnaeus who lay inert at his feet. He crouched and let her run into his knife, delivering a fatal blow.

The woman shrieked, crumpled in a heap and Marcus quickly ensured she was dead with a nudge of his foot. Marcus turned to leave when he saw the young boy who had watched the fight. He had forgotten all about him and Marcus quickly realized he had just created a future enemy. The boy was on the verge of tears and eyed Marcus with scorn before turning and fleeing down the alley. Unwilling to harm the child, Marcus turned and ran in the direction he had come from, unsure of exactly what to do for the moment. At present however, he had to tell Vibius their friend was dead; his flesh wound could wait.

XXV

The fire had consumed much of what it could, and only the houses around the upper plaza were still ablaze. The fighting was mostly over, with only a few pockets of resistance left. Those remaining Britons were surrounded and given the option to surrender but, unsurprisingly, few chose to do so. Finding it more honorable to die fighting in their homes than be executed or taken prisoner to finish off their days in slavery, the last defenders fought bravely and always to the death. Many Roman soldiers were busy tending to the wounded and recovering the dead, while others rounded up the few prisoners who had chosen potential life over certain death.

Marcus had managed to emerge onto the main street, and he began to walk up the avenue, passing dozens of Romans lying against the burnt-out homes and in the streets. He gazed in wonder at the carnage that surrounded him. Dead men littered the streets, while damaged houses and men lined them. The sky was dark, and the overpowering smell of blood and rot lingered over the village. Captured wagons were being brought in from the surrounding farms to ferry the wounded back to camp. Marcus watched in pity as his fellow brother-in-arms were lifted off the cold ground in pain and he was shaken out of his trance when Vibius called out his name.

"Marcus! I see you made it," the big man said, putting his paw on Marcus' shoulder.

"I can't believe it. Look at the mess we've made," he said, looking around him.

Vibius followed Marcus' gaze and then looked back at his friend.

"It was them or us. Personally, I'm not too displeased with how it turned out," he answered with a small laugh.

"No complaints either, apart from one," Marcus said. "Cnaeus didn't make it."

"What?"

"Cnaeus was killed," Marcus repeated.

Vibius began to answer but was cut short when Claudius approached.

"Congratulations, men!"

Marcus and Vibius looked up at the general.

"Thank you, sir," Vibius answered.

"You all did a good job here today, and I just wanted to congratulate you for another victory!"

"Thank you again, sir. I didn't like what one of these men said about my mother back at camp," Vibius said with a grin. "I think I may have gotten a bit carried away, though."

The centurion laughed. "Well, as long as Caesar doesn't curse your mother, I don't think he'll mind your volatility!"

Claudius' glanced at Marcus' arm, grimacing at the sight.

"I would get a doctor to check that cut out, son. Don't want that thing to get infected ..." Claudius let the recommendation hang in the air.

"How is the attack going up top?" Vibius asked.

"Not well. There're about two hundred men or so with their families grouped around the town center. Our legionnaires are having a tough time with them. These barbarians are obviously willing to fight to the death and that includes their women and children."

"Have we gotten their chief yet?"

"Androvic? Not yet. We believe him to be among the survivors up there." Claudius looked up the slope. Through the passing smoke and moving men he could see the Romans gathered around the square. The sound of battle was somewhat muted by the creaking of the wagon wheels and rummaging of men.

"Looks like we're not quite ready to break out the wine amphorae yet—is that right, sir?" Vibius grinned, looking up the large street.

"Not yet, but I'm guessing it won't take very much longer," Claudius said with a wicked smile.

"What do you mean, sir?"

Claudius looked each man in the eyes in turn. "Let's just say things are going to get *hot* up there shortly."

XXVI

Androvic was out of breath. His skin was covered in blood as were his clothes and armor, and his arms felt like lead weights when he tried to move them. As a chief, he knew he couldn't expect much mercy from the Romans if he opted to surrender, not that the choice crossed his mind. He would rather fall on his sword than allow those Roman heathens to lay their hands on him and cart him to Rome to die a humiliating, public death surrounded by the approving cheers of thousands of spectators. He thought of his fate if he were to be captured and a menacing chill ran down his spine. *Gods, allow me to kill several more of these Roman pests before I join you in the afterlife*, he prayed.

He slashed his long sword across the tops of the Roman shields in front of him and watched as the blade glanced off the helmeted heads. He wished much worse than to only scratch their helmets. Behind his large shield, he bellowed for his men to push outwards, to expand their ranks, but the Romans were overpowering them and squeezing their formation ever tighter by the minute. Soon, he wouldn't even be able to breath, much less fight. Suddenly he was pulled backward, and one of his soldiers took his place.

"Sir, you must remain in the center. I fear for you in the front lines," the man said before resuming the fight in Androvic's place.

Across the circle, Ludovic was struggling to stay alive as well. He had been wounded several times already, and the loss of blood was beginning to affect his judgment. Striking aside a Roman sword, he quickly returned the blow, slashing his sword across the man's face. The tip of the sword cut through the man's eyes and nose, and the Roman shrieked in pain. Watching him fall, Ludovic prepared for the next man to step up. Just as he expected, a Roman advanced with a thrust of his shield, which collided into his and struck him in the mouth. Ludovic's teeth cracked under the blow, and he spat out bloody pieces before starting to fight again. He was about to plunge his sword into the man's exposed neck when suddenly he felt a sharp pain in his back, below the base of his neck.

Ludovic saw flashing lights, and blood began to pool in the back of his throat as he tried in vain to breathe. He gagged, gargled, and began to stagger, wide-eyed, as his life ebbed slowly from him. Within milliseconds, the Roman legionnaire plunged his sword into the dying Briton's abdomen and put him out of his misery.

Dozens of additional arrows flew past and began to rain down on the encircled Britons.

"Archers!" cried the frightened survivors as they realized their luck had run dry.

Men, women, and children were struck indiscriminately as the arrows impaled whatever was in their way. Shrieks erupted as Britons were struck and then trampled as others attempted to maneuver and evade the archer-fire. As if that wasn't enough, the Roman archers began to light their arrows on fire before shooting them into the crowd.

Many were struck and killed on impact, while the less fortunate caught fire when the flaming barb struck their clothing. Those in the center pushed outward to escape the arrows, while those on the perimeter pulled back to escape the Roman infantry. As if in a vice, the Britons were squeezed together as the Roman infantry exploited the gaps and tightened the noose around the Britons more than ever. Both sides knew the fight would be over in minutes.

Androvic felt a knot form in his throat. Even when he had first been surrounded, he had clung to the hope that he might somehow win the fight. But now, encircled by blades and under a rain of fire, all hope of survival had faded. Death, at this point, was certain.

He sheathed his sword and pulled out his knife to cut the straps that held his armor around his chest before the Romans could reach him. Because of the archers, the Roman legionnaires were making headway faster than ever. Frantically, he began to slash at the ties that trapped him and let out a sigh of relief as the last tie was severed and the armor fell in a clang to the ground. His chest felt unrestrained for the first time in hours.

Around him, chaos reigned, as swords and spears pierced flesh relentlessly. Pushed around by the terrified; Androvic fumbled for his sword and unsheathed it from its scabbard for the ultimate time. For the first time that day, he took notice of what it felt like to be alive. The smell, although pungent, let him know his heart was still beating; the air, although thick and stale, made him realize he *was* alive. It was at that point that he realized no man felt more alive than one who was about to die.

He felt certain euphoria at the thought that soon, all his problems would be over. The thought to go on living just a while longer crossed his mind, but he quickly realized that much could still go wrong between now and when he took his own life. What if he thought about it too much and persuaded himself not to do it? What if he was wounded and could not manage to fall on his sword? He would be damned if he'd let the Romans have the honor of killing him, or, worse, take him alive. He had no intention of dying nailed to a cross, exposed like dirty laundry.

Turning the sword so the tip was up, he lowered it so the tip was just below his sternum. In the maelstrom, he found it difficult to keep the sword steady and had to tighten his grip around the handle to keep it from being knocked around much. He wondered once more if he was doing the right thing, when suddenly the man in front of him was struck by a flaming arrow and began to shriek as the flames enveloped him slowly.

It was now or never.

With a deep breath, he pulled upwards on the hilt, the sword piercing his flesh and digging into his heart in the blink of an eye. For what seemed like eternity, the pain was unbearable, and he found himself unable to breathe.

A thousand thoughts and images flashed through his mind as his life ebbed away. Staring without seeing, his knees began to buckle, and the bear-of-a-man crumbled. The Briton chief was now no different from any other corpse littering the streets. The last thought that crossed his mind before he departed for the afterlife was how he had succeeded in cheating the Romans. Now they wouldn't get the pleasure of tormenting *him* before his death, as they had done with so many other chiefs and prisoners of war in times gone by.

XXVII

Caesar was ebullient. Two men from the opposing tribe knelt at his feet while he sat in his chair sipping wine from a silver goblet, bathing himself in their misery and contempt. He took special pleasure in tormenting his defeated foes when they came to surrender. After weeks of campaigning in this foreign land and having lost many good men, Caesar was keen on returning to Gaul. They were already into winter and nowhere near enough food was in stock for his army.

He had to get back to Gaul ... *fast.*

The Roman commander looked over at Volusenus and his two generals, Claudius and Lucius, with a one-sided grin on his face; victory was officially at hand. With a swig of his wine, he set the empty goblet on the wooden stand at his side and placed his attention back on the two men cowered at his feet. He crossed his arms and pointed his chin at the two British men, looking down at them over his prominent cheekbones.

"Caesar, we have come to offer our surrender," said the first man as he raised his head off the floor, his face ugly with sorrow and scars. The Briton was stout and the teeth in his mouth were more rotten than a dead tree in a swamp.

"Surrender. Does this word have any meaning to your people?" Caesar asked sarcastically.

"Pardon?" the man asked, wide-eyed.

"Somehow, this conversation seems like an echo. It was not very long ago we had this same conversation, am I correct?"

"Yes, sir, but ..." the man began.

"Of course I am," Caesar replied curtly as he looked down at his fingernails. The ends were all rough. He had a nasty habit of chewing his nails when stressed, and despite his many attempts to quit, he never could. He had defeated countless enemy armies and conquered innumerable regions, but the one enemy he could not surmount was his own sense of doubt. He glanced down at the foe at his feet again.

"I will accept your surrender, Briton. But under several conditions."

At this point the second man joined in. He was dark-skinned, his long and tangled hair circling the bald spot that had appeared with age. The top half of his right ear had been cut, and a large scar continued both front and back, an unsightly memento of a previous encounter with a now-dead enemy.

"O great Caesar, we but aspire to fulfill your wishes. We have acted like beasts, futilely attempting to resist you and your great army. Please find it in your heart to accept our submission to you, and ..." there was a pause as the man's lips quivered in suppressed anger and grief, "and to Rome."

Caesar watched the man attentively. He leaned forward in his chair atop the dais, his body still several feet away from the envoys. The skin under the Briton's eyes was swollen and dark, as was most of his face, the consequence of long nights spent conspiring against him, Caesar guessed. While waiting for Caesar to respond, the man rested on his knees at the Roman's feet like a sack of grain, a pile of trash. Like a slave.

Volusenus watched silently from his corner of the room. He sat next to a small table covered in succulent grapes and wine, but he had not taken a bite since entering the room. He twirled his thumbs incessantly; the tension in the room was so thick he was surprised he could even breathe.

As Caesar studied his vanquished foe, there was relative silence, with the exception of the mild drumming of the rain on the tent and the howling wind. Still huddled on the cold ground, the vanquished men sweated lightly with nervous tension despite the cold that seeped through the few fissures in the tent's walls. On the sidelines, the two Legion commanders watched without uttering a word, waiting for Caesar to impose his conditions.

Before accepting surrender, Caesar always had flashbacks of the previous engagements that had led to this moment. Scenes of previous battles flashed through his mind. He saw himself riding in the field outside his fort, the many dead lying on the cold, wet ground. Then he saw the ships floundering in the waves. Then, the men who found themselves ambushed and surrounded in the wheat field. He smelled the smoke of the burning village; saw the crumbled buildings, the men slain in the streets. Remembering all the torment the Britons had put him through, Caesar felt no pity for those begging forgiveness at his feet.

Caesar leaned back in his chair and looked up at the ceiling.

"I want twice as many men as the last time," Caesar spoke, as if to himself. "Four hundred men before winter is out are to be delivered to me."

The half-eared man simply nodded as he listened.

"I want you to pledge your loyalty to Rome and to never raise arms against her again," Caesar said, knowing such promises didn't count for much with barbarians. But still, it was the act of stating submission and the coupled humiliation that mattered.

Caesar lowered his head to look at the man and unfolded his arms to place them on the armrests.

"I will do so. I give you my word," the fat man said

"Your word," Caesar snickered.

"I may have been your enemy, Caesar, but I still have honor. I give you my word that the prisoners will be handed over to you swiftly," he replied.

"I want them sailed to Gaul," Caesar said, standing up.

"To Gaul? You do not want to wait here while we return them to you?" he asked, inquisitively.

"No," Caesar answered with a sarcastic grin. "Your land is an acquired taste, and I desire to return to Gaul for the moment being. It is unfortunate my trip had to be cut short. Not to worry though, I will come back to visit soon. There is still *much* of your country that I have yet to see."

The Britons stared at him with repressed anger and loathing.

"Remember. Four hundred men. In Gaul. Before winter," Caesar said as simply as he could.

"They will be delivered to you in Gaul, Caesar," the first man answered with a diplomatic bow of his head.

"I dearly hope so. I guarantee you won't particularly enjoy the related consequences if you are late," Caesar growled.

The two men nodded and stood up slowly, and Caesar stood to approach them.

"Be on your way now. The sooner you go, the sooner I get my men." The Roman waved them away.

"Yes, sir. And may you all have a most pleasant evening," said the fat man as he turned to leave.

"I'll pass your good wishes on to my soldiers as I make a round in the hospitals tonight," Caesar answered with bitterness.

The stout man pursed his lips and halted before nodding slowly and finally walking away. The two Britons walked out of the tent and were escorted through the now-torrential rain to the gate.

Caesar turned to his men and stretched his arms out before him.

"Men, the time has come for us to return home," he said with a warm smile.

Volusenus flinched as he walked past the cold draft let in by the slit that constituted the doorway. He shook off the chill that ran up his spine and both men grasped forearms.

"Rome vanquishes again," Volusenus said proudly as the two generals joined in.

Caesar smiled warmly again and put his other hand on Volusenus' shoulder. "I could not have done it without you, my friend. I owe the success of this expedition to you."

"No, sir. I was just fulfilling your orders," Volusenus said modestly.

"Thank you in any case," Caesar replied before letting go and turning to Claudius.

"General, without you and your men, this invasion would have been a disaster," he turned to Lucius. "The same goes to you, General. You and your men were invaluable to this operation. I owe much of my success to the both of you as well."

"Thank you, sir," the general said with a slight bow.

"Men, our task here is far from complete, but I do believe we can find three minutes in our busy schedule to celebrate this victory," Caesar said as he walked to his table and removed the cork from a wine-filled amphora.

"I won't say no to a little wine," Claudius confessed.

The men laughed in unison as they gathered around the table. Caesar poured three goblets of wine for him and his two generals.

"Still don't drink, Volusenus?"

"No, sir, I've been sober for thirty-nine years. I couldn't bring myself to break the streak *now*," he said with a laugh.

"Well, you can go ahead and settle for the water in the amphora there," Caesar joked. "If you're looking for something a little stronger we've got some grape *juice* in that amphora though. It's not fermented, so it's no good to me."

"Not much of a manly drink, but we'll let it slip this time," Lucius teased him.

Volusenus laughed as he poured himself a glass of water. "Thank you for your kindness."

The four men brought their goblets together with a dull click. For the first time in ages, the officers relaxed temporarily and discussed things other than war.

XXVIII

The rain hindered the dismantling of the fort. Marcus protected his face from the thrashing wind as he tried to pull the picks that held the tent to the ground out of the muddy soil. He remembered the proverb "Great rains generally fall after extraordinary battles" and had found that it was generally true. As if to wash away the blood and death of battle, the skies had opened up, and torrential rains had fallen since the village had been seized. Two days of incessant rain had passed since the Britons had been crushed. During that time, every man had been busy repairing the last of the ships and collecting the dead from the field, forest, and burnt-out village.

The wounded had immediately been brought back to the infirmary, where they had been tended to in great quantities. Now the evacuation was at hand, although no one called it so. The enemy had been decimated, as had the countryside, leaving the Romans meager amounts of food, forcing them to sail back to Gaul, where their food stocks were plentiful. Caesar *had* floated the idea of venturing deeper into enemy territory, but he quickly realized he couldn't afford to do so. He had too many wounded, and with food reserves running low, it was safer to return another time. Besides, it wasn't polite to overstay one's invitation.

Throughout the camp, the men had packed their belongings and were now in the process of breaking camp. The men always found it a boring and strenuous task, but with the rain, it was downright miserable.

With a final heave, Marcus finally removed the pick from the cold suction of the viscous mud and cleaned it in a bucket nearby. He watched as clumps of mud loosened and fell to the bottom of the container. He shook off the excess water as best he could and handed it to Vibius. The latter placed it in a pack under the tent, protected from the rain outside.

The collapsed tent flapped slightly in the brisk breeze, seeming eager to be packed up and removed from the rain. The men quickly folded the tent and placed it in the bag meant to contain it. Within minutes, they were done.

Stretching backward, Marcus looked around the camp and found it to be a weird sight. Several weeks ago, sweat had been put into building the fort, and now more sweat was spent taking it down.

Packing the last of their belongings, Marcus noticed a centurion walking in their direction up the street, stopping every now and then to talk to the legionnaires. Through the dense sheets of rain, Marcus did not recognize him at first, and only upon hearing his voice did he identify the man as Severus.

"You men are doing a good job. Caesar would like to sail out as soon as possible, and it seems that we will have favorable tides in roughly six to eight hours. Our plan is to make it out then. Are you boys capable of making that work?" he shouted over the drumming sound of the plummeting rain.

"Yes, sir. In fact, all of our personal gear is already put away, and we were setting out to lend a hand elsewhere," Marcus shouted back.

"Hell if I'm staying here! I wouldn't stop working if I lost both my arms!" Vibius shouted with a grin.

The centurion laughed. "Well, let's not put that to the test, shall we?"

Vibius nodded with a smile.

"Instead of lending a hand to the others, I want you men to get down to the ships and drop off your gear. Caesar wants the men on board as quickly as possible so we're ready to sail."

"What about the fort? Are we not to disassemble it?" Vibius asked.

"No, it is to be burnt down before our departure," Severus answered. "If this damn rain hasn't saturated the wood."

"I hear that, sir!"

"Keep up the good work," Severus said before setting off down the avenue.

Marcus picked up a length of rope that was lying on the ground, coiled it, and handed it to Vibius who slung it around one shoulder and picked up the pack with his other arm. With Marcus' help, the pack was slung over his back, and Marcus then put his own pack on. Securing the straps tightly, he checked his men and the ground they had once called home. Ensuring nothing was left behind, he began to march down the street toward the Porta Praetoria, closely followed by his men. He slowed to let his men past and turned around to look at the busy street one final time. He didn't know why, but this fort had meant something to him. It held a special place in his heart. Maybe it had been the sole beacon of light in an otherwise dark and ominous land. Maybe it was something else entirely but Marcus still looked in sadness at the rapidly dwindling constructions. Maybe it was the fact that three of his friends had left Gaul never to return. Suddenly, out of the corner of his eye, he saw Brutus approaching him, leaning forward against the heavy wind.

"Marcus," he shouted upwind, waving to get the man's attention, "I've been looking for you."

Marcus turned and took several steps toward the centurion. Brutus's leg had been amputated after the ill-fated forage, and he now depended on a crutch to transport himself.

"Yes, sir?" Marcus asked.

"Listen, I just wanted to congratulate you and thank you once again for everything you have done. I am in extreme debt to you."

"Well, it's no problem, sir; I was just doing my job as a soldier," Marcus answered humbly.

"Listen to you ... You're a modest man, Marcus. That's a rare trait. You're also brave and smart." Brutus let his observations hang in the humid air for a second before going on. "You would make a great centurion."

Marcus had always wanted to lead men but felt like he would be abandoning his comrades with whom he had shared so much. He had always regretted having turned the assignment down after the ambush but now the Gods were offering him a second chance.

"Well, sir, I don't think I'm ready for the post."

"Nonsense. You saved those men in the ambush, Marcus. We are all alive as a result of your quick thinking. You have great capability, and you could do so much more for your men as a centurion than as a simple legionnaire ..."

Brutus let his sentence hang for several seconds before continuing.

"So? Do you accept this promotion?" he asked impatiently, eager to hear Marcus' response.

Marcus turned to look at his friends from his contubernium. He would miss them, it was true, but he knew that he would still be fighting alongside of them, just on a different part of the battlefield. With luck and a good word from Brutus, maybe he could even be assigned command of his former unit.

After debating for several seconds, Marcus finally accepted.

"Thank you, Marcus. I can rest assured my men will be looked after properly now."

"I guarantee it, sir."

Marcus smiled and thanked the man one last time before beginning to walk away. Brutus suddenly shouted out for him one final time.

"Marcus!"

He turned at the sound of his name.

"I'm afraid you might have to wait until we get back to Gaul before the official ceremony."

"That is fine, sir," Marcus answered with a smile before turning away.

"Oh, and Marcus!"

"Yes, sir?"

"Drop the 'sir' when you talk to me. I'm no longer your superior, my friend," Brutus said with a grin.

As Marcus turned to rejoin his contubernium, uncertainty became near-jubilation. He would finally live up to his destiny. He would finally lead men in combat.

"So, did you accept?" Vibius asked when Marcus finally caught up with him.

"Accept what?" Marcus asked with a sly grin.

"Oh, come on! You know we know what you were talking about ... So, were you promoted?"

"I was,"

"Congratulations," the men said in turn as they began to walk down the slick slope to the beach, their feet sloshing in the deep, sticky mud.

Mud turned to sand as the men continued to descend the hill. Quickly, the sound of waves mixed into the sound of falling rain. Most of the boats were anchored a short way away from the beach; a few others were beached with ramps that led up to the deck. The five men approached the ships and assessed the quality of the repairs on the ships. The repairs were coarse, and no one knew for sure how the makeshift work would hold in the channel waters, but all were willing to attempt the risky voyage back to Gaul before they were trapped in Britannia by the onset of winter.

Five ships were beached in a row, and the men stopped at the first one they reached. There, a centurion motioned them over, and the men filed up to him.

"You men may board any of the last two ships. The first three are reserved for the wounded."

Marcus nodded and thanked the man and regarded the two ships he could choose between. The fourth one down the line was a trireme and the fifth was a bireme. Having sailed on a bireme on the trip over, he selected a sturdier and smoother ride home aboard the larger of the two types of vessels. He proceeded past the first three vessels and walked up the access ramp that led to the trireme's deck, as small waves began to pool around the wooden ramp, signaling the approaching tide.

It didn't take long for his contubernium to climb the ramp and find a spot on deck. It was not surprise that the stern of the vessel was more crowded than the bow, the lessons of the first trip still fresh in the legionnaires' minds. Spotting an open section at the stern, Marcus and his men made their way through the huddled men, set their belongings down, and settled on the sodden deck.

Marcus kept his helmet on as a shield against the incessant rain. Restless, he stood and leaned against the ship's railing to watch his men set their equipment down and organize themselves for the voyage home, like a father watches over his sons. Counting the men, the tally stopped at five. Three men were no longer present in the flesh. Two men he had fought alongside for years were now dead, and the third, his newest recruit, had not survived his first month in the army.

"Marcus, there was nothing you could have done," Vibius said, placing a hand on Marcus' shoulder.

Marcus looked at his friend and nodded slowly. After years spent living, fighting, and bleeding together, Vibius could read Marcus like a book. The jubilation from having been promoted had been replaced by sorrow because three of his brothers-in-arms had died on the expedition.

"I know," Marcus whispered. "I know."

As the deck continued to fill, the men at first did not notice that the rain had abated, though the skies remained overcast.

The trail of legionnaires that stretched from the Porta Praetoria and Porta Dextra to the ships like a line of ants did not convey the glorious image that the soldiers had been lulled into believing when they were first conscripted. The sun did not reflect from their armor. The men did not sing in unison about their exploits, past and present. No birds circled their camp, a propitious omen of times to come. Nothing in any way resembled glory. The sky was gray, the men's faces morose, and their bodies and gear dirty and broken. The sole joy came from the thought of going home. And by home, they meant their home away from home; Portius Itius. None of the legionnaires had seen their families since joining the army.

Wounded and fit alike pinned hopes on the prospect of one day seeing their families, although Marcus believed many wouldn't survive even the return trip back to Gaul. Within the long line of legionnaires were stretcher-bearers transporting the mutilated to the beached ships, which were both overcrowded and damaged.

Suddenly the trireme shifted as the ramp was raised onto the boat's deck with a loud clank. Marcus peered down at the wet beach below. Soldiers had moved into position alongside the beached vessel and were in the process of digging out the cold sand from beneath the ship. Slowly, as water and man worked symbiotically, the vessel began to inch backward into the channel waters. When the trireme backed out far enough, a bireme rowed into the empty spot left by Marcus' vessel. In a matter of minutes, the bireme was in position, and the ramp was lowered onto the beach to allow men up. All along the beach, vessels had pulled up and been beached to allow the legionnaires onto their decks

Peering over the side, Marcus examined the work that had been done on the trireme's hull. The repair efforts were evident, and Marcus did not trust the refurbished ship farther than he could throw its anchor. But it was all he had. Every ship had been damaged in the relentless storm, and while some fared better than others, not a single one had been spared the onslaught.

As time passed, the sky grew darker, finally turning pitch black as the sun set on the far side of the island. Ships were made ready in record time—loading men and provisions had never been carried out so quickly.

Marcus glanced at the fort and spotted several torches lit at different locations along the walls. Evidently, they were getting ready to burn the place down. Marcus turned his attention back to the beach and was not surprised to find that he could no longer discern individual soldiers anymore. In fact, with darkness reigning, the only evidence of life on shore came from the innumerable torches moving about the crowded beach.

Below the deck, the oarsmen paddled relentlessly against the waves as they headed for open sea. Marcus noticed the clouds threatened to open again, and he sincerely hoped they would reach Gaul before the rain began to fall once more. He was sure there was nothing worse than being out in the open aboard a compromised ship in a rainstorm.

XXIX

Caesar held a lit torch in his hand. He looked down at the dancing flame and watched as the reddish orange light danced off his armor. Fire intrigued him. Its ability to entirely reduce everything to ash in such a brief time enthralled him. He knew of nothing else capable of destroying a thing as completely and swiftly as fire. Despite his general's wishes that he board a ship and get off the island, Caesar wanted to be among the last to leave. In fact, to display his fearlessness, he had taken the responsibility of burning the fort down himself along with a few others. Among those in the fort with him was Volusenus who held a torch of his own.

"Haven't you ever wondered, Volusenus, how fire consumes matter the way it does?" Caesar asked his friend, admiring the torch's flame.

Volusenus looked at Caesar quizzically.

"Well, in all honesty," he started, "I can't say that I have. Why do you ask?"

"Have you not ever wondered how fire spreads? How does it go from a spark to a raging inferno nothing can withstand?" Caesar asked as he looked up toward his friend.

Volusenus smirked and raised his shoulders.

"The thought had never crossed my mind."

"It's intriguing, is it not?"

"It is indeed," Volusenus replied.

Then Volusenus watched in silence as Caesar studied the torch flickering in the strong wind.

"What is this world we live in, Volusenus, this world where things take so long to grow but are so quickly destroyed?"

He remained silent. Volusenus knew Caesar was asking this question without actually expecting an answer from his friend. Caesar, still captivated by the dancing light, spoke again.

"A life takes nine months to develop yet is taken away by nothing more than the thrust of a sword. A civilization takes decades, even centuries, to grow but can be destroyed in a day," Caesar said with a vacant stare.

Suddenly, he lowered the torch and studied the empty fort around him. He regarded the structure from top to bottom, studying every little nook and cranny.

"All the time spent living here, working here, and it must all go," he said softly, almost to himself.

Volusenus nodded slowly behind him; he also felt saddened whenever they abandoned a fort. After all, it was the closest thing to a home the men had during their time in the army.

"Come, Volusenus. It is time to end this," Caesar said as he began to walk toward the Porta Decumana at the far side of the fort. Volusenus watched as Caesar moved off into the shadows, his shadow a dancing flicker of light opposite the flame.

At the Porta Sinistra, Volusenus held the torch to the dry wood on the threshold of the covered gateway. At first the wood resisted the heat, but gradually, the wood turned black and began to char. Then, in a blink, the wood ignited, and the flames grew instantaneously. He took several steps back and watched as the flames devoured the wood like vultures on a corpse.

Meanwhile, Caesar torched the far gate, while the others lit the surrounding walls on fire. Hurrying back to the main gate, the men waited for all to return so they could all march to the beach together. Each man was captivated by the brutal efficiency of fire. The flames spread quickly and were devouring the fort like famished dogs. After a quick head count, the men walked down to the beach, where several ships were still being boarded by legionnaires. When Caesar reached his flagship, the farthest boat of all, he boarded it hurriedly and walked to the stern, where many onboard were admiring the raging inferno atop the cliff to their left.

"Caesar! What are your orders? Are we to set sail?" the ship's captain asked.

"Yes," Caesar said, leaning against the railing on the starboard side. "Head for Portius Itius."

Around him, the men began to shout orders as the vessel retreated from the beach and began to turn for open sea.

XXX

The majority of the soldiers stood at the railings, watching their fort break apart under the heat, as the vessels sailed away. The far gate had already collapsed, and the other gates were on the verge of crumbling as well. The sky above the fort was orange, and pitch-black smoke entwined itself with the rain clouds floating above. The legionnaires watched helplessly as what had once been their home disintegrated into cinders. As the ships set sail for Gaul, the overcast skies began to clear, and soon every man was captivated by the stunning beauty of the stars and moon above. As if the clouds themselves had been the source of discontent, the legionnaires felt at peace once they emerged from the cloud cover into the clear night sky. They had left the land of savagery and devastation and were now on their way back to a land so much more familiar. The Britons, however, would be aching for revenge more than ever once the news reached the other villages. More men would be sent to Gaul. More children would be taught from birth to despise the Romans. If anything, many thought, this expedition had only compounded already existing problems.

But what did a simple soldier's opinion count for, anyway?

On his trireme, Marcus resolved to sit with his knees to his chest at the stern of the ship while the bow moved up and down with the waves, splashing the men huddled there. He observed as the men complained and tried to protect themselves from the cold waters, to no avail. Then he began to laugh, slowly at first, then louder. Soon others were turning to face him.

"Cnaeus, my friend, you were right!" he said, speaking to his departed friend.

Vibius watched his friend as he laughed for the first time in over a week. Smiling himself, he pulled the blanket over his head and fell fast asleep.

Feeling more alive than ever, Marcus stood up and leaned against the railing and inhaled the cold air around him. The sea was only mildly agitated, the innumerable stars shone brightly, and the cold wind felt heavenly. He smiled to himself as he closed his eyes and realized anew how great a feeling it was to be alive.

www.ingramcontent.com/pod-product-compliance
Lightning Source LLC
Chambersburg PA
CBHW050517260626
47157CB00004B/1363